THE ENTITY OF CAMP DEVILS LAKE

ANTHONY R. GURULE

ISBN: 0692683178
ISBN 13: 9780692683170
Library of Congress Control Number: 2016911339
Anthony R. Gurule

The Entity

of

Camp Devils

Lake

Love Hurts

As my heart aches at the sight of her
She looks at me like a fool
She doesn't see me, yet I ache for her

When I walk, I see her in a lovable blur
The pain she brings on me is so cruel
She doesn't see me, yet I ache for her

As I try to talk to her, my words come to a slur
At times I feel like a huge fool; it's so cruel
She doesn't see me, yet I ache for her

How I long to tell her I love her
There is not a trickle of drool, yet my heart aches at the sight of her; it's so cruel
She doesn't see me, yet I ache for her

As I see her, I think if only it were
This is when I use my own self-inflicted pain as a tool
I love her, I love her, but how to tell her I love her

If I love her, then why can't I tell her my heart's true desire
The lovable pain she gives me is so cruel
But as I look at her in a lovable blur
She doesn't see me, yet I ache for her

For you, my love.
Magaly Torres

To my brother, my sister, my mom and dad, my family, my friends, and all the students and staff, past and present, at Polk Middle School.

Believe in your dreams, and do what needs to be done to make them a reality.

Grandma and Grandpa Gurule, thank you for everything!

Rodger,

Thank you for offering to be our grandfather and always being so loving toward our family. Aragon family, please know I have always held this close to my heart, and have the deepest respect for Rodger. Nino and Nina, thank you for always being there for me and supporting me in my dreams and ambitions.

CONTENTS

CHAPTER 1

DARKNESS AWAKENS

It was 2008, and our school was off by bus to Camp Devils Lake for two weeks. It was going to be great! The high school students would each have their own private quarters, while we, the middle school students, would have to share.

When we got to the camp, it was seven in the evening. After being assigned our bunks, we unpacked and then went down to the cafeteria to meet up with the camp director. "Mr. Satan himself—in the flesh!" he joked with us. We never did find out his real name. "I'll meet you all down at the lake, where I can introduce myself to you by the campfire," was all he said.

So we all trekked down to the lake, where a large bonfire was already ablaze. But when the camp director came out that night, all fun and games were over. We knew we were all doomed.

We found him bleeding from the face and screaming horribly—oh, those screams! It sounded as if he was possessed by something dark and evil, and I felt my spine begin to tingle. The man fell twice and got up again, and then he said in a loud, eerie voice, "He comes to feast upon all your souls." Then he keeled right over, but before he died, his body twisted and jerked as if he was fighting whatever was possessing him. We were terrified; some of the younger kids even wet their pants. The spectacle was hard to watch—and even harder to believe. What had happened to him? Why had his voice changed, sounding as if a dark force had possessed him?

We all gathered around and looked at his limp body, twisted and mangled. There was no movement; he just lay there motionless. It took a lot of force to ravage a body like that, so how had this happened? In shock, we all stared at the corpse. The most frightening thing about it was the face. It had holes and gashes, and his eyes burned a fire-like red. They were wide open and ideally positioned to stare back at everyone. Blood gushed from the holes in his face, forming a pool around the body.

All at once, the whole school started to panic. Now the adults at the camp were aware of what was going on, and they gasped at the sight of the mutilated camp director. One lady said, "He looks horrible!" The adults then cleared the students from the site so that we could no longer see the dead body, taking us all to our quarters for the night. So began the true horror we were about to face at Camp Devils Lake.

Those firelit eyes and that demonic voice stayed in my head, his words repeating over and over until the morning—"He comes to feast upon all your souls." I got up when the loudspeaker sounded, calling everyone to report to the cafeteria for breakfast. Not surprisingly, we all looked as if we didn't get an ounce of sleep at all that night. Both staff and students had the appearance of the walking dead. No one in the room dared speak of the previous evening's event. It was a horrible tragedy, and the adults looked stunned, wondering how the camp director had gotten that way so quickly. They had seen him an hour before his gruesome demise, and he'd been happy and joking around.

We got our food and sat down, but just before we were about to eat, the loudspeaker came on again and broadcast in that same eerie voice, "He comes to feast upon all your souls." Panic set in again as everyone, adults and students alike, began to run toward the doors and out to the buses, but when we got there, the buses were gone! The teachers, shocked and scared, resolved to go call for help. They went up to the radio house to summon the buses, but to their surprise, the phone was smashed and destroyed. Shaken, one of the teachers cried, "How is that possible? We called the ambulance last night to come and get Mr. Satan. That was just a couple of hours ago! How on earth is all this happening?"

We spent the rest of the day trying to make sure the camp was safe and secure so that another event like the one from the night before would not occur. That was when the loudspeaker came on again. This time, hideous laughter blared out, followed by a dire warning.

"He-he-he-he, ha-ha-ha-ha! I'll swallow your souls and make you feel as if you're cold-to-the-bone dead. Then I'll possess your body and wreak havoc upon all your friends! The fun begins tonight. I will take flight and eat the weakest of you from the inside, making you turn against your friends until you're all dead." We looked at each other in astonishment. We were all going to die!

That eerie voice was starting to make the adults angry, and my fellow students were all cowering in fear. I, on the other hand, had a different feeling about this entity. I wanted it to try to come for me. I would be ready and waiting. It was not as if it could take the sun away—or was I speaking too soon? Time always has a way of working against you. We had only three hours until sundown, and I thought of this as the countdown to our doom. But then I got a bright idea. I proposed to a teacher that if we were to wait in the room where the loudspeaker was, we could catch this evil entity. It was sure to use the intercom again soon. The teachers all got together and agreed that this might be the best approach—we could be trapped here for two weeks, and they needed to keep all us kids safe.

Sundown came, and as predicted, the entity came over the PA system again, threatening, "Let the mere mortals' deaths begin!" We all knew that our two biggest and strongest male teachers were standing ready to knock this guy out, but then the loudspeaker turned off, and we didn't hear anything. All stayed quiet and calm. It was so eerily quiet and peaceful that my peers and I were mute in anticipation, impatiently waiting.

Then it happened. Both teachers came out, their bodies shaking and pus coming out of their mouths, walking toward the center of both quarters so we could all see them. We all stared, paralyzed with fear. I was so scared that my hands were trembling, and I could feel the warmth of my urine as it trickled down my pant leg. Both men were suffering—you could see the pain in their eyes as their bodies from the waist up began to twist all the way around. The flesh started to tear as they got a quarter of the way around, and then halfway, and finally all the way. We all screamed as blood squirted all over the floor and splashed the windows. Their eyes, that same fiery red as those of the camp director the night before, terrified all of us. Then their bodies fell over dead and limp, their eyes the same as Satan in the flesh. Fear turned our bones cold, and we knew we had come face-to-face with death.

We all screamed, as what happened next was sickening. A flow of red, yellow, and black oozed from their bodies over to bunks of the high school students, targeting the kids there. They were all screaming in fear as they all started to shake, their bodies turning blue and purple as if their bones were as cold as ice! In another moment, pus and blood began to pour out of their mouths, and they all screamed in pain.

At that point, the loudspeaker came on again, and we heard, "You are all weak! The pain each of you feels is the pain caused by your own heart's wicked deeds. I will eat you from the inside now and cause you horrible pain!"

The faces of the unfortunate kids started to swell up. It was difficult to watch—they were still throwing up blood and pus, but then their eyes exploded, and their shaking bodies fell to the floor in a giant heap. At that moment, everyone in my quarters started to panic.

It was survival of the fittest. I pulled my eyes from the high school kids and looked at the mass chaos happening where I was standing. The adults were trying to get out the door and run away. But to where? I didn't know, but the door would not budge. We were trapped! Doomed! That thing was coming for us next, and we felt we would have no hope of surviving the rest of the night.

I don't know how long we were trapped in there, but finally the sun came up, and the chaos stopped. The door opened, and we all ran out, many of us throwing up. I was sick to my stomach. I reeked of urine, and my body was so weak that it felt numb. I thought I was about to fall over dead. We all had raccoon eyes and were deathly pale.

Gathering around in a big circle, we discussed what we were going to do about the high school students and teachers. They were all still alive—how, I didn't know—but their faces looked mutilated, and where their eyes used to be lurked a tornado-like fire that whirled around and around, as if the entity itself had possessed them all. They all had a pulse, but it was rapid, and it remained that way. Their faces looked horrible, and the blood seeping out of their eyes was being slowly cooked by the fiery red burning. It was nasty.

We decided to pick up the high school students and take them to our quarters, a gruesome, frightening task indeed. When we picked them up, they were either mumbling inanely or screeching out loud in otherworldly voices, but if you listened carefully, you could hear the humans inside screaming in pain. It started out softly, but then the human voices all started screaming in unison—but their mouths were not moving. The sound was coming from their eyes! Those scary-looking eyes were burned all around—the students were not able to close them. This entity was pure evil.

Ms. Honeycutt suggested that we should all try to do an activity to ease our minds of the current situation. She asked for volunteers, and everyone except a few wanted to stay. Ms. Chacon offered to stay and watch the other children. She was never good at watching us, and she always let us do whatever we wanted. I, on the other hand, decided I wanted to explore the campgrounds, and I set out by myself, going throughout the outer portions of the quarters and checking the outside walls and doors. They all seemed dark and gave me an eerie feeling. I next walked to the building that housed the intercom and circled it twice. To my surprise, I found nothing unusual about it. My mind was racing. I had no explanation for how or why these events had occurred—they just had.

I started up the stairs to check inside. I hesitated. My body was weak, trembling, and I could feel the fear rising in my heart as I walked up the stairs and opened the door. *Boom, boom, boom!* I could hear and feel my heartbeat start to race. The door creaked open with a low moan. I was terrified, ready to faint. After a deep breath, I took one step, then another, and then another.

Then—it happened. The loudspeaker came on, and I was standing not more than four feet from it! My knees became weaker and weaker until they buckled, and I collapsed and fell hard to the floor. Dazed, I heard the entity's voice say, "I want to eat every one of your souls! I will burn them out of your bodies to make my presence known to all! I am the being that will destroy the human body and destroy you all! I have tricked the devil himself, and I will do what he cannot! I will destroy what was created by dirt and make you feel my wrath!"

With all the energy I had left, I forced my body up and started to run as fast as I could to get out of there. I ran all the way to our quarters, where everyone, having heard the terrifying announcement, was trembling in fear.

That night, we all prepared for the worst. The high school students were still in our quarters. Their eyes burned that same fiery red, and you could see the flames burning around and around. It was sickening, awful. The smell of the burning flesh and blood made all of us gag, and their screams of pain from the fire in their eyes, which was cooking them from the inside out, sent chills through us. One girl kept crying out about how cold she was, but I found this very hard to believe—how could that be? The fire in her eyes was constantly burning, and her flesh and blood were slowly being cooked! Her dripping face was disgusting—it looked as if we were at a barbecue, watching the fat of a burger drip off the grill onto the floor. I then realized why she was cold—she was about to die.

And then it happened again. The loudspeaker came on, and that same eerie voice said, "You all shall see!" The speaker crackled into silence, and we all stayed quiet as we became aware of a spine-tingling presence in the room with us. The air got terribly cold, and the lights started to flicker on and off. Then the lights died completely, and we all screamed. Now the combusting high school students were our only light source. Their eyes burned bright, and as we looked at them, the fire in their eyes shot out and up into the air, forming an enormous ball of fire. It seemed their flesh started to cook faster and faster until their faces were burned to a crisp. It didn't stop there—their heads exploded, and then their bodies disintegrated, becoming part of the massive ball of fire in the center of the room, which took the form of a perfect sphere. It remained in place, circling. We gasped, hearing the high school students screaming in pain and agony. Our panic peaking once again, we all ran outside and down to the lake, where we had met the first night we arrived. It was dark, and we couldn't see a thing until the huge ball of fire, having destroyed the building, started to roll down toward the lake. It was coming to get us, and we had no hope of surviving.

In the cold darkness of that night, we were aware of the creatures of the forest lurking all around us. Wolves howled in the distance, and every leaf scraping the ground caused us all to jump. Then, suddenly, all was quiet. The wind stopped, and the night was still. It was time. A dense fog formed all around us, and all we could see were the creatures of the night staring at us, as if passing judgment, their eyes burning with the same red fire we had seen in our fellow students! We cowered in fear as those scary-looking eyes never left us, moving all around without a sound—just the eyes hovered in the distance. Then we heard the animals cry out in pain, and then bursts of fire came from their eyes and shot directly over our heads. The fog cleared, and we knew we were doomed. That huge ball of fire was ten times the size it had been, and we could hear the screams of demons coming from inside it. The screams were deathly, and I could see all my friends and teachers shaking with fear. All of us were staring transfixed at the huge ball of fire.

With a horrendous cracking sound, streams of light started to shoot down into the eyes of the students around me, cooking their bodies from the inside out. Their bodies shook, and pus and blood shot out of their mouths. Then their heads began to explode, and their bodies ignited into flames. As their lifeless bodies continued being cooked from the inside out, they were pulled up into the huge ball of fire and were disintegrated inside!

I started to run as fast as I could toward the road. I didn't know why, but I had a feeling that if I made it to the road, everything would be fine. I could still feel the presence of evil all around me, but I just kept running as fast and as hard as my legs would let me. I got to where the buses had dropped us off, and I saw a car with its lights on and its motor running at low idle, and to my surprise, no one was in the vehicle.

Figuring this would be my best bet to get out of there, I got inside the car and hid in the backseat. Before long, I heard footsteps in the brush outside, and the owner of the vehicle got into the car and started to drive. As he peeled out and accelerated rapidly, the pebbles from the rocky road bounced off the inner fender well. I began to wonder why it was getting brighter and brighter, and I looked up. There it was—this huge ball of fire chasing us! I couldn't move. My body was trembling in fear, and I could feel my heart pounding. I tried to scream but couldn't. I asked, "Why me?" I knew we were doomed.

To my astonishment, the car radio started to change stations all on its own, causing the driver of the vehicle to start to freak out. The same eerie voice came on and said, "I want your soul! You cannot escape me, boy!" Then the old Michael Jackson song "Thriller" started playing at full volume, and the owner of the vehicle turned the radio off. The guy was so scared that he pushed down even harder on the gas pedal. I was still in shock at the sight of the huge ball of fire. We were halfway down the mountain when the ball of fire burst into the form of a huge dog.

The flaming dog was gaining speed, running faster and faster toward the car and catching up with us enough to start hitting the back of the car with its giant nose, trying to flip the car over. It was horrible! The entity was going to kill us and swallow our souls whole. Biting the trunk of the car, the dog tore a big chunk off, but as it did this, it lost its balance and fell hard to the ground. The man in the car continued to drive as fast as he could down the mountain, but the dog on fire got up and started to run after us yet again. He was gaining speed, but we were nearing the bottom of the mountain. The farther away we got, the more it began to shrink, until finally the dog was no more.

***

But the story doesn't end there. The driver of the car that night had looked into his mirror, and when he did, the entity had possessed him. The man's eyes began to glow that fire-like red, and the boy who had thought he was safe died that night. His soul was swallowed whole, and his body was burned to a crisp. When they found him, he was in the backseat of the car, those fire-like eyes burning bright.

CHAPTER 2

MYSTERIOUS DEATH

It had been six days since we'd found the boy in the car, and the most horrifying thing about his body was the condition of his eyes. When I was first called to the scene, I'd arrived to find it clean—no fingerprints, no gasoline, and no matches to light the boy on fire. I'd walked down to the car and found that the boy inside was dead, his body burned to a crisp, but his eyes were still on fire. When the EMS team took the corpse to the coroner to be examined for cause of death, I got an eerie feeling in my stomach.

Now, six days later, the coroner's office called me. In a monotone, the male voice on the phone said, "This is Pablo, and I am calling in regard to the little boy that was brought in six days, six hours, and six minutes ago."

I looked at the clock, and to my surprise it was 6:06 a.m. It was odd that the coroner's office would call me this early in the morning. I asked whether they'd been able to determine anything about the cause of death, and Pablo replied, "You have got to come down here as soon as possible."

"Why?"

"Rodger, it's the boy. He's...he's...I can't explain. Just come down to the coroner's office, and I will show you."

I got up and started to head for the shower, but then I decided the case was significant enough to skip my morning ritual. I opened a drawer and pulled clothes out, getting dressed as I made my way toward the garage. The morning air hit my nose as I opened the garage door. Unlocking the car using the button on the remote, I got in and started her up. The engine roared with might as I depressed the gas pedal, looked into the rearview mirror, and backed out of my driveway.

When I reached the coroner's office, I met Pablo at the front door and immediately noticed that something wasn't right about his eyes. They burned a fire-like red, and in a horrible voice, he croaked, "He comes to feast upon all your souls."

Sweat trickled down his face, and the fire glowed in his eyes. I looked at him and asked, "What is wrong with you?" Getting no response, I shook him and asked again. He proceeded to grab his pen, which he lifted up into the air, about to stab himself in the chest, but I reacted in just enough time to stop him. My reaction, though, was not proper—I punched him hard in the face, so hard that I knocked him out.

Picking Pablo up, I laid him on one of the gurneys in the back. I got some water and poured it on his face to wake him, which he did, gasping for air and yelling out. I gave him a few minutes to pull himself together. He wiggled his jaw a bit, making sure I had not broken it.

"All right, lad," I said. "Why did you call me down here? What is so important that it had to have my immediate attention?"

"Rodger, I am sorry. I called to tell you that the boy's eyes will not turn off."

"What are you trying to say?"

"The boy, Rodger! His eyes, those firelit eyes, will not turn off! We've tried everything—everything—and they still will not turn off. They light up the room at night. I poured water on them, and they will not stop burning. I just don't have an explanation as to why the eyes will not turn off."

Impatiently, I said, "What do you mean?"

"I'll show you." He led me to where the boy's body was and pulled the sheet off the body, but even before he did so, I could see the glow coming from underneath. I gasped at the sight of the crisp body lying there motionless on the table, those eyes still burning bright. Taking matters into my own hands, I went to the sink, filled a cup with water, and poured the water into the boy's eyes. The water and the fire met, and steam started to rise, but to my surprise, the fire in his eyes kept burning!

I was shocked. How could this be true? What had caused this boy's death?

"Pablo, has anyone else been in this room?"

"Just my staff," Pablo replied. "Why?"

My mind started to race as I thought about every aspect and possibility as to the boy's cause of death. I had just now witnessed the most horrifying thing I had ever seen in my life. Or perhaps I was speaking too soon. The coroner now pulled out another dead body, laying it right next to that of the boy, whose eyes still burned. It became hard for me to look at, and I started to feel sick.

Rather than diminishing, the fire from the boy's eyes danced ever more intensely for a while longer, and then in a terrifying instant, it crossed over to the other body. What happened next was so terrible, it made me puke. The body was dead, but once the fire reached its eyes, the corpse started to twitch and crumple like foil. Suddenly, embalming fluid began to gush out its mouth, nose, and ears, shooting up toward the ceiling and walls of the room.

I was still in shock, starting to feel chills creep down my back. The bones of the corpse began to break, each of them popping as the body crushed itself into a ball. The only parts sticking out were the head and neck. The head became animated, starting to look in all directions as if searching for someone or something. Reaching me, it stopped, its eyes closed. There I was, in shock, staring at the dead body. I had no explanation as to why this was happening. Then, to my horror, the eyes shot open, and the same fire that had been in the boy's eyes was pointed directly at me. I was sick, and my heart was pounding. The fire in the dead body's eyes whirled around and around.

Have you ever heard people say that the dead speak out in pain? Well, I wasn't a believer until that moment. As the fire in the corpse's eyes lit the whole body on fire and the flames grew higher and higher, its face started moving from side to side, and a loud, eerie voice screeched at the top of the corpse's lungs. It was a sight to see. I ran out into the corridor and puked my guts out.

I wanted to get the hell out of there as soon as I could, but as I started for the outer door, Pablo stopped me.

"Are you all right?"

"No," I stated. "What the hell just happened in there?"

He told me to relax, that this was one of the tests they had done on the boy. I looked at him incredulously and asked, "Relax? Relax? You want me to relax? That was the most horrifying thing I have ever seen, and you expect me to relax?"

He then told me that earlier, in the course of their normal work, they had placed a body right next to the boy's, and this same thing had happened, just not in the same order. "OK, Rodger, pull yourself together," I told myself. I waited a minute, put two and two together, and then told Pablo I was going in to see the body again, by myself this time.

I went to where the body was laid out and looked at it very carefully. I walked around it twice, studying it, trying not to look into the eyes. I grew very interested in figuring out who this boy was and how he'd come to be this way. As I walked around the corpse for the last time, I peeked at those horrifying eyes, and for a brief moment, my body felt warm, as if I were being taken in by the fire whirling round and round in his eyes. I quickly made my way out of there.

I decided my next step was to go down to the police impound yard to examine the car. Once I located it among the assorted vehicles, I saw that the trunk had been burned, and it looked as if a chunk of the car had melted off. I thought, "Why does the trunk of the car look like it's missing a piece?" I walked around the car and found that the driver's seat showed burn marks similar to the burn marks on the backseat. Odd that the burn marks were larger and that the roof of the car showed smoke damage in these two spots. It became apparent to me that there had been two people in the car, and judging by the size of the burn marks in the front, the driver had been an adult male, probably in his midthirties. The burn marks were pear shaped, and it was evident that he'd clearly been overweight. I took a closer look at the length of the burn marks on the seat and found the burn marks ended high in the seat, so the killer's height must have been around five feet eleven. The fact that he was overweight and tall and had a broad body structure ideally gave me an idea of what his age could be. I searched inside the car and looked in the many different storage units, such as the center console and glove compartment. I found a picture of a little girl. The date on the back of the picture was recent, and she seemed to be in middle school. What was his motive, and why was he and the boy found at the bottom of the mountain?

Where had these guys been going? How was I supposed to figure out how this boy had died? Had the man in the front seat caused the boy's death? The burn marks looked as if the guy in the car had reached around behind and killed the boy by smothering him with the fire. If so, what had been his motive? This was all I could think about.

"Think, Rodger," I mused to myself. "Why did he kill the child, and why is he missing? Where is the other body?"

It then hit me. We had found the body at the bottom of the mountain. The only way in and out of that mountain was that road. I had a hunch that would change my life forever.

I stopped in at my local café on the way back to my office, as I did most afternoons, and noticed a story on the front page of the paper I was about to leaf through about the outcry from multiple families against a school principal. The headline proclaimed, "Field Trip Goes Horribly Wrong." I sat in my usual booth, drinking a cup of coffee with two sugars and cream while reading the article in more detail. Apparently, the school had gone on a field trip to Camp Devils Lake and never returned. The students and staff had vanished, and the school principal was under investigation. The superintendent of the school had suspended the director of the school, who was put on paid administrative leave while under investigation. Reading on, I wasn't too surprised to discover that the story was linked to the murder scene I was investigating. The department was under pressure from the media, families, and the mayor. I picked my eyes up off the paper for a moment and looked out the window and noticed the clouds were dark, threateningly purple.

I continued to read the rest of the story. The journalist had found an eyewitness to the scene and therefore had a primary source of information.

"The car at the bottom of the mountain was burning from inside," claimed the local man. He'd reported the accident as he was driving past the base of the mountain. The reporter emphasized how the local man had shakily stated, "I saw a man wandering through the woods, but his eyes were on fire! When I got to the car, a body was still burning in the backseat, and the driver's door was wide open."

To me, the man was obviously delusional. The paper went on to list the names of all the 150 students and 20 staff that were missing. It occurred to me as I saw these names that perhaps the boy had been on this trip. Had he been trying to escape from someone? I decided to drive up to the mountain to look for clues.

I drove slowly, looking at the beautiful yet eerie scenery. The gravel road was rough on the tires and seemed to get narrower the deeper I went into the forest. As I looked carefully on all sides of the road for anything unusual, I soon came upon a large chunk of black metal dangling from the branches of a tree, hanging ten feet from the ground. I pulled over and approached it, finally jumping up and punching it with my fist. It fell off the tree, hitting the ground with a dull thud. It looked like metal melted from the car in the impound station—its large indentations seemed to match. It became apparent that whatever had happened that night, something enormous had been after the boy and the driver. I picked up the piece of metal and placed it carefully in the trunk of my car.

From there, I made my way up to Camp Devils Lake. When I arrived, I got out of my car and walked down to the lake. Everything seemed dark, eerie, and black as death. The seaweed looked dead and rotted, and as the current pushed against it, the bottom of the lake moved, making me feel depressed and putting my heart and mind in a dark place. It was the kind of darkness that swallows the light and makes you feel trapped in nothingness, where the only way out is to light up the darkness.

As I started to walk to the camp, the trees too gave me an eerie feeling that crept slowly down my spine. Looking up at the vast forest, I realized that the trees were all black. The scene continued to make me uneasy, as if this whole forest was dead. I began walking around the camp, looking at all the buildings. Pine needles carpeted the path that led toward the main building. I was hoping to encounter someone whom I could talk to about the camp, ask whether the person knew anything about a boy and a man having been there, but

I found no one. The camp was empty and abandoned. Where were the police investigators and the CSI unit?

I walked up to the radio tower and noticed the door was open. Chills crept down my spine as I made my way up the stairs. Reaching the door, I was about to go in when I was startled by the harsh cawing of a crow, making me jump. Giving myself a moment to recover, I ventured inside. The crow outside the window continued to caw, bobbing its head at me as I looked all around the room. I found that both the radio and the tower had been smashed up, destroyed—by what, I couldn't tell, but the place was a massive mess.

I walked up to the desk, where some forms were scattered— they were for the James K. Polk High School and Junior High School. They listed the dates the schools would be at the camp and who their guide was to be for the trip. I started to think, listening to the cawing crow outside.

What the hell had happened here? The school had come down to the camp on a field trip—and then it hit me. The newspaper from this morning had described exactly what I had just found. I started piecing together all the available evidence in this puzzling case. As I moved toward the door, all of a sudden the loudspeaker came to life. A voice eerily intoned, "He comes to feast upon your soul." I turned quickly around and noticed that the loudspeaker was right on top of the desk. Feeling a cold draft on my back, I couldn't believe my eyes as I saw the button pop back up all by itself. The hair on my arms started to rise, and my heart began to pound. Summoning my courage, I hurried outside and headed toward the cawing crow.

A number of cawing crows had gathered, many more than before. I walked out toward the sleeping quarters—it looked as if one of the buildings had been blown up. Not far away, I found the skeletal remains of two bodies, each ripped in half. Crows were all around, and I made the assumption that these damn scavengers had eaten every last scrap of meat from these bones. The skeletons lay there with their mouths wide open. It was a gruesome scene that made my stomach curl.

As I looked at where their eyes had once been, I noticed large rings of black around the sockets. Both bodies had similar directional burns in this area, and it looked as if the bone had melted—there were severe fragmentation and moderate fracturing around the eyes. The heat must have been extreme, because the structural integrity of the bone had been distorted, causing what looked like facial deformation. The probable cause of this was the dehydration of the collagen in the bone, making it evident that heat likely caused the distortion and severe fragmentation.

The bodies looked masculine, and from what I could tell, they had been adults somewhere in their thirties. They must have been staff members of the school. It seemed the men had died quickly and had been slaughtered brutally. Their spines exhibited multiple fractures, which was likely the reason they died—from what I could tell, their spines had been twisted right around.

Inside the sleeping quarters that were still standing, the walls and windows were splattered with blood. I pulled out my camera and started to take pictures of the crime scene, trying as I worked to find a footprint or something—anything—that would help me identify a killer. What had been the motive? What weapon had been used?

Just then, I heard a loud bang from inside the building. I drew my gun and walked cautiously around to the front. Hanging from two chains mounted to the pitched roof at the front was a wooden sign with a name burned into it. I couldn't tell what the name said, but I was beginning to feel very uneasy about the eeriness of the mountain, and the camp.

Ascending the porch walkway to the door, I turned the knob. No luck. The door was locked. "Damn!" I thought to myself. "Now I have to break down the door." I pointed my gun at the lock, getting ready to blow it away, but just as I was about to pull the trigger, a crow landed on my gun. Startled, I slapped at the crow with my other hand, and it flew over to the side railing of the porch, where it continued to eye me curiously. "What the hell?" I thought to myself.

I heard the loud bang again coming from inside, so I kicked the door with all my might, and it burst open, hitting the inside wall and then bouncing back a little as a result of the force I'd exerted. As it swung slowly back, it creaked for what seemed like an eternity. Behind me, the crow began to caw loudly. I started to get creeped out—the goose bumps started, and the hair on my arms began to rise once more.

I stepped inside and was greeted by a smell of rotten blood so strong that it stung my nose as I breathed. I walked toward the middle of the large room and found tables, chairs, and other furniture thrown all over the floor. The crime scene started to feel eerie and spooky as I got to the other end of the room, where I encountered a small wolf, which immediately began to growl. My gun was still drawn, so I pointed it at the wolf and waited. Continuing to growl, the wolf arched its shoulders. I didn't want to shoot the animal, but if it attacked, I would have no choice. I kept my finger on the trigger as I stared into its eyes. After a lengthy stalemate, the wolf eventually backed away, sprinting toward a large hole in the adjoining wall.

I took a deep breath in relief. My nerves were shocked, and I felt I was going to puke. Glancing around, I noticed large pools of blood and what looked like pus all over the floor. I pulled out my camera and started taking more pictures of the gruesome crime scene. The fact that I saw no bodies lying around was a surprise to me. Where were all the bodies? So many questions swirled in my head.

As I turned and looked out the window, I saw that it was close to sundown. "Rodger," I told myself, "call it a day." I closed the door as I left the place and headed out toward the main building and the forest beyond. No more than ten feet in front of me, a crow cawed harshly. Looking up at the trees, I saw only darkness, but I heard twigs snapping on the ground—something was coming at me from within the dense brush ahead of me. In a moment, I spotted another wolf, this time a huge one, moseying toward me. The wolf stopped and sat down, put its head down, and then arched its shoulders. Suddenly raising its head, it let loose with a ferocious howl, which startled me. The wolf was about three hundred feet away from me, but it felt as if it were right in front of me. The wolf remained seated, staring at me from a distance. The howl had caused a reaction in the trees, which scared the hell out of me. The trees began to fly up toward the sky. Under my breath, I said, "Those aren't leaves—they're crows!"

I started to run toward my car as fast as I could. I was a cop, but not an out-of-shape one. As I ran, I couldn't resist looking back, and what I saw gave me another shock—all the trees were dead. The crows were flying around me in a frenzy, attacking me and tearing at my skin. These scavengers would devour my body—and my soul. I regretted coming among these creatures.

I finally made it to my car. Having unlocked the doors with my remote, I dived in, slamming the door closed behind me. Momentarily safe from the deadly birds, I took a few deep breaths before putting the key in the ignition. As soon as the car started, I hightailed it back down the mountain as fast as I could. My tires gripped the gravel road as I accelerated and sent rocks flying. Looking into my rearview mirror, I could see the massive swarm of crows flocking toward me. When this flock began forming a gigantic black dog, I started to panic. The crows were out to kill, and it seemed I was their next target. In my rearview mirror, the huge black dog took on immense proportions and jolted swiftly toward me. I could feel my heart pounding as it gained speed and started catching up to me. In another stride or two, the dog, its darkness gone, burst into flames, the fires surrounding its massive body incredible.

I damn near shit my pants as I got to the bottom of the mountain, where another flock of black crows swarmed around my windshield. They met a gruesome demise as they flew into the glass, cracking it and deafening me in the process. My heart jumped with each feathery impact, and I could see blood and guts splatter as they died. I pressed onward, even though my heart felt as if it were about to beat out of my chest. Since I couldn't see anything through my windshield, I found myself peering through my rearview mirror, which was filled with the massive flaming dog still charging at full speed.

Brainstorming quickly, I decided to pop my car in reverse and nail the fucking thing with my car. I shifted the gear and started to drive in reverse, and although the dog could see my change of direction, it kept running toward the car. I floored the gas pedal and kept on driving, slamming hard into the dog. As I did so, the car started to feel scorching hot, and flames surrounded the car. The last thing I remembered was smoldering fire all around me and hearing an eerie voice saying, "I want your soul! You cannot escape me."

CHAPTER 3

QUESTIONS AND BELIEF

I awoke to find my windshield cracked, bloody, and smelling like cooked blood. I gagged, and I looked all around my car, trying to see whether I could find the huge dog. But I saw nothing, just darkness. I looked at my wristwatch—it was 3:33 a.m. I was extremely confused, and my ears were ringing. I peered into my rearview mirror and saw that the back window was pitch black. I could not see anything behind me or in front of me.

I opened the door and instantly felt the cold, crisp night air on my face. Walking around the car, I found that the back of the vehicle was burned, certain parts of the bumper almost melted.

As I gazed at the mutilated metal, something on the ground caught my eye—just off to the side was a huge paw print, the sand inside its borders auburn red and sweltering hot. Then I spied another, and another. Following them back toward the top of the mountain, I saw a whole trail of dog prints lighting up the road like luminarias around Christmastime.

I reached into my pocket for my cell phone and dialed 411 to have a tow truck come to the mountain. The female voice on the phone asked for my location.

"I'm at the bottom of the mountain near Devils Lake," I answered.

"There's a towing company about a mile from there. I'll get them to send someone your way."

I said OK and waited, trying to be patient. Before too long, a tow truck arrived and drove slowly up to my car.

The stocky man who got out of the truck with his clipboard made me kind of chuckle. He was hobbling because he was half-asleep.

"What seems to be the problem tonight, sir?"

The fellow standing before me shakily looked at the car and asked if I was all right.

Trying to sound as casual as I could, I told him, "Yeah, I'm all right."

With that, he walked over to the front end of the car and gasped.

"My God, sir, what happened?"

"You wouldn't believe me if I told you."

He seemed suspicious and somewhat scared at this point, but he proceeded to get his strap and chains and started to connect the front of the car to his tow truck. Sliding under the car, he put the first strap around the frame of the car. With this accomplished, he went to the other side of the car, and while he was underneath that side, he said, "Sir?"

"What do you need, *sir*?" I replied sarcastically. I did not like to be called sir. He didn't answer.

I walked over to where he was lying and asked again what he needed.

"I…" the man started to say, and then he grunted.

"Is something wrong?" I asked.

He grunted again, shifted his body to the right, and sent out a scream. This was followed closely by a sigh of relief. I put my hand on my gun just in case. He came out from underneath the car a bloody mess. His face was covered in thick red blood, and he spit on the ground to get it off his lips. From his hand dangled some sort of creature.

Looking at me pointedly, he asked, "Do you want to tell me the story now, sir?"

"What are you holding in your hand?"

"It's a dead crow, and there are about ten of them stuck in your radiator," he told me. "I pulled this one out, but at first the damn thing wouldn't come loose."

I looked at the crow and noticed the head was missing. The man had pulled at the damn crow until the body had separated from the head, snapping back at him. He was no longer mystified at the blood on the windshield. I told him the birds had just started flying into my car, and that's what had caused me to stop. I covered my ass by telling him the car must have died because of the crows fucking up my radiator. Had I told him what had actually happened, he would have called the psych ward.

He looked uphill into the forest, saying that as he'd been driving up to get me, he had seen spots of fire coming down the mountain. I looked at the dirt road and found that the dog prints had cooled down and were no longer flaming red. The guy looked at me, worry all over his face. I glanced at the name tag on his jacket.

"Theodoro, can you tell me exactly what you saw when you saw the spots of fire coming down the mountain?"

"Sure," he said. "The flames disappeared one by one until I got to this location."

"Is that unusual around here?"

"This mountain scares everyone who comes up here," Theodoro replied. "When I was called to pick you up, I was informed that a police officer was stranded."

How had they known that? Glancing at my phone, I realized that as an agent, I must have been in the database. Theodoro went on to say that if I hadn't been a police officer, he would have let it wait until the morning. He told me that the stories he'd heard about the mountain were always dark and scary and that as a religious man, he was going to have to pray when he got home. Rolling my eyes, I said, "Let's get away from this mountain."

When I finally got home, I stood at my door shakily looking at the dead bolt as I got out my keys. I turned the key and went inside, and as I did, the light above my head flickered, which I thought was odd—there were no bugs around the door. I looked at my wristwatch to see what time it was—5:50 a.m. In the kitchen, I warmed up some coffee that was left over from the previous morning, a habit I'd formed during the time my wife, Irene, had still lived with me.

I got my coffee and went into the living room, where I turned on the television. The room was still dark, and I could see the solid oak floor shimmer in the electric glow of the screen. My mind roamed back to thoughts about the day and how I'd been attacked by the crows and then by the dog. Flipping idly through the channels, I found nothing exciting to watch.

As I sat there on the couch, I suddenly felt liquid dripping down my face.

"What the fuck happened today?" I asked myself.

I got up and headed to the bathroom, and as I turned the light on, the sound from the television suddenly and loudly exploded into the harsh cawing of a crow. It made me jump, and the hair on my arms started to rise. Shaking it off, I looked into the mirror and discovered many small cuts on my face where the crows had clawed and bit at me, and the drips I'd felt were blood. I grabbed a towel and started to clean up the cuts. When I'd finished, I made myself feel better by looking at my reflection in the mirror one more time and saying, "Damn, you look sexy!"

I walked out into the hallway toward my bedroom to get a clean set of clothes. As I changed, I looked over toward my daughter's bed. I sighed and returned to the living room.

CHAPTER 4

LIES, SANITY, OR INSANITY

My head ached, and I was sleep deprived, but I felt OK enough to go in to work. I went into the garage and pulled the cover off my Barracuda and drove down to the local café. In my usual booth, I started in on today's paper, and a headline immediately caught my eye: "Mysterious Fire Trails Down Mountain."

I read on and learned that many of the locals were calling it an act of God. The news article went into depth, relating a complete "he said, she said" about what these emotional folks actually thought they'd seen. I kept thinking to myself, "Yeah, but what if you'd *lived* it?"

I rolled my eyes and decided to go down to the police station to further investigate the boy's cause of death. When I arrived, I was met at the door by the commissioner and the chief of police.

"Detective, how are you doing today?"

Looking at the chief, I said, "I'm fine, sir."

He eyed me suspiciously and asked, "How did you get those cuts on your face?"

Looking into his eyes, I said, "You wouldn't believe me if I told you."

"Sure I would." His voice stayed calm. I realized I was in trouble.

We entered the building and walked past a long stretch of cubicles. Everyone in the room looked up but remained quiet as I walked by with the two senior officers. We arrived at the chief's office, and I was immediately instructed to have a seat. I sat down.

As calmly as possible, the commissioner asked, "What happened last night?"

I took a deep breath and began to tell the story, hiding some of the details and facts to prevent my being thrown into the psych ward. The commissioner listened thoroughly to my explanation and became intrigued about what had happened on the mountain. I could tell because his eyebrows kept moving as I told him about my discovery of the dead bodies and my investigation into the pools of blood and pus on the floor of the still-standing sleeping quarters at Camp Devils Lake.

The chief listened with alarmed concern, and he too became drawn into the investigation. They both asked whether I was feeling all right, and again I assured them that I was fine.

The commissioner then asked bluntly, "Why is your car totaled?"

I then realized why I was in the office. They were going to either get rid of me because of the damage done to the car, or reprimand me. Damn! So I told both the commissioner and the chief that the birds had kept flying into my windshield and that when they did, I could no longer see through my window. I told them I stopped when my car had started to feel really hot.

In a more serious voice, the chief asked, "Why did the car get hot?"

"I think the car probably overheated because the birds clogged the radiator."

He looked puzzled but then replied, "The back end of the car had burn marks and was melted on certain parts of the bumper."

"What burn marks on the bumper?" I asked innocently.

He pulled out a folder that contained photos of the car, which he told me to take a look at. The photos were of the rear end of the car. I knew the car looked melted, but it hadn't looked that bad in the dark. I focused on the burn marks on the car and realized they were impressions of the dog's two massive legs. I looked up at the chief and the commissioner and felt ambushed. I couldn't explain how the damn car had gotten burned. I started to open my mouth, but the commissioner cut into my explanation.

"Rodger, how long have you worked for the department?"

With a glance over at the commissioner, I said, "Nineteen years. Why?"

He looked at me with a puzzled yet questioning look. I could see his eyebrows scrunch in confusion. Irritated, I got up and told them that if they were going to fire me for the damn car being damaged, they should stop asking all these questions and fire me already. The commissioner and the chief looked stunned and confused. With a stern voice, the chief told me to sit down. I did as I was told.

The chief reached over and turned off the lights, instructing me to watch the video he had queued up and ready to go. The TV screen on his credenza flickered on, and I watched myself drive down the mountain, all the birds flying around my car. The commissioner told me that the camera had been put there the day before yesterday because of what had happened to the missing staff and students of Polk.

Looking into my eyes, the chief said, "You won't be fired, but when asked to tell the truth, you need to be honest, no matter how out of the ordinary the truth might be."

As I continued to watch, I asked, "Why didn't you show me this footage when we first got into the office?"

The video was crystal clear—all the birds flying to their gruesome demise as they hit my car. The only distorted image was the dog bursting into flames—the camera had caught only the back end of the dog.

The tape came to an end, and we all sat in the room speechless for a few moments.

The commissioner then asked me again to explain what happened while I was driving down the mountain. His face was pale, and he gulped as he looked at my surprised expression. I felt as if I were on trial. The atmosphere in the room was dark now, and the flickering of the light made the scene more intense. The commissioner, sweating profusely at this point, wiped perspiration from his forehead as he waited for me to explain to them what had happened. I thought for another minute and then decided to give them the information they wanted.

"I had heard a noise coming from the quarters. It was a loud bang. It must have been the wolf that was in the room," I told them. I explained how I'd walked into the quarters and smelled the god-awful odor of pus and blood on the floor. The commissioner and the chief were now on the edges of their seats. I went on.

"I noticed it was getting dark, and as I was starting to leave, I saw another wolf out in the distance. The wolf stared for a moment, and then it howled, lifting its neck high up."

I could tell from the commissioner's eyes that he was getting impatient, so I decided to give him the short version. I explained that the wolf had howled and that all the crows started flying up from the trees.

"What happened next?"

"I got out of there as fast as I could. I got into my car and started to drive down the mountain."

Looking puzzled and in awe, the commissioner said, "I've heard enough. I understand why the people are scared to go into the mountain. It sounds to me like it's haunted."

With that, the commissioner put some papers down in front of me and told me to sign on the dotted line. His hand shook as he handed me the pen.

"What's this?" I asked. He bluntly told me not to question his authority. So I signed, not even reading the document. He then went to the chief's desk and handed me a pair of keys, telling me to be careful with the investigation and not get myself killed.

"Be safe on the road, and remember…what we talked about here—none of it leaves this room," he said in a pissed-off tone. His final sarcastic remark was, "Have a beautiful day."

I got a weird feeling about his reaction to my story. I walked over to the commissioner and shook his hand and then turned to the chief and did the same. The chief looked stunned, but it seemed he wanted to say more. He remained quiet, however.

I walked out the door and ran into Angela just passing the chief's door. Angela was not more than four feet ten and weighed about 120 pounds. She was an extremely attractive woman with long, dark hair.

"Hey, Rodger. Are you all right?"

"I'm fine."

"I could hear the commissioner's deep voice in there, but the conversation was so muffled coming through the wall that I couldn't eavesdrop."

I smiled and asked how Irene was doing. She smiled back at me, her beautiful blue-green eyes flashing, and replied, "She's doing well. You know she still loves you, right?"

I smiled and started to walk toward the underground garage, and Angela followed. With a smirk, she said, "You love her too. I can see it in your eyes. You can't hide the truth from your eyes. They sparkle as I talk to you about her."

"Angela! What do you want?"

"For you to go speak to Irene and make things right."

"I will in time, but now is neither the time nor the place to rekindle our relationship."

Angela sighed and shook her head. "You are a good man. Don't let your mistakes from the past ruin your life and your relationship."

I smiled and said, "Tell Irene that I love her very much. I'll give her a call, and we can meet to have coffee and catch up."

"Rodger, the divorce papers haven't been signed, so legally you are still married."

"I know that, Angela," I told her. "We still have a chance to save our relationship, but first I have got to finish this investigation."

"You've got to stop running from the past." Angela had followed me all the way to my car. I looked at her angrily as I hit the button to unlock the doors. The lights flickered.

"Bingo," I said, and climbed in. Continuing to jabber on about my wife, Angela followed and got into the front passenger seat. I looked over at her and asked, "What are you doing?" With a meaningful glare, she told me she was coming with me. I told her to get out of the car.

With a triumphant gleam in her eye, she said, "You know that little piece of paper you signed in the chief's office?"

I thought back and realized I'd signed the document without reading the juicy details. It must have been a way for the commissioner and the chief to keep an eye on me. A bit confused, I asked, "Why did you volunteer for the partnership?"

With some hesitation, she said, "I didn't sign up to be your partner."

"What?"

She smiled. "I volunteered to aid you in your investigation. You signed the papers allowing me to learn from your techniques as a detective."

My eye was beginning to twitch as I became intensely frustrated with the situation. This day couldn't get any worse.

CHAPTER 5

ANGELA

I started to drive out of the parking structure, having decided to go back to Camp Devils Lake. Angela started asking a lot of questions about what had happened last night.

"How did your car end up melted on the back end?"

"It was just the bumper."

"Yeah, that thing. How did you get cut?"

"When I crashed, I got the cut." I was not a good liar.

"When do you sleep?"

"When I am at home long enough to relax."

"Did you sleep?"

"No!"

It felt as if I had an annoying little sister in the car with me who kept saying, "Are we there yet?" Angela was in fact my wife's sister, and right now she was the most annoying little thing on the planet. She had told me once before that she wanted to join the force and become a detective. It seemed to me she was de-escalating herself, which seemed fine as long as she finished quickly.

We were nearing the foothills of the mountain, and soon we took the exit that would lead us up to Camp Devils Lake. Angela got tense at this point. I asked her what was wrong, and she confessed that she was scared of the mountain because so many people had told her different stories about the evil lurking in the woods and the mysterious disappearances of adults and children, of how they were never seen again once the mountain devoured their bodies. She said that every time she had to engage in a call to the mountain, it gave her goose bumps, and she would tell another officer to take the call.

"Do you want me to turn around and take you back?"

"As long as I'm with someone, I should be OK."

"What stories have you heard about the mountain?"

She mumbled something under her breath.

"Angela, if you're uncomfortable, I'll understand." With a quick glance over at me, she gathered her courage and started telling one of the tales.

On a dark and stormy night, the winds howled and pranced a dangerous game. The ground shook and quaked as the devil's wings thrashed upon the earth. The tail of the serpent grabbed hold and snatched both the wicked and the righteous, stripping their flesh from their bodies. Their deathly screams howled through the night when the demons came to feast. The devil, delighted with the suffering humans, pounded the earth with his mighty wings. The winds of torment filled the air, and the demons roamed free to infect and desecrate the land. The children screamed in despair, desperate from the loss of their loved ones, and bowed to the devil. The devil, embracing their screams and pain and delighting in his dark intentions, said, "This is how it should be, but to him, all around and all-knowing, I am forced to bow to you, you minuscule little creatures."

The children, confused, looked up, and as they did, the devil looked into their eyes and bowed, not taking his eyes off them. The subtle look in the devil's all-seeing eyes made the children cower and look away. The devil was not pleased at this and yelled out in a demonic voice, "Look at me, you little heathens!" And as he said this, the children looked directly into his eyes, and he possessed them all. He infected and changed them. He devoured their souls, chewed their bodies, and spit out their skin and bones. The creature then reanimated their bodies to do its bidding. These lost, soulless children wreaked havoc on the townsfolk, slaughtering all the cruel and heartless people. These lost, cruel children ran amok upon the earth, devouring flesh and biting into the souls of the sinners, the greedy, the gluttonous, the sick, and the weak.

The devil, who had made the children in his own image, was amazed by the countless souls sent to the darkness of his dwellings in hell. The children were lost forever but had been created in the image of a beautiful yet deceptively cruel, evil creature. These children were born on the mountain of Camp Devils Lake. The town in which these children were brought up in the world was now a desolate wasteland of dead trees, the lair of enormous unknown creatures said to be the demons of the earth. Beware the mountain! Beware the fruit of his children, for they bring wrath upon the land.

Camp Devils Lake had originally been located near the bottom of the mountain because many people were too scared to venture into its higher elevations. The town's mayor had moved the camp near the lake and made a generous contribution to restructuring the camp.

"The legend of the children of the damned souls has been told many times in the past but is now being forgotten by the new generations," Angela concluded. She seemed exhausted after telling the story of the origins of Camp Devils Lake.

"We heard the stories about the mountain when we were kids." Looking up, she suddenly noticed that we were on the gravel road and heading deep into the mountain. Trying to get her bearings and focus on her surroundings, Angela suddenly froze as she spotted a great many serpents on the sides of the road.

Worriedly, she asked, "Do you know what kinds of snakes are up here?"

"Timberland rattlesnakes and northern water snakes," I replied.
"Is that all of them?"

"Yes, besides the million other species I don't know. Why?"

"Look on the sides of the road."

It looked as if the snakes were all congregating toward the road. They slithered their way to the edges and coiled themselves, positioning their heads upward toward the car. As we passed, their heads swiveled to follow us with their eyes.

"It was weird seeing those snakes do that, Rodger. What do you think of this mountain?" Angela asked.

I told her I thought of it as a place that was misunderstood by everyone living in the town. She threw me a quick glance and then rolled her eyes.

"Yeah, right."

My wife, Angela, and their friends had played at the bottom of the mountain when they were younger and had heard horror stories from the people who had tried to live on it. Angela told me she and the family thought the mountain was haunted with evil sorcery.

"This mountain creeps me out, Rodger. Why are you intent on coming here?"

"Listen, Angela, I know I'm not supposed to tell you about anything that was said in the meeting with the commissioner and the chief, but when I was explaining to them what had happened, they didn't seem scared about the situation. They seemed surprised I was still alive. The last thing they said was 'Try not to get killed.' To me, they seemed in shock to see me alive and walking around with just a couple of scratches. It felt as if they knew that something is happening on the mountain. Angela, what do you think?"

She looked at me as if I were insane. "Rodger, I think they were interested in the mountain as much as you are right now. They were constantly talking about the car this morning. The investigator was telling the chief that the burns to your car were not like anything he had ever encountered. He looked baffled and confused."

"Mike was looking at the car?"

"Yes. He was trying to figure out what happened with the bumper. He told the chief and the commissioner that it looked like something had run into your car. The commissioner was shocked and told Mike to have the car scrapped."

I looked into Angela's eyes and told her that I'd had in my trunk a piece of the vehicle I found at the bottom of the mountain. Stunned and confused, she told me they hadn't found anything in the trunk of the car.

"What the fuck?" I said, enraged. "It sounds like they're covering up the investigation!"

Angela was in wonder at the whole idea of the commissioner and the chief somehow covering up my investigation. She turned to the lake then and was in absolute amazement, gazing at it excitedly.

"How beautiful, Rodger," she said. If she noticed that the clouds were a deep, dark purple, she didn't mention it.

"From experience," I said, "the scenery is utterly beautiful, but it's deadly and deceptive, Angela. I was here yesterday and found a million or more crows trying to eat me alive. No trees are living in the camp. They're just old, dead wood. Angela, follow my instructions while at the camp—promise?"

Hesitant at first, Angela played with the idea of being in complete danger the whole time at the camp. But she agreed. "Sure, Rodger."

As we neared the camp entrance, she excitedly read aloud the sign on the road: "Welcome to Camp Devils Lake." We arrived to find multiple police officers scanning and investigating the campground. The commissioner and the chief were both there, presently doing what they did best—coordinating the whole operation.

"They're just standing there doing nothing," Angela said as if reading my thoughts.

"You took the words right out of my head."

She gave me a weird look and smiled. "Rodger, did you know the commissioner and the chief were going to be here?"

Surprised, I replied, "No, I did *not* know they were going to be here. It's amazing how fast they got up here and started corrupting my investigation."

Angela and I walked over to the chief and the commissioner, who at the time were both talking to the coroner. The shocked look on the commissioner's face as we walked up surprised me. He paused momentarily and then shook my hand, asking in a serious voice, "What are you two doing here?"

I looked into the man's eyes and said, "I am continuing my investigation. Why, sir?"

"The story you gave us this morning was so interesting that we felt it necessary to take a more active role. Now, if you will excuse me, Rodger." The commissioner turned and walked back over to the chief. They were collaborating and gathering evidence, discussing the two dead bodies and seemingly shocked about how their spines were twisted right around at the waist.

Angela was walking around the camp in utter amazement. She had never seen the police department act on an investigation so fast—CSI, FBI, and a whole bunch of other agencies were working on the crime scene, and members of the media were hovering nearby. She noticed the trees and the gray clouds above, observing also that the forest was dead and that the trees looked ancient.

The sound of a helicopter startled us all. The mayor had arrived at the crime scene in an S-76C helicopter, a machine made for the wealthy—it was extremely expensive. The mayor made his way out of the chopper and was instantly surrounded by the media. Like most politicians seeking to increase their standings in the polls, he gave some brief, unanswerable statements on the investigation and made a few false promises, following the age-old tradition of politicians providing snippets of small but tangible progress, enough to move them off the radar and cover up the broken promises.

Boldly, Angela walked over to the political giant and asked him why he was there. The mayor seemed surprised by the question, stating that he was there to see what had gone wrong with the James K. Polk High School and Junior High School field trip. Angela appeared in utter shock at this response because now media, police, and the mayor were here to show they were taking action, but before, no one wanted go near the mountain. She seemed to be contemplating what was going on.

The commissioner and the chief were both walking around the camp, pointing out the eerie yet beautiful scenery and noting that the trees all seemed to be dead. I trailed behind them, looking at them as if they were stupid, trying to eavesdrop. The commissioner, the chief, and I then decided to head toward the radio tower. Angela was out of sight, caught up in the mess with the media and the mayor. I could no longer see her.

All of a sudden, the camp's loudspeaker activated, and a loud, eerie voice intoned, "He comes to feast upon your souls!"

The commissioner and the chief looked at each other and in unison said, "What the fuck?"

The hair on my arms started to rise again, and I could feel the cold breeze on my neck as the wind began to pick up. From within the crowd of media broadcasters, a person started to yell as hundreds of timberland rattlers emerged from the forest and swiftly slithered toward the camp. The mayor ran toward his chopper and had the pilot fly his party to safety. The camera crews, too, all rapidly moved toward their vehicles, trying to get away from the snakes.

But the snakes were too fast. The first scream we heard was from a female news anchor. She'd been bitten in the leg and fell hard to the ground. The rattlesnakes attacked the victim all at once, and the poor lady died within seconds of the multiple deadly strikes as the poison circulated quickly throughout her bloodstream.

The commissioner pulled out his gun and started shooting into the air. I looked at him curiously as he pulled the trigger for the third time. The snakes seemed to move in units and were out to kill. The shots made no difference. The commissioner and the chief pulled back and went for cover in the radio tower. I fell back and followed. I had a sour taste in my mouth and felt a sudden pain shoot up my leg and right up into my brain. Thinking I'd been bitten, I turned and looked down, and I was amazed to see Angela behind me, slashing at the snakes with a butcher knife. I shouted to her to fall back and follow me into the radio tower building, and she obeyed without question.

Joining the commissioner and the chief in the radio room and slamming the door shut, we ran to the windows and saw that the snakes were congregating around the tower, all of them coiled up and vibrating their rattles in unison. Their tongues flicked in and out as they smelled the air.

Angela rummaged through a supply closet and found six small propane tanks, eighteen flares, a flare gun, and a lot of bandages. The closet was huge and also contained a medical kit, which had some vials at the bottom. We all looked at the package and read the label: "*Crotalus horridus*—Timberland Rattlesnake Antivenom."

The commissioner and the chief looked at each other and sighed.

Angela looked at them and asked, "What's wrong?"

The chief lifted his pant leg, revealing that he'd been bitten. He was starting to feel the effects of the poison running throughout his veins. The commissioner grabbed the vial of antivenom, pulled out a pocketknife, and cut the plastic off the bag. Pulling a syringe out of the other package, he inserted the needle into the vial and drew up the antivenom. Holding the needle ready to give the injection, he then told the chief to pull up his pant leg again so he could administer it.

The chief was in pain. I could see Angela reacting to the expression in the chief's eyes, squirming at the face he made as he received the shot. With that accomplished, the commissioner took the syringe to the sharps container and disposed of it. He turned around and walked toward the window.

"Rodger," the commissioner called.

"Yes, sir?"

The commissioner waited a couple of seconds before asking, "How are we going to get out of this mess?"

I looked out the window and was amazed to see thousands of snakes coiled up below with their rattles rattling. The sound was getting louder and louder, and my head was starting to hurt.

The chief, seated in a nearby chair and starting to recover, looked at his wristwatch and declared, "It's been three hours!"

His head was probably throbbing because of the loud rattling, but Angela didn't seem fazed by the noise and was rummaging through the kit we had found, setting individual items out on the floor. In amazement, I watched her work. With the propane tanks and flares, she was starting to make what looked like a mini explosive device. She took off her belt and used it to attach two of the propane tanks together. Without blinking, she asked the chief and the commissioner for their belts, which they willingly provided, puzzled but going along with her plan.

She made three of these devices and then taped a flare between the tanks on each of them.

"Angela, what do you plan on doing with these explosives?" the commissioner asked.

Her disgust evident in her face, she replied, "This will serve as a diversion so we can get to Rodger's car."

"How are we going to get those outside?" the chief asked with concern. Suddenly his mouth gaped open at a timberland rattler staring at him through the window.

"Rodger, look!" the commissioner shouted. "The rattlesnakes are all making their way up the tower!"

I looked around and found the inner ladder that led up to the top of the tower. The sound of the damn rattles was making my head pound. I looked over at Angela and told her I was going up to see why the snakes were all heading to the top of the tower. With a very direct stare, she nodded as if she understood my motive. I grabbed the bombs from her, saying that when I got to the top, I would start throwing them and shooting the flares. The commissioner and the chief said they would stay inside while Angela got the car.

I began to climb at a steady pace, trying to be extremely careful, anxious to avoid slipping and falling, breaking a leg or blowing off a limb. As I neared the top of the tower, the sound of the snakes dimmed. Finally, some relief—my ears felt better. I came to a stop and analyzed the latch of the door to the outside. The lever said to pull down to release and push up to open. I followed the instructions, and as I pushed the lever up to climb out onto a small, narrow gated walkway, the rattling became deafening again, making my ears ring. I noticed there were many crows flying over my head as I made my way through to the walkway.

The tower was high, and I could see the snakes trying to climb up the tower, but for the most part, they kept falling. I grabbed the first bomb and looked toward my car. Judging carefully, I dropped the bomb about five feet from the door of the tower and aimed the flare. Before the bomb could hit the ground, I took a shot. *Boom!* The bomb ignited, and after a couple of seconds, Angela ran out the door at full speed. The rattlesnakes all scattered.

Angela was in incredible shape and extremely fast. Her hair danced back and forth as she bolted toward my car. I threw the second bomb a little further from Angela, and again the snakes scattered and splattered. Angela had now reached my car and was trying to open the door. I still had the third and final bomb to throw and decided I would wait till she was about to drive up so that the commissioner and the chief would be able to get out safely.

I looked at my car and wondered what Angela was doing. It looked as if she was going to break the window of the car. Damn! I still had the keys, and she was unable to open the door. I reached into my pants pocket and pulled out my remote. The Barracuda was a sweet ride, but with the new upgrades, luckily it had an automatic start. I pushed a button on the remote, and the alarm beeped twice as the doors unlocked.

Angela was kicking at the snakes below and pulling them off the top of the car before she was able to get in and close the door. I could see her rifling through the car, trying to find my spare keys. At last, pulling the center console up, she extracted the other remote. I could tell she was pissed off. She started the car, revved the engine, and began to drive toward the tower. I hurried toward the door of the tower, but as I did so, I got attacked by a set of crows. The crows were cawing, but their sound was soft compared to the rattlesnakes.

The crows clawed and scratched at my face as they flew around me, trying to kill me. I still had my gun and the last bomb in my hand. Raising my arm above my head with the weapon in my hand, I fired a shot into the air. The crows scattered and flew away but then circled around and began to attack my face again. I was getting really tired of these damn crows attacking me. Already exhausted, I was now fighting to survive. I shot into the air twice more, reholstered the gun, and made my way to the door.

Squeezing my way back inside, I slammed the door shut, inadvertently catching one of the crows following me in close pursuit and ripping its head right off. The blood splattered all over my face and soaked my hair. I gagged and spit but continued fighting—crows were still clawing at me as I made my way down to where the commissioner and chief were waiting for me to shoot the last bomb. By the time I got to the bottom, I was a bloody mess. I entered the room with three crows attacking my face and neck, and the commissioner, immediately drawing his gun, shot all three crows without hesitation, killing them instantly. Blood in my eyes from the crow I'd killed at the top of the tower had made it hard for me to make it down the ladder with the other crows clawing and attacking, but when the commissioner and chief saw my face, they gasped.

"Are you all right?" they both asked.

I nodded briefly and looked toward the door, pulling forward the last homemade bomb. I grabbed my gun and walked toward the tower's entrance. I was pissed—my blood was boiling with anger, and I could feel its intensity overwhelming my insides. Opening the outer door, I started shooting at the damn snakes, unloading my clip and then reloading. Having cleared a bit of a path, I walked out five feet from the building and set the bomb down. The commissioner and the chief were right behind me. Angela by now had driven up and positioned the car with its passenger side toward us. I always liked her integrity and consideration for others—she'd always been very smart, ready for action.

The commissioner and the chief were now shooting at the snakes as they again slithered toward us. As I yanked open the door of the car, I heard a yell and turned to see that the chief had fallen to the ground. He was trying to get up as the commissioner unloaded a set of rounds at all the snakes that had started to surround the chief. With a mighty lurch, the chief managed to get up and hobble in the direction of the car—he'd twisted his ankle and was now a desperate man.

Finally both men clambered into the backseat, and I slammed the door after them, grabbed my gun, and slid into the front passenger seat. Lowering the window of the Barracuda, I aimed for the bomb and shot my weapon.

I was impressed by the number of snakes on the mountain—when the bomb went off, it seemed as if thousands of snakes were flying in all directions, their bodies blown apart and scattered.

From behind me, the commissioner reached forward and put his hand on my shoulder.

"You, my friend, will be branded a hero in this city. Thank you."

Turning around, I looked him dead in the eyes, about to tell him off, but as I opened my mouth, the ground beneath us started to shake. I yelled out in surprise. Angela looked over at me, beginning to freak out. I took several deep breaths to calm down. In the rearview mirror, I could see the ground now shaping itself into the form of a serpent. The immense snake made the earth shake as all the trees around us started to fall toward the car.

I was getting really pissed off, my heart pounding with sheer anger. I reined it in as best I could, calmly telling Angela to keep driving but to stop the car when we got to the bottom of the mountain. She was transfixed by the sight of the serpent dropping the trees. Everyone in the car remained silent as we hurtled down the road. The mountain was monstrous, deadly, and very supernatural. The people who lived here had always said that strange yet beautiful things happened here. The serpent, now as huge as a building, was showing its might—the might of something that could not possibly be destroyed. We all watched in amazement as we bolted down the mountain.

I now understood the tale of Camp Devils Lake and had a newfound respect for the mountain, but what I did not know was that the mountain's impact on my life would increase exponentially throughout my investigation. It would even bring out my deepest, darkest secrets and wreak havoc upon the very foundations of my soul.

When we got to the bottom, Angela slammed on the brakes, put the car in park, and exited, puking all over the side of the road. Then, to our dismay, the car radio began changing stations all on its own, finally tuning in to an eerily spooky voice that made the hair on my arms rise. A rattlesnake rattle filled the airwaves, and then the eerie voice slowly and deliberately said, "I want your souls—you cannot escape me!" It almost sounded as if the serpent were talking. In the backseat, the commissioner and the chief were both in shock.

I got out of the car and walked over to see whether Angela was all right. She was breathing heavily and seemed to be going into shock. Looking down at her leg, I noticed she was hurt.

"Angela, what happened? How did you get hurt?"

She turned around, looked me dead in the eyes, and passed out. I pulled her uniform's pant leg up to her knee and noticed she had been bitten in the leg. When had she been bitten? I lowered Angela gently to the ground and went over to the commissioner for the antivenom. He pulled the small kit out and handed it to me so that I could give her the shot.

I first had to fill the syringe. I pulled the plunger, filling it with air equal to the exact amount of fluid I would need, and then, holding the vial upside down, I inserted the needle into it. I then pushed the plunger down, injecting all of the air from the syringe into the vial. This done, I started to pull the plunger out to withdraw the fluid. As I did this, I began to think of my wife, Irene, and how much I loved her and our family. Angela was her sister, and I knew Irene would be devastated if she lost another of her relatives because of my actions on the job.

I got the alcohol swab and dabbed it on her skin to ensure a sterile site. Holding Angela's leg with my free hand, I inserted the needle quickly and carefully at a forty-five-degree angle. Her skin was clammy, and she was starting to look extremely pale. The chief and the commissioner watched me as I pulled the plunger out slightly to determine whether there was blood in the syringe. If there was, I would have to carefully remove the needle and then find a different spot to administer the injection.

But it was my lucky day—no blood in the syringe. I finished giving Angela the shot, and the chief came over and handed me the first aid kit from the car. Pulling out a large roll of gauze, I started to wrap her leg, finally tying the bandage securely. Both the commissioner and the chief helped me put Angela into the front passenger seat of the car.

The whole time I'd been working on Angela's leg, I'd been thinking of my wife and the turmoil our lives had gone through. The thought of losing another loved one to my job was killing me inside. My heart dropped as I again noted Angela's clammy hands and pale face. She was out cold but alive—she was going to make it. My heart was still uneasy, though—scared not for Angela but for myself and especially my wife, who had already gone through so much torment.

The radio in the car came to life again. It was that same eerie voice.

"He comes to feast upon your soul!"

The commissioner and the chief caught eyes and shook their heads. I looked at both of them and asked whether they knew anything about the radio or what was going on. The commissioner, who was staring at me with an ashen face, appeared to also be questioning what had just happened.

Realizing we had to get Angela to the hospital, I told the commissioner and the chief to get back in the car. I knew in my heart that once the news got out that Angela was in the hospital, my wife would immediately race over. I didn't think I could handle the burden of seeing her heart break again, her agony at seeing another loved one dying because of our jobs.

We sped over to the hospital and watched as the nurses and medical personnel took Angela into the emergency room.

CHAPTER 6

PERCEPTION AND APPEARANCE

Both the commissioner and the chief, still in shock, were being checked out by the doctors. The chief showed the doctor his leg and asked whether he would be all right. After a quick examination, the doctor said the leg was in good shape and that he should make a speedy recovery.

The doctors were stunned to hear that the mountain had now caused even more deaths. The commissioner was on the phone talking to the right authorities, arranging for them to go up and retrieve the dead bodies and clean up the mess at Camp Devils Lake. The scene at the camp was a horrendous tragedy for the poor families who had lost all their loved ones.

It wasn't long before I spied Irene coming into the hospital's lobby. I looked at her and felt my heartbeat increase with excitement. She was a beautiful woman with brown hair and brown eyes, in every aspect the perfect woman for any man, the definition of a loving, caring, and heartbroken mother. Her life had been full of constant worry for her family, but she never gave up, and she always followed through with her plans. She saw me and walked over to me, her tears overflowing.

I gave her a huge hug and held her close. Shakily, she asked in a whisper, "What happened on that mountain?"

"A timberland rattlesnake bit Angela." I went on to explain how Angela had driven all the way down the mountain, saving us, but that we'd all been unaware she had a bite on her leg.

Irene backed away, looking into my eyes and turning red with anger. I could tell—her shoulders started to rise, and she slapped me hard in the face. Regaining control a moment later, she asked more calmly, "Is my sister going to make it?"

I looked into her eyes and felt my pulse increase again. The attraction was there, and as I gazed at her red lips, my natural instinct was to kiss her. I struggled to maintain control over my emotions.

"I worked hard on her leg and got the antivenom into her bloodstream in time."

Irene came in close and gave me a hug, holding me even tighter this time. My ear on the side she'd slapped me was still ringing, but I felt I deserved every ounce of her anger. Her touch and gentleness ignited my heart with love.

The chief ruined the moment, though, when he came over and asked me to speak with the mayor. The mayor was an entrepreneur and considered an influential political power.

Breaking away from my wife, I said, "Sure, I will talk to the mayor. Irene, I'll be right back." She rolled her eyes and walked toward her sister's room.

The chief took me by the elbow and walked me toward the mayor, who at that moment was introducing himself to the camera crews. A huge man, he told them that his name was Jaquez Grolet and that his family's last name had been changed five hundred years ago from Grolet to Gurule, which had then passed down through the family for generations. His family tree had originated in France, and he was a good person and a great politician. He'd recently changed his name back to Grolet to honor his French origins.

I never did like getting involved with politics because of the massive amounts of pressure from all aspects of the media as well as from individual, self-serving parties. I thought of media in government as a very poisonous spider stinging its prey, as the public servants worked hard to gain recognition from the public just to be knocked down, belittled, and ridiculed for choices and decisions that were not entirely within their control. The poison was the media, and they were always focusing on the latest fad or drama about an individual political person or party and publicizing any harmless secret or condescending humiliation.

The number of media people surrounding the mayor was extreme, and photographers weaved about, all madly snapping pictures. Spying me, the mayor walked toward me and shook my hand. This sparked a frenzy, the media anxious to capture images of the mayor with the so-called hero—a hero tormented by his woes, his wife unable to forgive and forget the horrible tragedy of the past. The mayor asked many questions, and I talked with him as the video crews kept rolling. The flashes from the cameras were making my eyes hurt.

Averting them momentarily and glancing down the hallway, I noticed a dark figure walking into Angela's room. Its face was black, and its eyes were glowing red. I abruptly bolted down the hall to Angela's room and burst inside.

Angela's monitor was still beeping, but my heart nearly stopped when I turned to where my wife was sitting. The black figure was standing right next to Irene, its red, burning eyes glaring at me as it shifted and jolted toward Angela. It darted toward her lifeless body and pried her mouth open. She was helpless and unable to defend herself from the evil creature. Its face, slimy and scaly, shifted in my direction again. Jagged spikes served as its hair, and two long pointed horns curved out and upward from its forehead. Its presence was pure evil. It was going to attack and kill Angela if I didn't do something.

The lights started to flicker, and the floor began to quake. The black creature was now softly whispering a chant. At first I couldn't tell what it was saying, but then it became clearer.

"The human soul soars through this life, which will eventually soothe the soul's purpose of searching for God. I wish to share with you the depths of darkness and the everlasting horrors of our dwellings. I want your soul—you cannot escape me."

It repeated this four times, and as it did this, it pulled the hair on Angela's head backward and forward to make her head nod as it asked her whether she wanted it to take her soul. She was nonresponsive, so it just swayed her head back and forth as if she were a rag doll.

I pulled my gun out, but before I could shoot the beast, the hospital priest walked in and, reacting quickly, drove his crucifix against the creature's chest. This caused the room to quiver as the monster yelled out in pain and agony.

The priest shouted, "Be gone, demon, be gone! In the name of Jesus Christ, be gone!"

This made the demon furious. The beast started to back away from the crucifix, glaring at me with its dark, red eyes.

"Look at my teeth! Look at my teeth!" it growled.

I couldn't resist doing so as the demon's mouth opened wide. Its teeth were razor sharp, and black fluid dripped from them as its mouth opened up like a snake's. Its image resembled nothing I had ever seen before. It looked hideous. Its presence felt like death. The priest and I could tell it was lethal and ready to kill.

It danced away from the cross, chuckling as it asked the priest to turn the light down because it burned its eyes and laughing sadistically as it looked at the cross. Under its stare, the crucifix started to melt, burning deep into the priest's hands. The priest screamed in agony.

The beast began to speak with a snakelike hiss, saying, "Your faith cannot help you, for the whole world revolves around the presence of evil. It gives me strength, and since you have sinned, Father, I can't help but feel the need to swallow all your souls, make you feel cold-to-the-bone dead, and make you suffer in the dark depths below.

"Priest, I will tell you that the light of God is very beautiful, yet the fires of hell delight me more. I feel your pain and agony, as I too was burned by the cross. The pain I feel on my chest makes me feel stronger. It feeds my strength in this pathetic soul this body has and feeds my purpose of existence."

The priest, crying out in pain, muttered some verses from the Bible, exorcism passages, which sent the demon on an even bigger rampage. At that moment, the mayor, who was unaware of the demon, walked into the room. As the demon laughed cynically, its roar shook the room and caused Angela to come out of her slumber. She screamed, but the demon did not care. It turned its attention to the mayor, who was in shock at the sight of the dark image standing before him. Looking into the mayor's eyes, the demon smiled, its eyes turning from red to black. As this transformation concluded, the beast itself turned into a cloud of gray, black, and blue smoke that appeared to be on fire from the inside. The smoke hovered in place for a couple of seconds and then flashed toward the mayor, who began to shake and salivate as the smoke entered his mouth, nose, and eyes.

Unable to protect himself from the demon, the mayor screamed in pain, his arms and face slumping toward the floor. Still standing there slumped down, he mechanically reached into his pocket and pulled out a large tarot card. As he gazed upon the card, his cheeks started to rise with a big smile. The tarot card had the number fifteen on it. In a demonic voice, the mayor said, "Lucifer."

Sadistically, the demon in possession of the mayor's body then chanted Lucifer's name fifteen times.

When its chant ended, the demon looked up and gazed upon Angela. Its eyes were black with deep, red pupils—seemingly purely evil. It looked at the card and said, "This symbol gives me hope and fuels my power."

Continuing to stare at Angela, the demon continued, "If you repeat his name fifteen times, I warn you to beware the power you will be granted, for if you go through with the chant, he will forever be burned into your soul."

The whole situation was frightening, but the demon possessing the mayor now stood and stared into my eyes. I felt frozen and couldn't move. The whole time I was standing there, I felt taken in by the power I felt coming from the mayor's eyes—or rather the demon's eyes. The beast started to change the mayor's eyes from black to a flaming red, evidencing the power of the being now in control of the mayor's body. In the background, the news crews and anchors were getting all of the action on tape.

The demon had the full attention of its audience. Its eyes were looking directly into my eyes. The mayor's face exhibited a steady, solemn stare that gradually turned into a direct, constant smile. The demon was in my head—it started to voice my own thoughts, speaking out loud in a soft, demonic voice.

"What the fuck are you? What the hell are you? What do you want?"

The last question stopped the demon as it looked into my eyes. I felt it was staring directly into my soul. The beast started to laugh in a high-pitched voice as if I'd tickled it. Then it spoke angrily.

"Seriously, I cannot possess your tormented soul."

"Why, you little prick?"

"You have blood on your hands," the demon said.

My heart started to beat extremely fast. Its power was extreme and could be felt as it talked. The demon now started expressing itself in a different language.

"*Feliz dia de los muertos*, right, Rodger? Rodger, look at me when I am talking to you! Respect your elders, Rodger. I am centuries older than you, but your mom is in here with me. Do you want to speak to her?"

And then I heard my mother's voice. "Rodger dear, join us, sweetie. Embrace us, baby. Raise hell with us, son. Raise the dead in your soul, Rodger. La-la-la, la-la-la, la-la," she sang. "What are you waiting for, Rodger?"

I felt heat start to fill the room, making the mayor's jacket steam. The demon was not happy with me and was going to try to kill me. I looked into the demon's scary-looking eyes and could see the fires burning there.

"Why are you here?" I asked it.

The demon suddenly replied, "I want your souls. You cannot escape me."

It looked over at Angela and began making its way toward her bed again. I jolted to the front of her bed and told the son of a bitch it was not going anywhere near her. The demon picked me up by my shirt with ease and held me above the ground. I knew this was not good. My hand went for my gun, and I succeeded in retrieving it from its holster. The gun now in my hand, I pulled the hammer back and shot the demon in the leg.

The beast did not move. It didn't even flinch. It just stared back at me with those scary-looking eyes. I was in shock, amazed. Brutally, the demon said, "Look, Rodger, my leg is not even damaged."

Scanning where I thought my bullet had hit, I saw that it had never even penetrated its leg.

"But how?" I asked.

The demon looked over at the camera crew and said to one of the men standing in front, "I am sorry, Tom, for your soul is mine now."

Tom looked down at his chest and noticed the blood gushing down his shirt.

"Rodger, do you want to try again? You little shit. I could break your neck right now, you little fuck!"

I thought about what the demon was saying and got the impression I was going to die, but at that moment, the priest pulled out a vial of holy water and threw some of it onto the mayor's face. The demon responded by dropping me down to the floor and grabbing at its own face, pissed now and not at all happy with the priest.

"You will pay for that!" the demon yelled, and as those last words slipped from its mouth, the smoldering smokelike substance made its way out of the mayor's body, hovered for a few moments, and then shot into the priest's body. The priest reacted by running toward the door near the media, but he was stopped five steps outside the room.

The vial of holy water was on the floor now. I picked it up and started to head toward the priest. The demon-possessed priest was now looking for the receptionist.

I called to the priest, saying, "Hey, asshole!" I walked over in a hurry, and let the demon have it, splattering the holy water all over the priest's face. I watched as the demon cried out in pain. The media and news crews were all in shock at the steam rising from the priest's face after the holy water hit it. The demon pulled itself back, looked at me for a moment with the intent to kill, and then released the priest from possession. The black smoke appeared again, and this time I threw what little holy water remained at the smoke. The demon laughed and started to scream. The camera crews were all watching as the massive amount of black smoke began to get bigger and bigger. Then, moments later, the smoke started to shrink, and as it did, a demonic baby's voice said, "I will feast upon all your souls! Mark my words—you all will pay and suffer as I have. I will start by eating the weakest from the inside first and wreak havoc on all of your tormented souls. The fun begins tonight. I will take flight. You all shall see."

The black smoke then vanished, and the demon was no more.

Good thing, too, because I was out of ideas. I turned around and saw that the mayor had come out of Angela's room. He was disoriented and in utter shock. The priest, who had fallen to the floor as the demon exited his body, was rolling around, saying, "My eyes, my eyes! What's happened to my eyes?"

I looked at the priest and noticed that his eyes were on fire and burning a deep, dark red. As he put his hands up to them, he burned his hands badly. In unison, the priest and the mayor said, "What in God's name?" Together they started to pray as loudly as they could.

I'd turned around and started toward Angela's room when the mayor grabbed my hand and told me she was out cold. That didn't stop me, though. I continued in that direction, and the mayor, confused, yelled, "Aren't you going to help me get the priest up and into a hospital bed?"

I knew the medical staff here could have assisted the mayor, but I turned around and helped him get the priest up off the ground, and together we made our way to a hospital bed with him. His eyes were like those of the little boy in the morgue—they would not turn off.

"What does it mean?" I kept asking in the back of my head. "How does a boy go out into the middle of the woods and suffer the fate of being burned to death? How do his eyes *still* burn even though there is nothing to keep the fire going? That boy's death has caused me so much trouble. What is this demon after, and what does it want?"

The priest mumbled something and then started screeching, which caused me to turn back and tell him to shut up. But I noticed that his mouth wasn't moving. His eyes were still burning, and he smelled like sulfur.

"Father, are you all right?" The priest did not answer. He was dead silent.

"Father, are you all right?" I asked again. Still no reply. Suddenly, though, the priest, with impressive strength, picked both me and the mayor up off the floor. He opened his mouth but paused for a moment, his eyes swirling around and around.

"Rodger, I am going to take great pleasure in killing you slowly. Your heart is so corrupt with torment, it sickens me, yet the thought of possessing you fuels me, as it will cause your family horrible pain."

Suspended beside me, the mayor grunted because he couldn't breathe. He was trying to loosen the priest's grip by pounding at his hands. The priest twitched his head in the mayor's direction and said, "You're going to rot, Mr. Mayor, because you are a believer in the darkness, and we like the taste of your demented, lying soul. Mayor, you are not going to die just yet, but didn't you promise to ensure the safety of all the families who were under quarantine? Remember, Mr. Mayor? Oh, yes, you do, Mr. Mayor. And what happened to all of those families?"

"I don't know what you're talking about!" the mayor croaked. I could feel the grip of the priest start to loosen. Was he perhaps weakening? He dropped me to the floor, maintaining his grip on the mayor. I got up, and within two seconds, the chief had drawn his gun and shot at the priest three times consecutively. The bullets penetrated the skin of the priest but had no effect. The news crews were still getting all the action and were all focused on the mayor, who was still being held in midair by the priest.

"I know all your dirty little secrets…"

The lights started to flicker on and off. I could see the priest's eyes as the lights went out.

"You are not going to be able to lie to me, for I will not judge you but embrace your character and your actions as just. You are a great man, an evil man, and an excellent model citizen, but you're just a little shit, and now I am going to swallow your soul."

The mayor was crying and sobbing with fear. His piss was dripping all over the floor, and his honor had been shot down by the demonic creature now in charge of his fate. The demon smiled, amused by the mayor's response. It bellowed a spine-tingling shriek and then said to the mayor, "You had the military forces kill all those poor, innocent people, and then you washed your hands of it by choosing particular families from other parts of the world to live in the city. You and your campaign paid them well to keep all their mouths shut. There now—your dirty little secret is out. You and your campaign are tarnished. You little shit!"

The priest opened his mouth again, and this time he had super-sharp teeth that looked like razors. The mayor begged for forgiveness and cried out for help. The lights were still flickering, making the scene even more intense. The priest, his hands on the mayor's neck, now curled them backward, exposing the mayor's throat, and then bit into it hard, killing him instantly. The demon possessing the priest's body ripped the mayor's trachea right out. The priest and the mayor both dropped to the floor, and their lifeless bodies lay there with those firelit eyes burning bright.

The chief ran toward me right away as the camera crews went deathly silent, shocked at the sight of the mayor being murdered in front of them. Both the chief and the commissioner came to my aid while I was still pulling my thoughts together. I had fallen when the priest had dropped me, and I'd hit my head pretty hard. When I got to my feet, it was like looking at something from out of a horror flick.

CHAPTER 7

EVIL SPIRITS EXIST

I arrived home after being briefed by the commissioner and the chief of police and spending some time with my wife and her sister at the hospital. Angela was awake now and had caught up on events by watching the media footage on the news. When she saw what had happened, she was in as much shock as I had been.

Everyone was calling it a freak accident. Members of the media were questioning the other priests in the hospital, asking them what they thought about the creature. When being interviewed, the archdeacon said that he'd been present in the hospital but had been unaware of what was going on. As I watched him on the television at home, he stated, "The entity that we witnessed is very real, so tread cautiously if you feel you are a target of an evil presence. The entity is neither living nor dead; it is a being of dark, cruel, and wicked intentions."

As the archdeacon droned on about the creature, I started to fall into a deep sleep. Then I began to dream—it started out very foggy at first, but with time, the dream became more detailed. It was about a man who was a real badass, someone who didn't give a fuck about the world and was always up to no good. This man was a tough son of a bitch. His whores had to worship the ground he walked on. The man was so bad that his parents had had to disown him. His life of crime, which started with breaking windows and progressed to theft, arson, rape, and assault with a deadly weapon, left them devastated and bankrupt. He had been to prison on multiple occasions, and never did he care about the consequences. Each time he went back to jail, he would come out with a new tat symbolizing that he'd either killed someone or hurt them really badly. The man's attitude was so fucked up that he made everyone hate him. He intimidated everyone around him, his whores and his girlfriend included, to get what he wanted. The man was relentlessly evil, always thinking purely of himself alone.

One All Hallows' Eve, his bad intentions and evil ways finally caught up with him. He was in an alley not far from where we lived today, and on that night, he stole a basket from a homeless bum. The man forcefully took the bum's basket of junk and beat the poor old guy within an inch of his life. Through broken teeth and a busted jaw, the bum told the evil man, "Beware the child that bears no mark, for it will swallow your soul and send you into the depths of hell, where you will burn for all eternity."

Not giving a fuck, with a smirk on his face, the man said, "Whatever, you fucking excuse for a human being."

Proudly and with attitude, he pulled out his .44 Magnum. He kissed the piece and then put it to the old man's head, saying, "Shut the fuck up." And with no further hesitation, he shot the bum's head off. Blood splattered everywhere. The man watched as eight to ten pints of it rapidly shot out onto the asphalt and then said, "Fuck your basket, you piece of shit."

It was a gruesome scene. The man tucked his gun away and started to strut slyly down that cold, dark alley. He walked with attitude, his hand by his piece and his pants sagging below his ass.

The alley was dark and eerie. His spine tingled as he heard the leaves of autumn scrape against the pavement. The man continued walking toward the end of the alley, not giving a shit about what had just happened, but then he hesitated when he heard the whimpering of a crying baby somewhere nearby. Goose bumps began to creep up his arms, sending chills down his back and raising the hairs on his neck. The crying baby started making the badass edgy. The man got his gun out and shot twice into the distance in the direction of the sound. The baby wailed louder.

The man was getting paranoid. Now extremely pissed off, he ran toward the cries, found the baby, and picked it up, and as he did, the baby stopped crying. As the man pulled the blanket off the child's head, the child looked into the man's eyes angrily and said, "Look at my teeth. Look at my teeth." The baby's face was dark and eerie, and its teeth were long and sharp, dripping an acid-like fluid. Spooked by that, the man dropped the baby. In the back of his head, he could hear the bum's voice again. "Beware the child that bears no mark." Remembering this, he started to run, and as he began to run, he heard the growl of a dog.

He looked back and saw a huge dog. It was dark and had massive muscles shaped like human skulls; its teeth were razor sharp and, like the baby's, had an acid-like fluid dripping from them. Starting to run again, the man pulled up his pants, got out his piece, and started shooting at the hellhound. The dog arched its massive shoulders and thrust its head into a downward position, growling like nothing the man had ever heard before. The dog, pissed off, began to run hard and fast toward the man. The massive hellhound was gaining speed, and when the man saw this, he too started to run harder and faster, his heart pounding in fear. The man's adrenaline kicked in when the big dog burst into flames, its pursuit of the man leaving a trail of flaming dog prints in its wake. The hellhound's howl made the ground tremble and quake. The man, running as fast and as hard as he could, managed to escape the hellhound's fury and make his way back home.

At his house, the man thought he was safe, but when he went to bed that night, he started to hear the cries of the baby that bears no mark. He pulled the covers over his head and listened to the wailing baby. He could hear the loud thudding of his heartbeat, and he shakily tugged the covers more securely over his head. The cries continued until the man got so pissed off that he got out of bed and went from room to room, trying to figure out where the cries were coming from. Finally, he came upon the baby. The man shakily picked it up, and as he did this, the child looked into the man's eyes and said, "Look at my teeth. Look at my teeth."

The man almost shit his pants. He was so pissed off and scared that he shook and flailed the baby as hard as he could, all the while yelling at the child, "You fucking piece of shit—die already!"

The baby was not even winded. It laughed and then replied, "Look at my teeth. Look at my teeth," and with that, the baby opened its mouth wide, displaying those sharp, razor-like teeth. The acid dripping onto the man's neck caused him to scream out in pain. The baby that bears no mark then bit into the man's neck repeatedly, inflicting excruciating pain with each bite. For the terrified man, this brought to his mind all the horrible, gruesome images and memories of all the bad deeds he'd committed in his life. That night, the screams of the man resounded, and the baby who was biting into the man's soul sent him into the depths of hell. It was said that the man would spend eternity burning in hell and suffering for his soul's bad deeds. Live an honest, healthy life, and try hard not to get into trouble, for if you do, the baby that bears no mark will return and swallow your soul, sending you into the depths of the darkest abyss.

The dream was short but incredibly frightening. I was still seeing the man being eaten by the baby when I heard a growl coming from behind me. I turned to see that same big, dark dog towering over me, growling with extreme animosity and starting to burn a fire-like red. The flames were scorching hot, and I could feel the heat emanating in my direction. I could not run or speak—my body was frozen in fear. As I looked at the dog, its gigantic head met mine, and it began to growl louder, arching its shoulders as if it were about to attack. In another quivering moment, it had launched itself high into the air directly above me. Still frozen, I looked up as the hellhound descended, and the fire from its eyes shot directly into mine and started cooking me from the inside out. It hurt a lot, and I felt as if I were dying.

I thought to myself, "If I die in my sleep, I'll never wake up."

I awoke screaming, kicking, and flailing as the nightmare came to an end. My head was pounding. As I sat there in bed, I could see my reflection in the television screen. My eyes were ablaze. I shut them and covered them with my hands, and when I again opened my eyes, everything was back to normal. In my head, I could hear a very faint voice, there for just a split second, saying, "He comes to feast upon your soul."

My heart was racing, and I was drenched in sweat. To myself, I said, "What the hell was that, and why did it hurt to come out of the dream?"

I got up and went to the shower. I got a funny feeling in my stomach as I stood there with the water dripping down my back—faintness and weakness, as if my body were fighting me from the inside. I felt I was going to puke. Looking down in horror, I saw spots of blood and pus on my chest. It was coming from my mouth! I was puking up blood and pus. Trembling, I stayed in the shower until the water had rinsed it all away. I kept thinking about the blood and pus, though, and how its forceful exit had hurt my esophagus. It stung like hell and made me feel as if I were going to die.

Stepping out of the shower, I started to dry my body with the white cotton towel hanging on the towel rack. I felt sick and weak, and my face, hands, and chest looked pale white. I could not understand why I felt like this. The events of yesterday must have drained my body—seeing the priest with his eyes lit on fire or perhaps the very presence of the demon that had killed the priest and the mayor. I sensed I was going to puke again.

I looked into the bathroom mirror and found that my body had changed significantly in the past two days. I looked dead and raccoon eyed—the bags under my eyes were immense. I glanced in the mirror one more time and thought I saw the image of the...what had the archdeacon said the demon was? Some entity? The archdeacon, who was an old man, was sure scared last night as he was questioned by the media. Those media people always had a way of exploiting their version of the truth, of never looking at the good in a person. That person may have become a political giant, but given one piece of evidence that the person had led them astray under certain circumstances, they always exploited the monster. Just as the entity had been using the monster in the mayor but also saw the good in the man, saying it was the character of the man it wanted—not the man but his presence, power, and being.

It had sought the mayor's power over the people and their choices. It had intended to head into government and destroy the very groundwork forged by our founding fathers, but it had not been successful. The demon had made the mistake of leaving itself out in the open, but it had been a genius at the timing of getting the public to notice and believe in its existence. It had a believer in me, yet I still doubted the foundations of my belief and refused to acknowledge that there were forces we are not supposed to know about in this world.

The dream of the baby that bears no mark scared the hell out of me and made me very anxious. The child, with its dark, demonic eyes, was hideous, and what made it worse was that the monstrosity had devoured the man's soul right in front of me. Thoughts of the blood and his scream came back to my mind repeatedly, the dream haunting me, but it was better not to dwell on it. It did invite the idea of the supernatural, though.

What was going on with my investigation? It had turned into a sideshow, the crazy turns of events leading me to witness multiple near-death experiences.

I finished getting dressed and walked out into the living room just as the doorbell rang. I peeked out and saw my wife waiting on the porch. I opened the door immediately, and the moment I saw her eyes, I knew she was scared. She was shaking and in shock.

"Irene! What's wrong?"

She gave me an enormous hug and stayed there in my arms for a long time. I was a bit mystified—I had just seen her yesterday at the hospital, but now I felt the warmth of her tears seeping through my shirt.

I held her in my arms and gently brushed her hair to the back of her ear as she continued to cry. She was quietly sobbing.

"What is going on, Irene? Why are you crying?"

She looked up at me, her eyes glazed over. Her pupils were pitch black because of the tears, which continued to bead down her face. For some reason, it made me think of the baby from my dream last night.

Irene cut into my thoughts by saying to me in a low voice, "Rodger, she's dead!"

"What?"

"She's dead!"

"Who's dead, Irene?"

Irene looked into my eyes furiously and said, "Angela is dead!"

My heart jumped, and my body turned cold, going into shock.

"Wha...what?"

"She was asleep," Irene said through her tears, "in the hospital room last night. The hospital was quiet, but the lights in her room would not stop flickering."

"Irene, what do you mean she's dead?" I just couldn't comprehend this.

She was still holding me tightly. "Angela started to get all clammy and pale as she was sleeping, and her forehead was sweating like crazy. Then she started screaming out in pain. The doctors told us it was due to the remaining poison that was still in her system and that she was fighting the infection. But they were wrong. She was in that hospital bed, yelling and screaming at the top of her lungs, and for a long time, I couldn't make out the words she was screaming. But then I heard, 'He is swallowing my soul!'"

Her face suffused with anger, Irene looked into my eyes and said, "Promise me you will kill that son of a bitch!"

"What happened, Irene?" I said, deeply concerned.

With another meaningful gaze, she said, "He comes to feast upon your soul!"

My heart dropped. I knew what this meant. She was gone. Irene sobbed and told me Angela had been tossing and turning in the hospital bed, her eyes shut at first, and then, when she opened them, they were on fire. The demon in Angela's body was pointing out to Irene her past and the imminent future. She trembled in my arms as she started telling me the story.

After I'd left yesterday, Irene stayed in her sister's room, watching over Angela as she slept and making sure she was OK after the rattlesnake bite the previous night. Irene was the eldest of the siblings and was stronger by far than any of her brothers or sisters. She was the most energetic girl I knew. This had been one of the many reasons I married her in the first place.

Irene, still holding on to me, pulled me closer and continued. I could see that it pained her heart to tell me what had happened.

"Angela had been in an enormous amount of pain. She was sweaty and clammy, and it looked like she was dreaming, but judging by the way she thrashed about and groaned in her sleep, the dream must have been gruesome and bloody. Her body was showing signs of torture. The doctors were trying to say it was just the poison from the snakebite and the antivenom reacting in her body. Angela continued to toss and turn on the bed."

Irene went on to say that the hospital officials had finally decided to strap her body down because the staff could not control her movements. They administered meds to calm her, but Irene stated that Angela had still been erratic, tossing her arms and legs forward and squirming even though her limbs had been tied down. Her eyes were closed, and the doctor determined that her condition was worsening. Her body was fighting the poison, and she was reacting to the venom running through her veins. Her mouth kept moving and mumbling in pain, short sentences escaping as she was lying there—"He comes to feast upon your soul."

It was then that Irene realized she and her sister were not alone in the room.

"Angela kept moving and thrashing. It looked as if she was trying to run from something or someone in her dream, Rodger. She was moving her arm as if she was shooting her fingers. It looked like she was holding a gun, and as she held the gun, Rodger, she would turn her head back as if running from something. She was scared and running as hard as she could. Her face turned red as she took deep breaths. Her breathing was extremely fast. The heart monitor started to go crazy. The doctors looked at the machine and administered more meds to help her calm down.

"Rodger, she began to frantically move her head from side to side, the whole time mumbling and repeating, 'I will swallow your soul and make you feel cold-to-the-bone dead and wreak havoc upon all your friends. He comes to feast upon your soul.'

"Her wrists were starting to bruise, and her leg where she'd been bitten was extremely red and swollen. It was hard to watch my sister go through so much pain. Rodger, I was so scared for Angela, and I felt my heart drop, because I knew she was not doing well. By then, Angela had woken up and was consciously aware of what was going on when the entity made his escape. She was so freaked out and scared when she saw what happened to the priest and then the mayor as they were being possessed. Rodger, she kept crying like a baby, and she kept saying, 'Look at my teeth. Look at my teeth.' Her mouth would open, and her teeth would show. There was nothing I could do for her; she was fighting a battle in her head.

"The lights in her room started to flicker on and off, and suddenly the whole hospital went black. Angela was still moving from side to side. Just as rapidly as the hospital had gone dark, it became silent for a while. The room we were in started to shake, and the machines were all moving toward the walls. The couch I was on, Rodger, moved toward the front of the room and slammed hard into the glass. It didn't break, but it got cracked in a million places. I was now positioned facing my sister, and I could see her lying there with her head in my direction. She was staring at me, crying. Then she put her head down, and that's when I heard the son of a bitch come out full force. Her head slowly came back up, but she was laughing in a sinister male voice. Her eyes were on fire! The entity said through my sister, 'Irene, you have been a good mother all your life. I have someone who wants to talk to you. Would you like to speak to this person? She has been waiting to talk to you.'

"I shouted at the entity, 'No! I will not talk to this person. Where is my sister?'

"It said, 'She has already…how would you say? Bit the dust.' The entity continued its sinister laughing as it used her body to look into my eyes. Her eyes were on fire—they were lighting up the room! The lights were still off, and I could feel the temperature drop. I could see my breath as I exhaled, it was so cold, and as the entity looked into my eyes, it seemed pleased. I couldn't move. I felt drawn to the power of the demonic presence.

"The entity, using my sister's voice, then asked if I remembered playing at the bottom of Camp Devils Lake and if I felt any regret about letting my father down when we would lie to him about sneaking farther up the mountain. It told me my dad was there with it, and that his soul was rotting in a field of hungry babies who were all stripping him of his flesh and wreaking havoc on his soul. It said that every day brought a new form of torture to ensure that his soulless body would remind him of the promise kept and the deal he broke. Deals with the afterlife are hard to break and will always come back to haunt you.

"He offered me a deal, Rodger. He offered to spare you and Angela if you would leave the case alone. It was a deal I could not refuse, but it told me that my soul would belong to it if I accepted. It offered me its hand and gestured that it was the only way. The emotions that ran through my body made me feel I was going to die. My heart fluttered at the mere thought of getting back what we'd lost. I picked up my arm, put my hand out, and then dropped my arm down.

"Defeated, I looked at the being now in control of my sister's body. Her hair and nails were all pitch black, and so were her lips, the filthy drool dripping down onto her hospital clothes. Her eyes, Rodger, were red, on fire, and they looked hideous. Her whole face was dark and no longer in my sister's image. Angela's face and body had started to change into the entity's image. Her face began to bleed as horns ripped through her forehead, and her mouth started to tear and elongate as the entity's teeth emerged. Angela's teeth were falling to the floor, and the entity's eyes were fixated on me—my reactions must have pleased it. I squirmed as my sister's face was being transformed before my very eyes. The entity smiled with delight and made its offer again. I could see its sharp teeth as it smiled, but the creature was curious as to why I had not accepted its offer. My sister was no longer herself. Her image was now a hideous monstrosity, and her skin was barely hanging off the entity's face. It was extremely bloody. It looked like the metamorphosis of a butterfly, but this was disgusting and pure evil.

"The demon pushed the horns out slowly so I could see the blood squirt and then drip down her face. Some of the blood hit me, and I started to feel tears fall from my eyes. My heart throbbed with pain and agony. I was so scared, Rodger—its eyes never blinked, and it stayed there talking to me in her voice. It said, 'Irene, what's going on? Where am I? It's so dark and cold in here.' I looked at the entity and noticed that its horns were on fire, and its eyes were a dark red color. I was terrified the whole time. The fear turned my body cold, and I couldn't move. Its eyes were fixed on mine, and it was trying to pull me into its trap. It was attempting to possess me. I could see Angela in its eyes as it watched me carefully. The entity in her body was very demanding as I watched my sister scream out into the darkness. She was crying and trying to figure out if she was dead or alive.

"The entity was very devious, and by then was getting really pissed off at me. Going back to its thick, deep voice, it started yelling, 'You fucking bitch, answer me! What is wrong with you? Don't you want to rescue your sister?' Then its voice started to taunt me again with Angela's voice. 'Help me, Irene! It's dark in here and freezing. Help me, Irene!'

"I looked at it with all the hatred in the world and said, 'No, I will *not* take your deal!' The entity, not pleased with my decision, growled ferociously, and as it did, its growl shattered the rest of the window glass into tiny little pieces. I felt the room get even colder, and my body started to tremble. The glass fell to the floor, but the entity picked up two of Angela's fingers and flung them into the air—and there they remained. The entity started to chuckle. 'Irene,' it said in a low-pitched voice. 'When you look at yourself in today's society, how do you think they portray you? You are poor and living away from your husband. He loves you more than anything in the whole world, but you continue to live without him. Why, Irene?'"

At this point, Irene paused in her relation of the story. She seemed exhausted, but she was doggedly determined to tell me everything. By now we had moved into my living room and were sitting on the couch.

At the entity's last remark touching on her relationship with me, Irene had frantically yelled at the entity to stop.

"Answer the fucking question, Irene!" it had said.

"I can't," Irene replied.

"Why?"

"I just can't."

"Irene, I think you are afraid to face your fears, but consider—you are already in your final stage of spiritual evolution. Your society is corrupt and is inspired by total control of the lower-level humans. You are not part of this class, because your husband is an intelligent and extremely wealthy man. He has a good job, money, a gun, and a badge. It's interesting how you continue to blame him for—"

"Stop! Stop! Stop!" Irene had screamed.

"Hmmpphh!" the entity grunted, and the whole room had started to shake.

Irene took a deep breath before continuing. "Rodger, I began to tremble, and my bones felt extremely cold. I felt my stomach burn inside, and I threw up pus and blood."

I remembered my own episode from the shower this morning and could relate to Irene's pain.

"It hurt, Rodger. The entity smiled and was excited, like a little kid getting candy. It was thrilled." Irene wiped her eyes.

The entity had then stated, "Irene, you grew up on the mountain of Camp Devils Lake, right?" The entity had seemed delighted with its attitude.

Irene had answered slowly, trembling, "Yes. Yes, I did. Why?"

"You little bitch! *I* will ask all the questions! It is said that the children of the damned lie on those grounds. The spawns of Lucifer himself lie on that mountain. You want to know a little secret?" the demon had demanded in a soft, conspiratorial whisper. Then it had bellowed, "I am one of those children! And I want everyone's soul to suffer as I have suffered. I am what you would call one of the shadow people. The dark matter in the world no one can get rid of. This is why we were created. We are known as the children of the damned. We have caused many of the souls to rot, tormented countless lives, and ripped families apart, but recently we have taken a step back and waited in silence.

"The times have changed, and the earth has changed. You humans are now destroying yourselves, and it is quite entertaining. It all started with an idea, a theory devised by a man who was interested in the evolution of species and how the species adapt to survive. Your society sees you as being poor right now, Irene, and the fact that you are still married and not living with your husband is a disgrace to you and your religion. Since you are choosing to be in the low-ranking class and are considered to be so by your government, you are now categorized as being a lesser human. Since you are primitive, you deserve to end your suffering. I can stop your pain, but it delights me to ensure that you stay alive long enough for me to rip Rodger apart. I will grasp at his innermost fears and torment his soul.

"You were offered a deal. Why did you refuse my deal? Wouldn't you like to have back what you've lost? I would, if I were you. But you refused, and now I get to torment your soul and kill Rodger slowly while you rot in the same house you grew up in on Camp Devils Lake. My brothers are waiting in silence, as God too waits in silence. He is very crafty and will soon find that the light is no match for the spawn of Lucifer. The dark matter of the world will soon destroy the light and swallow the earth in darkness. We are the beings that will destroy what was created by dirt and consume countless souls as the earth plummets into a new age. These souls will then be created in *our* image and be a better, superior breed of evolution.

"Irene, are you understanding what I am telling you? You little bitch! I'm just describing why your world will never work. The theory of the superior race will haunt this world and corrupt it, destroy it, and cause countless wars. We have rested for quite some time and are now ready to play with all your children and their children's children. Your God feels he knows what is best for his children, but when we torment the humans, making you cry out in agony, he does nothing. His word to help and guide you is bullshit.

"The Bible you read is written by man, and the church is blind to the idea of evolution. It is sickening how the church continues to say that evolution is wrong. If this were the case, would you believe the church is lying when they strike fear into people, forcefully adding religion into politics to strike fear into everybody willing to listen? I wouldn't. Countless people are already fighting to survive, and yet by their status, they are considered less than their birthright. Ha-ha-ha-ha-ha! Your lives are puzzle pieces connecting the world with conspiracy and falsities. This is the kind of manipulation we grovel in—it enhances our hunger for knowing what makes you so-called superior images better than us. I can understand why I am going to let you live, but it will be fun to see how Rodger feels once he knows you know what he did.

"The evening he found out about the son of a bitch and knew he'd been killed, Rodger went to the coroner's office, pulled his gun out, and unloaded all the rounds into the man. He was already dead, but he lied to you that night and said he was at the cemetery. How do you feel about your husband now, Irene? It must haunt you so much to know that neither you nor your husband could do anything to save—"

At that point, Irene had yelled with all her fury, "Shut the hell up, you fucking evil creature!"

The entity, even more delighted, had said, "OK. Have it your way. I will leave you now, Irene, with a gift to clean up."

And reverting back to Angela's voice, it had said, "Please, Irene. Help me!"

"With a great roar, the entity then dropped all the glass to the floor and smiled at me," Irene said. "Its teeth were super sharp and looked nasty with all the black foamy liquid dripping from them. 'Now I lay me down to sleep. I pray the darkness within me creeps. I pray the entity my soul to eat. For when I die before I rest in peace, the entity shall show no mercy to my soul's defeat.' It said that in Angela's voice, Rodger. The son of a bitch said it in her voice."

Then it had said, "I will leave you now, but watch as I cook your sister from the inside out. Her eyes will burn a dark red that will eventually kill her. She is dead, but she's alive in a vegetable state. Here is the question I pose to you, Irene. Will you do like society and end her suffering? End her life? Or will you let her suffer till she dies anyway? The choice is yours; it is your life. You were granted the choices of right and wrong, but you need to decide.

"Abortion of young—they die not by their choosing but by the killer's choice. The mother and father participate in the decision to bring on precious life, but once the child is known to have an illness, the mother and father choose to destroy what was created.

Your government allows this problem to continue, yet it pleases us so. The choice is yours."

Irene paused again and sighed. "It then gave a sinister laugh, and Angela's body started to shake and spew foam everywhere. The doctors ran to her and gasped—they couldn't believe their eyes. Angela's eyes were on fire. The entity didn't even keep its word—they tried everything to revive her, but she would not respond. The flames swirled around in a circle as she lay there. It would not turn off."

I thought of the boy in the morgue and took a deep breath. Anger had swelled in me as I was taking in all of Irene's information. She and I were both still sitting on the couch, our hands clasped, when the phone started to ring. I picked up the phone shakily, the anger penetrating right through my gut and heart.

"Hello?"

My heart sank as the man on the phone answered normally at first and then sounded demonic. "Hello, this is Pablo, and…he comes to feast upon your tormented souls!"

Then the phone clicked, and it sounded as if he'd popped out of it.

"Rodger! Angela was brought in dead last night—she was completely gone. But she started breathing again as soon as we put her on the table and were prepping her for embalming. She began to gasp for air! She is alive, but her eyes are exactly as they were last night."

"How were they last night, Pablo?" My stomach started to turn.

"They are on fire! They look exactly like that boy's eyes when he was brought in," Pablo explained. "What the hell is going on, Rodger?"

I was in shock. The story Irene had told me about her sister was real and not a lie. Now Pablo said they were sending Angela back to the hospital. I looked over at Irene, thanked Pablo, and hung up.

Stepping back to my wife, I gave her a big hug and a kiss and told her that Angela was alive and being transported back to the hospital. Irene gasped, her eyes filling with hope and disbelief.

"That was the coroner's office. They were shocked when she started gasping for air. She's alive, Irene. I promise you that no matter what happens, we will get rid of the entity of Camp Devils Lake, and we will show no mercy."

I started to think I was in way over my head, but as we drove to the hospital, I wondered about the entity and the way it had reacted to holy water and prayer. This thought intensified as I remembered those past experiences with the entity and the priest. "If it's a soul it wants," I thought, "and it really wants to torment me, then it will be in for a fight and a rude awakening."

CHAPTER 8

WALKING IN DARKNESS

Irene and I were sitting in the waiting room while we waited to see Angela. Her hands were shaking, and she was crying. I held her in my arms and told her everything would be OK. She looked up at me, her eyes glossy, and suddenly she started to puke. Moving quickly so I would not get puke on my shirt, I grabbed the trash can and held it for her, pulling her hair back as she expelled all the remaining vomit from her gut.

When she'd finished, she looked up at me and said, "Look into the trash can, Rodger!"

It was full of pus and blood. She wiped her lips with a Kleenex, which also came away tinged with blood, white goo streaked through it. My heart sank, but I wrapped my arms around her again and gave her an enormous hug. She was starting to cry as the doctors came over, but she pulled herself together so she could discuss with them the condition of her sister. They confessed that none of them had ever seen this type of case before. Apparently some of the medical staff were afraid to be in the same room as Angela because they didn't want to suffer the same fate. The doctors exchanged mystified glances and then addressed Irene.

"Markings have shown up on your sister's body. They look like messages to you and Rodger. The evil being inside her is causing her horrible pain, making her scream in agony."

"What were the messages?" I asked.

The doctor replied, "There's writing on her skin that says, 'He comes to feast upon your soul! I want your soul, Rodger! You are already dead! Stop fighting—it is inevitable!'"

Irene looked at me, her eyes welling up. I could see both the love and the fearful frustration of trying to comprehend what had transpired in the last two days. The doctor handed me some photos of the messages appearing on Angela's body. They looked like cuts, rips in her skin, but they were also burn marks. The words themselves eventually disappeared from her body, which turned my stomach. I felt my heart heat up like a furnace and my adrenaline spike.

"Irene, I would like to continue my investigation of the missing schoolchildren, the little boy we found at the bottom of the mountain at Camp Devils Lake, and of course your sister's condition, as she is now fighting for her life. I will find the entity and make it suffer for what it has done to our family."

Irene came toward me and gave me a hug, saying, "Kill the motherfucker, and don't show any mercy."

Her words of encouragement made me feel stronger. Love for her swelled in my heart, and the tension between us broke from my soul. It felt good, but no sooner had my strength returned to normal than the lights in the hospital blacked out. I held on to Irene as I looked around the total darkness, attempting to see. I turned, trying to figure out what had happened. Then we heard a sinister laugh coming from where the doctors had been standing a moment ago. The lights were still off, and the doctors were screaming out in fear.

"Rodger!" boomed a loud voice. "I've come to feast upon your soul!"

The doctors were all crying and cowering. Irene held me tighter. I could feel the warmth of the tears dripping off her face and the resulting wetness of my shirt.

"Where are you?" I asked calmly. The sinister laugh continued. I could not see, and the son of a bitch was laughing all around me. Raising my voice, I said confidently, "Come out, you bastard! Show yourself!"

The entity's laughing stopped. In the ensuing quiet, I felt the temperature drop. Irene held on tighter.

"Rodger!" the entity said in a sinister voice. "You found your courage! Your wife has renewed your soul's strength. This is interesting. I like the challenge. Thank you, Irene. This means Rodger will suffer even more.

"You want to see my face, Rodger? This is quite a challenge indeed," it roared. "Well, I do not wish to disappoint you. I am extremely sorry for the mess in the infirmary. I do hope you all will be able to salvage the children's body parts. I have created an image of me and my face, but before we do any of that, let's have some fun with the people who are trying to play God in their profession. Earlier, six doctors showed you images of me burning and slicing messages into your sister's flesh. This should enlighten your ideas of my power and the shadow people of the world."

Silence once again descended, and it remained cold in the room. I could feel Irene shivering as the cold began to creep down my spine as well. It felt as if we were freezing in the Arctic. We could not see anyone or anything—all we could do was listen. I heard someone throwing up in the distance. The vomit splashing onto the floor sounded nasty.

"What is that?" Irene asked as two fireballs flew toward us.

I told her I had no idea. It looked awful and was freaking Irene out. Now, out of the darkness, I caught the image of one of the doctors as he walked in our direction. His eyes were on fire! When he got to Irene and me, though, he just walked right past us. Then we were startled by a loud scream coming from one of the doctors. In the dim light, I could see that she was bleeding from her nose and pushing at her eyes. In a demonic voice, she screamed, "Rodger! I've come to feast upon your soul!"

In plain sight, she started to hover above the hospital floor, her palms showing as she glided through the air. She was going in the same direction as the first doctor, but what she said made my heart sink.

"My children!" she screamed. "Why have you devoured my kids?"

"Rodger," Irene whispered, "get that son of a bitch!"

I grabbed my cell phone and turned on its flashlight.

"Irene, go into your sister's room and lock the door." To make sure she got there safely, I guided her there myself, telling her to make sure she locked the door after me and to use the flashlight on her cell to light her way around the room. She nodded and said OK, but her eyes lingered on mine. I could see her lips move as the light bounced off her face, and I knew what she wanted. I leaned in and let her do the rest.

The warmth of her lips on mine, though it was cold all around us, ignited my heart and made my body feel incredibly warm. I felt the cold disappear, and as she gasped for air, I realized that I still truly loved Irene more than anything in the entire world. She was the fire that had kept me going and the light in my life that would never die. I grabbed Irene one more time and gave her the biggest kiss ever. It was long awaited and necessary for me to want her.

Her return kiss was soft, and it felt as if I had waited an eternity for it. All the love I'd once had for her returned—I had felt dead without her. It gave me the strength to want to fight so that I could be with her again. I broke the boundaries of life without her, which meant my death. It reminded me of how much I wanted my family back. I would not let her go ever again.

I left the room then, hearing the click of the lock as Irene closed the door behind me. It was still pitch black. When I made my way out of Angela's room, it was no longer freezing but still brisk.

I looked at the other people, all trying to find a way out of the darkness. Unable to see, they walked blindly toward the walls. One of the female staff was walking toward the circulation desk when she bumped into another medical colleague also trying to find his way around in the dark. Both were startled and jumped.

"Sorry," said the woman politely.

Grunting as if hurt, the gentleman said, "It's OK. I can't see a damn thing in here right now."

Groping in opposite directions, they both now saw the light coming from my phone, and they started walking toward me. As they approached, I noticed that their eyes were starting to turn red and become inflamed.

From behind me came the soft whimper of a little boy, and I could sense the kid was terrified of the two people walking toward me, now four feet away from me, and asking why it was so bright and hot in there. I could feel nothing but utter coldness as they both began to scream out in pain, as if someone was hurting them really badly from the inside. As they walked, I could see their skin start to blacken. They were dying, burning on the outside and cooking in the inside, and they were still trying to reach me, heading toward my light. I remained still, watching in amazement as the two finally burst into flames, screaming at the top of their lungs as they tried to escape their fate. My heart sank when they both fell to the floor. They were dead for sure.

I turned around, and with the light cast from the two flaming bodies, I could now see the little boy. He was cowering, curled into a fetal position on the floor. I went over to pick him up, and as I took him in my arms, I saw that his face was mutilated. He started to talk.

"Hello, Rodger. Look into my eyes. Look into my eyes."

I remembered the dream and the baby that bears no mark and immediately let him go, but before he dropped to the floor, he tried to bite my neck. I felt the splash of something hit my throat, and it burned badly. I grunted in pain, glaring at the boy as he hit the ground. Pissed off, I pulled out a vial of holy water and poured it on him. As it touched his skin, the boy immediately started to cry and scream out in pain.

Now angry, in a demonic voice, the boy said, "Rodger, you're a little bitch! Look into my eyes, Rodger. Look at my eyes."

I tried not to focus on the boy's eyes, and let the kid have it with the holy water once again. It packed its punch, because it was starting to burn the boy's face and body really badly.

The creature lay there motionless as its body went limp. I then heard a loud bang coming from the staircase, so I shone the light from my phone toward the door. I could see a lady being dragged into the staircase by a hideously evil creature, which was looking in my direction and flipping its middle finger. The creature looked like a child with a devilish, demonic face exhibiting black burns around the eyes, and the eyes themselves were on fire, burning a dark burgundy red around black pupils. Its mouth was torn and elongated toward the back of its jaw, looking like a monstrosity not of this world. I had never before seen a creature like that, and its image made my heart sink with fear. I felt the coldness of the boy's soulless body. I connected with it and felt the pain and despair of the differences in the flesh. The creature's flesh felt like death. It was cold, smelled of sulfur, and looked like a child, but like God's children, it too was damned to walk the earth, suffering internally while it wreaked havoc upon the land and eventually destroyed it. This was one of the reanimated children that had been chewed up and spit out on the mountain of Camp Devils Lake.

I felt empathy, sympathy, and remorse for the creature. While I was standing over the child, I felt a cool draft on my neck, and I turned around rapidly to see what was behind me. My light illuminated a woman, also looking down at the child. She looked scared and did not move. Softly she asked, "Did you kill it?"

Startled and stuttering as I spoke, I replied. "I...I believe it's dead."

She slowly lifted her head and looked into my eyes. "Rodger," she said, "you only stunned it."

I peered at her more closely and noticed she was not human at all. Her face looked beautiful, but it was formed in the image of a serpent lady. Her face looked like the black mamba snake, and I knew instantly that while she was beautiful, she was also lethal.

"Rodger," whispered a slithery voice, "how have you survived for so long? Is it love keeping your heart pure from the evils within?"

"No!"

"It's the child, isn't it? I believe you're hiding something deep within your soul. The very depths of your torment lie with the religion flowing through your blood, its foundations that allow you to connect so easily with the afterlife. Your soul is impure, Rodger. You lack the foundations to achieve your life's goal for perfection and seeing your creator. This is called the divine right to reach the goal you set out in life. The poison running through your veins, Rodger, is the blood of the created and destroyed. Your own actions caused this problem and made you into a monster. You're more of a monster than I am, Rodger.

"How shall I kill you, Rodger? Fire, water, wind—or perhaps all of them? Hmm. Rodger, your death will be great, unlike any other. I will start by giving the hospital light. Hell's fires burn for eternity. Here, creation plays with fate and acts as God. In my hands, I burn the corrupted, the sorrowful, and the brokenhearted. This place brings hearts to a stop, and the living have to endure the heartache of loved ones lost. It is the gate and portal to heaven and hell, and the pity you all share is disgraceful. Rodger, your pity and sorrow will tear you apart. Who are you really, Rodger? Why are you hiding behind your badge of shame? There is no honor in what you do, because it can be corrupt, just like the hospital.

"The darkness swallowed the hospital whole and made you feel like you were all alone in the dark, cold and scared, but you're much cleverer than average. Lucifer turned light into darkness and swallowed the souls of the lost children. I am one of those children, and I am going to give back the light—but it will be soulless light and shadows. You shall see the world through my eyes, Rodger, and feel the pain I have suffered.

"Earth, the hospital, is all hell, and you're designed to endure this hell no matter the consequences or the outcome of your choices. Prison would have made a better game and a better lesson for you, Rodger. Your heart wants to destroy us because we are all the entity—and united, we are unstoppable."

"What is your name, demon? I demand to know your name!" I yelled.

"You shall not know my name, for the name is cluttered in sin, and you will not live long enough to even know my name." She came up close to me and leaned in, and I could feel the hotness of the air around her as she whispered in my ear.

"Now view the world as I do, Rodger, and tell me if you still want to investigate the cause of the little boy's death. His eyes will never turn off, and his soul will be devoured by us and made in our image."

I could not move. Her eyes kept me frozen in place, and she hadn't blinked once. Her body had no legs—she was all snake, but her upper body had the build of a fully grown woman unclothed. I could feel the heat radiating from her body as she kept talking, and I felt as if I were already dead.

She moved her head away from my ear, and my eyes stayed focused on hers as she backed not more than six inches away from me.

"Rodger, view the world from my perspective." She moved her head back and opened her mouth wide. I could see the snake teeth coming down as she bit hard into my skin. I felt a rush of iciness go through my body. I felt as if I were dead. I was not able to move my body.

Suddenly, she backed away and screamed, "Rodger, you asshole! What have you done?" She repeated this as she hid her face from me. I looked down and noticed holy water dribbling down my uniform shirt. Her teeth must have pierced the vial in my pocket. I could feel the burn of the bite, but as the holy water touched it, I no longer felt the pain.

But I could see as she saw the world. I could see the fires of hell all around the hospital and the screaming of all the souls being sent to hell. The suffering of all the people being sent to the dark people. I could see the souls of the deceased being taken down into the pit. I suddenly felt sick and had to puke. The children were being tricked into going, and the dark people were enjoying their torment.

The mamba snake was now looking at me with her eyes on fire. I could see how deeply she yearned to kill me and take my soul. I patted down my shirt and moistened my hands with the holy water. I felt intrigued, as if I had all the power in the world.

Turning around, I heard a dog's growl. I felt the vibrations of its mighty roar as the dog pranced toward the mamba. My heart hit the floor as I saw they were making their way toward Angela's room. I reached for my gun, but it was missing from my holster.

"The little bitch!" I said to myself. She'd leaned in and taken it from me. I'd been so mesmerized by her eyes and her body she'd been able to deceive me. Well, I wouldn't fall for the entity's tricks again.

The pair was almost at the door of Angela's room when the entity's voice stopped them in their tracks.

"Fools! Don't worry about the girl—she is already dead. Kill Rodger. He needs to die!"

I looked toward both the hellhound and the mamba as they shifted their attention back to me. The mamba lifted her hand, showed me the gun, and smirked as she dropped it to the floor. Strangely, I could feel and see everything around me. She'd done something to me, but I couldn't tell what it was. I no longer noticed the cold; rather, I had adapted to it. But even though I was now immune to the cold, I could still see my breath every time I exhaled. It was freezing.

I then realized what she'd done. I could see as she did—as a snake. Looking down at my hands, I saw they were dry and forming scales.

The mamba looked at the dog and commanded, "Kill!"

I felt the raw power of the hound's giant paw hit my shoulder. It burned as its fiery claws ripped flesh from my arm. The wind was knocked out of me, and I gasped for air. It hurt terribly.

The mamba now made her way over to me and asked me whether I liked her body and whether I wanted to touch it. I cast her a disgusted look and fell back as they both proceeded toward me. My arm felt as if it was about to fall off. Reaching into my pocket, I drew out another vial of holy water and held it out toward the two. They were not impressed until I took the top off the vial and poured some of the water on my arm. The pain completely disappeared. As I stared the two of them down, other demons started flying around the hospital.

I could still see the way the mamba viewed the world. It was certainly easier to see in the dark—the images were all in infrared, and even though the demons were not alive, they still generated heat as they moved, so I was able to see them.

The mamba and the hound made their way toward me. Still holding the vial, I determined a way out. I was going to go down the flight of stairs. Trying to intimidate me, they slowly came closer. The dog was now on fire. I could see it as clear as day through the ability the mamba had given me. He looked amazing, dangerous, and I could feel the heat radiating around the room. It started to dry up the holy water in the vial I had in my hand.

I was almost to the staircase when I stepped in a pool of blood. It was from the lady that had been dragged below. Her head must have hit the ground really hard, because the blood looked splattered.

"Rodger, where do you think you are going?"

The mamba slithered her way toward me with lightning speed and socked me hard in the mouth. I hit the wall hard. As I shakily rose and tried to recover my balance, I moved my jaw around to make sure it wasn't broken. The dog remained in place, still staring. The mamba was swift in her attack, the way a snake strikes its prey. She held out her hands and forced her nails to grow longer, and I watched as blood dripped from their ends.

As her hand again went to slice my face, I ducked and let her have it with the holy water. I washed my hands in it and let her have fist after fist. She gasped as I hit her on the sides and in her face, leaving burned-in fist marks.

She screamed as if she was enjoying it. "Hit me again, Rodger. Is this how you treat a woman?"

Her face transformed into Irene's. I hesitated at first and turned toward the door, hearing a loud growl from the dog. It started to bark, but the mamba was relentless in her attack and ready to strike again. I felt the fury of her might hit me as she transformed back into the mamba. Stabbing her fingernails into my chest, she lifted me right off the ground. She was pissed and ready to kill. She smirked, her eyes on fire, as she slithered her way toward the staircase with me still impaled on her talons.

"Rodger," she said, "I hope you like it down there. It is waiting for you. I hope you like the children—they are waiting to feast upon your soul. I am going to hurt you badly now, but don't worry about Irene—she will be well taken care of."

I could feel the pain rise in my chest, and she flung me toward the door of the staircase so hard that I flew right through the door and down the stairs. I could hear the mamba laughing as I fell.

"I hope he breaks his neck," she said.

In combat training, I'd been taught to relax and let my body do all the work as I fell. Bracing oneself when falling creates a risk of breaking bones and possibly death. I hit the side wall and stopped with a giant thud. All the air left my lungs, and I began to gasp for air. My head throbbed, and my chest felt as if it were on fire. As the blackness closed in, I passed out from the pain. In the back of my head, all I could think about was Irene.

CHAPTER 9

FIGHTING THE UNKNOWN

"Angela? Angela, it will be all right, sweetie. Rodger is going to kill the entity, and everything will go back to normal," Irene said as she waited with Angela in the dark. Irene continued to explain to her sister what was going on in the hospital.

"It's pitch black and cold, and there are demons all around, possessing people," Irene said. Angela said nothing, her body lying motionless on the bed. She had no idea what was going on. The glow from her eyes lit the room just enough for Irene to look around. The room was square and had no windows. Irene thought how convenient it was for the hospital to hide her sister from everyone.

It pained Irene deeply to have her sister lying hurt in the hospital, her only hope of salvation being Rodger and the success of his quest. She felt a pang in her heart at the thought of losing her sister.

"She's an amazing, beautiful, hardworking woman who would never hurt anyone," Irene thought, the tears building up in her eyes.

Thinking about it, Irene came to the conclusion that the bite on Angela's leg had sealed her fate as the entity started to eat at her soul. The entity had corrupted it and taken it out of Angela's control. She was such a beautiful girl, always trying to do the best at her job.

As she reminisced about her sister's life and the events now past, Irene heard a loud bang, which startled her. She heard someone—or something—say "Rodger," and her heart sank to the floor.

She thought to herself, "My poor Rodger is fighting the unholy and doing it by himself. The understanding of the unholy, of religion, and why the world works in mysterious ways—what is valid? What is not? If we do not understand the concepts of the different faiths, we too will find ourselves adapting to the new and forgetting the old.

"Which Rodger is now fighting for his life, trying to understand the entity and the origins of the demons since he started to investigate the death of the child found at the bottom of the mountain at Camp Devils Lake. You took part in that investigation when you got involved, Angela. He is a good, honest man trying to right his past wrongs but has had trouble piecing back together the family, which he never truly lost. His intuition and judgment have always gone for the benefit of the people who became part of his life. Difficult to say why, but the knowledge and experience he had when we first met made me fall in love with him. He has always been so courageous and eager to help anyone.

"Funny, I can still remember how he always drove with the windows down and the air conditioner blasting. I would get so frustrated with him when we would go out, because I would get a mixture of both the hot air and the cold air blowing on me. He has always been different, somehow set apart from everyone else.

"His intentions for his family and the responsibility of caring for me and our departed caused me to feel weary and upset. How could he do such a thing? But I later realized he'd just been doing his job. He was trying to make an honest living and made a huge mistake. I hated him for it and left him to rot in the home where we'd lost everything. It drove me to walk away from the grief and all the torment life threw at us at the time.

"You were right, Angela. I love him so much, and I will love him until I expire from this life. But back then, I felt as if we were inside a butcher shop, and the meat—which was me at the time—

was being chopped up, mangled. A freight train had run into my heart, exploding with sheer sorrow and anger, hence my state of mind. I know now that Rodger had not meant for it to happen. It was circumstances and the fact that the man had taken his wallet, but—"

Knock, knock, knock.

Irene's eyes swiveled toward the door. She did not say a word, but judging from the sound, she assumed a child was at the door. Angela's eyes swirled faster and faster, her head rising slowly until she was looking right at Irene.

Irene noticed the light from behind her move, and she responded by jumping. Angela's eyes were fixated on her, the continuous gaze making Irene's spine tingle. The knock sounded again. Angela's face looked hideous from the encounter with the entity. The light emanating from her eyes was bright and growing ever brighter, causing Irene to squint. As she looked into the increasing light in her sister's eyes, Irene perceived an image walking toward her. It was coming from the light.

Irene's heart began to race, as she did not know what was going to come from the light. As the glow brightened, the room became warmer again. Briefly taking in all of Angela's form, Irene realized with surprise that her sister's body had returned to normal. Angela rose and walked over to Irene, gave her a huge hug, and then pointed toward a gateway.

"Angela, how?"

Angela just laughed and said, "It was him who brought me to this place. I feel no pain, just paradise. I was told to let go of my body and let the entity suffer in it. He wanted to trap the entity there in my body, but the entity escaped again and has left my body to the other shadow people."

Irene, looking puzzled, questioned what she was doing and what was going on.

"Who, Angela? Who told you?"

Angela looked at the floor and thought for a moment.

"It was a person whom I could not see. It was a person with a super-bright light who came to me and asked me to let go. He said that hope for the entity had been lost. His hope had been to trap the entity in my body to allow the spirit to suffer the spiritual needs of material life," Angela explained. "Evil spirits or the shadow people are spirits that have a strong attachment to the earth and the human way of life. Spirits in hell do not understand that they are spiritual beings or even know that they are dead. All they know is life in a physical body, so the evil spirits are consumed with the desire to satisfy their material needs. The evil spirits in hell know that reincarnation from hell is not possible, so the evilness in the spirits aims to possess a living person. By possessing human beings, evil spirits can feel just as if they have their own physical bodies, feeling physical sensations and satisfying desires for food, sex, money, and power.

"The only prerequisite for evil spirits to come and stay with a person living on earth is that they must find someone whose mind is on the same wavelength as theirs. If the individual is in a vulnerable state, like near death or full of hatred, sorrow, anger, or frustration, this makes it easier for the possession to occur. But it happens fastest if the person's mind is filled with hatred and anger, and as long as it stays that way for extended periods of time, it will attract evil spirits. A spirit being that is on the same wavelength can sneak into a person's mind and stay on earth for five, ten, or even many more years before the spirit has exhausted the person's energy.

"The entity, though, is not one of those spirits. The man in the light thought it would have the same effect on the spirit of the entity but has found the entity to be even more powerful than he expected."

Irene looked stunned as the tears ran down her face. Irene was so happy to see her sister not in pain.

"But help me understand, Angela," Irene pleaded. "How is all of this possible? How are you able to communicate with me right now?"

Angela chuckled. She seemed a million miles from that place. "Irene, you need to be careful. The entity is fighting to survive today in the modern world. It wants to make its presence known all around the world. The entity is not a proper spirit, because the origin of Camp Devils Lake is unique to when the fallen angel was brought upon the earth. It changed him, made him into the hideous creature he has become. He sought the domination of the land and its people in order to run a better society. The children suffered in the days that followed, and when they looked into Satan's eyes, he possessed them all. He infected them and changed them, devoured their souls, chewed their bodies, and spit out their skin and bones. The creature then reanimated their bodies to do his bidding. These lost, soulless children wreaked havoc on the townsfolk, slaughtering all the cruel and heartless people. These lost, cruel children ran amok upon the earth, devouring flesh and biting into the souls of the sinners, the greedy, the gluttonous, the sick, and the weak. The children were lost forever but had been created in the image of a beautiful yet deceptively cruel, evil creature. These children were born on the mountain of Camp Devils Lake, and although the devil sought his own intentions of greed, power, and manipulation of the earth and its people, he unknowingly created creatures of pure demonic power that have the ability to use their power on earth to make it desolate, barren. But what has happened now is that the entity is using its power to become known in the world and work toward creating its own society.

"The entity wants power and the ability to kill, hurt, and thrive on destruction and torment. It has found the perfect person to make its evil intentions known to the world and is building the anger, anguish, and sorrow to possess Rodger. It is using you and your family to rip him apart so it can move in to possess his soul and live life on earth. It has the power to tear societies apart and have people kill each other for pleasure. It is an abomination to the world and needs to be stopped, Irene. Rodger need only look to the light for guidance. His soul is firm, different, and the entity knows it is, so it looks to harness this energy. The entity will possess Rodger, and the devil will come to destroy his creation—but he will fail, because there is no stopping the entity once it has maintained the living.

"In other words, Rodger…" Angela was starting to fade away, darkness beginning to engulf her. The last words Irene heard were in pig Latin: "Ehay omescay otay eastfay uponyay ouryay oulssay." Angela was not the one speaking, though.

Irene was back in the hospital room. The heart monitor flatlined, and Irene looked at her sister lying there on the bed. The fire in her eyes was no longer swirling around and around, and Irene knew that her sister was dead. Her heart broke, but deep down, she knew that Angela was now in a better place, gazing upon the possibilities of the afterlife.

The room felt cold and crisp, and Irene cast about for the voice of the person or thing that had spoken the pig Latin and taken Angela from her sister. She scanned the room, looking for anything that was out of place. It was still dark, making it harder to see. Irene pulled out her phone and put the flashlight on. She was met by two hideous orange eyes with black slits for pupils, and a serpent's tongue licked Irene's face slowly, leaving a trail of saliva dripping from her cheek.

The head of the snake was huge. Horrified, Irene started to back away, moving slowly backward until she hit the wall. The snake pursued her all the way. Irene gasped for air, having lost her breath when she hit the wall, and dropped her phone, but its light remained on, shining upward toward the snake.

Gathering her courage, Irene looked into the eyes of the creature and was about to speak when the snake opened its mouth. The snakelike being had no legs but was long and petite toward its tail end, and from what Irene could tell, its upper half looked like a woman, her breasts—they looked like triple-Ds—moving with her as she glided across the floor. Her body was all natural, incredibly sexy, but it looked dangerous, and her arms were slimy all the way down to her hands, which were not human at all—they had claws that were razor sharp.

Irene, now in fear for her life, was shocked at the immenseness of the creature. The snakelike woman opened her mouth, and all the sharp, jagged teeth frightened Irene. Her heart dropped as she gazed at the creature. Feeling she was about to die, Irene reached into her pocket and grabbed a vial of holy water that Rodger had given her during their car ride to the hospital. Rodger had packed the car full of these little vials.

"He told me to use it if I absolutely needed to. This occasion counts," Irene said to herself, shuffling her hand through her pocket.

The snake woman sneered at her and said, "Why are you squirming like a little bitch?" Her voice was dark and petite, but her tone and body language were dangerous.

Irene looked up. "I'm not." She smiled and then flung the contents of the vial at the snake woman, who bellowed and screamed as soon as the water hit her face.

"Bitch! What the fuck? You stupid cunt, you ruined my face. But no matter. I will be able to recover. It's only holy water." She was relentless in her attack. Her face steamed as she turned toward Irene. The whole world seemed to stop when she put her hands down to attack. Her claws were sharp, and her hair was as shiny as silk.

"You like to burn me with holy water?" she screamed at the top of her lungs. "OK, you will suffer, Irene, suffer dearly. Your sister died because she chose the path of the righteous one. Cowardice is what I call it. She was trying to trap my brother in her body to die and set his spirit free. The entity has no soul and is unbound to the world when he chooses to possess. He can't be destroyed. He was created to be the most powerful being in the world. We are all Satan's creations, but what he doesn't understand is that we all have our own minds and would like to destroy the human image. We are like our father, but we too were born of this world and know how this world can treat a person. This is why we want all humans to die and perish. It would be nice if your kind would stop hoping, living, fighting for breath. Let the breath go, and die. The hope of mankind is over."

Irene quietly interrupted, saying, "You're wrong."

The snake woman, pissed now, looked at Irene, her hellish eyes on fire, making Irene's heart stop. She felt herself falling to the floor. She took in a breath and felt a tear fall.

The snake's eyes now illuminated the room and displayed the past for Irene, and the particular event she was forced to gaze upon crushed her heart. Angela, who was now dead, comforted Irene as she fell.

"Irene," Angela said. "It's one of the children on the mountain trying to inflict as much pain as possible to cause you to die. Fight it. For Rodger's sake, do not give in. He's down right now—he's hit his head really hard. The images of the night you lost your whole world—that's the entity's way of destroying you all over again. If you emulate the great Buddha and let it go, you will be able to release this pain, and you will win. But if you put yourself in hell, you have chosen to put yourself away from God. Bring him in, and release this darkness that is killing you from the inside. Irene, live on, and give peace to your soul."

Irene's eyes were closed for a brief moment, and then they opened. She took in a deep breath and sobbed, but then her eyes met those of the snake woman. She was truly beautiful but hideously evil, evil, evil—as in Hebrew, in which the number of times sayings are repeated represents the enormity of the meaning. She looked hideous—no, she looked more monstrous than hideous. Or better yet, she looked more horrible than ugly. Her eyes were burning, on fire.

Irene got up and boldly accosted the snake woman. "Go back to the mountain, bitch!"

"Aw, you have a sense of anger, Irene, that I like. You are sassy."

"No!" Irene said. "I'm no longer going to let you use my life as your personal plaything. What happened in the past has hurt me, but now, while it is not forgotten, it has been let go. The anger is projected at the very being that is you. The person and image you were is no longer here. You were made in the image of God, then the devil. You do not belong on this earth. You are no longer needed to make the world suffer."

With pure love and devotion to her family, expanded now she knew that Rodger was hurt, Irene grabbed the snake woman's face, pressing her thumbs into the snake woman's huge eyes, causing her to scream out in pain. But the snake woman's eyes were scorching and on fire. Irene, not caring about the burns, followed through, and it was now, as she looked toward the door of the room, that she was shocked to see the door shattered into two parts. The snake woman must have gone straight through the door. She was extremely powerful and intense. Irene could feel the claws digging into her arms, and she writhed in pain.

Irene knew the snake woman would not be able to follow her if she destroyed the snake woman's eyes. She could feel the blood fall to the floor and realized the reason all this existed was the Enlightenment. Irene understood that during the historical period called the Enlightenment, everything had changed, and now, everything she knew about the world changed. The Enlightenment changed the lives of people through science and understanding—if it could be proven through science, then it was real. But here and now, Irene was defying the possibilities of the physical world. The cuts in her arms should have killed her, and Irene knew this, but she held on and refused to fall to the evil creature.

Irene suddenly felt the claws of the snake woman release and her body fall toward the floor. Wary, Irene understood the snake lady could be faking her death, because some snakes play dead when they are near death. Irene continued to push down. The snake woman's body fell limply toward Irene, who struggled to maintain her balance as both started to topple. The snake woman fell to the floor, hitting her head hard. The snake woman must have weighed a ton, because Irene was having a hard time getting out from under her—the pressure was suffocating her.

Irene pushed as hard as she could to get the snake woman off her, and finally she managed to roll away and gasp for air. Irene crawled to the hospital bed, grabbed the upper sheet, and pulled it down from the bed, tearing large strips with which to wrap the cuts on her arms. The cuts were deep, and the blood was now all over her pants and shirt.

Irene got up from the floor, feeling dizzy and still winded from the fall. She was exhausted. Irene looked toward Angela's bed and told her sister she was sorry for everything. It was not Angela's fault she'd had to die.

"It was the entity and its evil intentions of attacking our family, and it took your life to get at Rodger and me. What does Rodger's investigation have to do with Camp Devils Lake? He said a boy's body was found at the bottom of the mountain. Who was this boy? What was his name?"

Irene made her way around the snake woman as she headed toward the door. The creature was long, slender, and slimy. Her skin reminded Irene of a timberland rattler. Her eyes were gouged out, and Irene realized that her own hands were still covered in the blood and juices that had shot out of the eyes. Once she'd gotten past the fire, she knew she'd hit the vitreous, which is the liquid of the eye. It had squirted everywhere and made the burns on her hands hurt.

Irene now examined her hands and found that the wounds were gone. On the floor, the snake woman was still lying in a pool of blood, both her own and Irene's. The snake woman was wicked, unlike anything she had ever seen.

Irene had just turned to leave when she heard the whimpering of a baby coming from behind her. Whipping around, she saw a baby on the bed right next to Angela's feet. It was crying.

Hesitant at first, Irene gathered her courage and, with a last look at the crying child, turned and headed for the door. The baby wailed louder. Irene was not looking back and so was startled when the snake woman's tail rose at her feet. Irene was focused on the end of the snake when the snake woman jumped up and came at her, pissed off.

"Irene, you little bitch! I am going to kill you!" With unbounded rage, the snake woman swung a right punch to Irene's face, hitting her hard on the left jaw.

Irene gasped as the room spun before her eyes. She fell to the floor and passed out. Satisfied, the snake woman grabbed Irene's foot and began to drag her over to the staircase. Opening the staircase door, she flung Irene's body down the stairs, and Irene tumbled down and landed next to Rodger. The snake woman slammed the door shut.

"I hope you're dead, bitch!" she said with profound darkness.

CHAPTER 10

NIGHTMARES

I found out later that I'd been asleep on the staircase, but I was dreaming that I was in my bedroom. I knew I was not at home, but the nightmare started out vividly, and I'd often noticed that as I slept, I would start tossing and turning as my dreams got more and more intense. I now tossed and turned on the stairs, even hitting the senseless Irene beside me.

As the nightmare progressed, detailed indoor and outdoor images appeared. It began with me sitting in my bed and watching television. The movie playing was a soft comedic genre involving love at first sight. The woman in the film had always doubted her ability to endure the hardships life had to offer, yet her actions pushed her career and her and her partner's lives forward, and her character, built by love and devotion to her significant other, symbolized the concept of yin and yang. When one was down, the other would set the harmonic balance and stabilize the bonds they shared, ensuring life would go on.

They soon married and had a wonderful daughter. She was the most beautiful girl they'd ever set eyes on. This little girl reminded me of my own daughter, and it made my heart throb with pain. Before long, I fell into remembering how I'd lost her at a young age as a result of a criminal investigation that had gone horribly wrong. The suspect was wanted for murder, and we'd gotten a lead that he was going to be at a local flea market. We devised a plan to approach and apprehend him.

When we got to the flea market, he already knew we were coming. He had planned to kill one of the officers, but instead, he and I got into a scuffle, and he got away. I later returned home and realized that my wallet was missing. My wife and I were in the dining room discussing our financial situation when we both heard our bedroom window shatter.

I remember our daughter had been in our room, playing with her toys and singing a lullaby: "One little, two little, three little munchkins, four little, five little, six little munchkins…" The shattering glass made our hearts burst in fear. Irene and I both leaped up and ran toward our room, but before we got there, we heard her screaming as the man butchered her. The door was locked, and all I could hear was my daughter, my flesh and blood, crying for Mommy and Daddy. But by the time I'd kicked the door down, my beautiful little Reyna had been stabbed and murdered with a jagged piece of glass.

Irene and I ran into the room and went straight to our daughter, our hearts plunging as we gazed upon her lifeless body. Her eyes were dark, and I sobbed as my wife shakily closed Reyna's eyes. The sick thing about her death was that using her finger, the murderer had etched on the floor, "I wanted the heart and soul of your life!"

What followed was too much for me to endure. I searched high and low for that son of a bitch that had taken my little girl's life. The investigation ended in a standoff, guns blazing in an alley not far from where we lived. The man I'd been after was shot and killed by multiple officers. When they retrieved his body and did DNA tests, they confirmed that he was the right suspect. He'd been shot twenty-three times and killed. The scars on his hand proved without a doubt that he was the murderer of my baby girl.

The movie was too mushy for my taste, so I changed the channel, disgusted with the fact that my daughter's memory had again made my heart break with pain and agony. She'd been an innocent, and my mistake as a rookie cop had gotten her killed.

I turned the television off and fell into a deep sleep, starting to dream immediately. I found myself back in my room. The TV station was playing the same love story. I began to look at the room more carefully, trying to focus on the surroundings. The bed was very soft, and the blankets were as white as the light coming from the open bathroom door. I looked at the other bed in the room with all its stuffed animals and thought of my daughter. But then...

"Oh, shit. The dog."

The massive black dog was on the bed a couple of feet away from me. I could see it staring at me with those fiery eyes, wagging its satanic tail. It remained on the bed, just staring at me. I wondered what was keeping it from attacking and killing me. It just stared and growled, and I moved my hand slowly toward the gun I knew was wedged under the mattress. In one swift move, I went for it, and the massive dog growled even louder, startling me. I stayed in place, not moving. Then I heard a voice.

The dog was still growling in the background, but the voice, snakelike, hissed, "Ssstay, boy." The voice was soft, but it made the dog cower in fear. I tried to focus on the petite figure that now walked toward me. I sat up, leaving the gun wedged between the mattress and box spring, not taking my eyes off the petite little girl. A smell of sulfur filled the room as she walked toward me, making me gag.

The little girl wore a white dress with bloodstains on her chest. She had long, dark hair, dark as the night sky. Her eyes were focused and trained on me.

"Who is this little girl?" I thought to myself. Then it hit me as hard as nails in my gut. The little girl was an impression of my daughter. Her eyes were pitch black at first, and they looked almost as if they were swimming in tears.

Looking at me, she said, "You cannot escape."

I looked over at the massive hellhound lying on the bed, which remained unmoving, just staring. I got chills as the dog's eyes met mine; I felt I was being taken in. The girl hovered above the bed, and as her feet touched the sheet, the television flickered on and off for a few seconds and then blew up. My heart started pounding as I was left in total darkness.

She came face-to-face with me, and with her soft voice, she at first whispered into my ear, "I love you, Daddy." Then, with rage, at the top of her demonic voice, she yelled, "I will swallow your soul and make you feel as if you were cold-to-the-bone dead, rip your heart out, and eat it in front of you while you slowly die watching me."

She was standing right next to me, smiling, her eyes still focused on me. She lifted her hand and rubbed her scaly fingers across my chest. This little girl was not human at all. Her eyes were dark and eerie, and they made me quiver.

"What's the matter?" she asked. "Oh, you're scared, aren't you?"

The girl, becoming highly impatient that I wasn't answering, pushed me hard toward the wall. I flew, hitting the bed frame with my back and landing hard, face first, on the mattress. It really hurt—it felt as if I'd broken my back.

Gasping for air, I rolled over to take a deep breath, and as I did this, the girl grabbed my leg with her scaly fingers and dragged me to the floor. With a sadistic air, she towered over me and said, "Have you ever heard the story of the man that was a real badass?"

I thought of my previous dream. Trying to breathe in spite of the agonizing pain running down my spine, I said, "The man that got his soul swallowed by the baby that bears no mark."

The demonic creature, shocked and a little disgruntled by what I had just said, gave me a very quaint look.

"How do you know about the baby that bears no mark? Answer me!"

She lifted her hand and looked at it, and as she did, I focused on her fingernails. Those scaly fingers were now huge claws. Her face was no longer the image of a little girl but that of a giant serpentlike dragon. It looked at me with those firelit eyes and in a demonic male voice yelled, "Tell me, you little shit!"

I tried to answer it, but the pain in my back increased, and I was left speechless. I attempted to tell myself this was only a dream and that the pain I felt wasn't really there, but it hurt—and bad.

Then, very faintly, I heard my name.

"Rodger. Answer him, Rodger."

I looked in the direction of the voice, and there he stood—the boy whose death had caused me so much agony since we'd found the car at the bottom of the mountain at Camp Devils Lake. There he was, right next to the bathroom door, his hand on the doorknob. He wore sneakers, blue Wranglers, and a button-up shirt. His eyes were bright reddish brown, and his hair was straight. He had freckles all over his face.

I looked up, only to find the massive hellhound and the serpentlike dragon looking down at me. I opened my mouth to scream, but nothing came out. With a swift swipe of its claws, the serpentlike creature cut into my chest, causing me to scream. Blood spattered all over the walls and ceiling of the room.

"Answer me," the serpentlike creature insisted.

I opened my mouth and gasped for air. The pain was excruciating. My chest felt as if it were on fire, and I knew I had broken ribs. I choked on the blood rising in my throat. I tried without success to turn over. The massive serpent claw was coming down once again, and I screamed, "It was in my dream that I saw the baby that bears no mark!"

The serpentlike dragon grabbed my head with its claws and picked me up, with ease holding me suspended. I could see red as its claws dug into my head. It hurt like hell and burned my skull. Blood dripped from my feet as I hung there, and I could hear its slow trickle hitting the floor. The hellhound arched its shoulders into an attack position.

"Tell me more," the serpent said.

I opened my mouth, but the blood flowing from my head wounds went directly into my mouth, making it hard for me to speak. The serpentlike dragon saw this and threw me to the floor.

"Answer me!" the serpent yelled.

I again opened my mouth, choking, and I spit the words out as the blood kept streaming down my face.

"In my dream, I could see the baby that bears no mark swallowing a man's soul and sending him into the depths of hell. The dog that is right before you was also in the dream."

The serpentlike dragon looked over at the hellhound with ferocious animosity. The dog, already in position, was ready to attack. The serpentlike creature grinned and concentrated its fiery eyes on the hellhound, which burst into flames and growled with the intent to kill. The dog began to bark loudly, and with a roar, the serpentlike dragon lifted its gigantic wings. The ground trembled, and the walls of the house shook. Its long, scaly tail swayed back and forth as if it were pacing. The tip of its tail was sharp, just like its claws.

In a hellacious voice, the serpentlike dragon said, "How dare you even try to attack me?"

The serpentlike dragon's head started to grow two large horns on its forehead, and many smaller ones sprouted around the two larger ones. Its huge eyes burned red hot like molten lava. The hellhound jumped onto the serpentlike dragon creature and slashed deep, burning claw marks into its massive chest. The serpent grinned. In a perverse way, the creature liked the pain.

The hellhound started to get the upper hand, though, and as it did, the serpent headed for the bathroom door. The hellhound's relentless attack caused the serpent to fall, and taking immediate advantage, the hellhound bit hard into the serpent's neck, twisting it and trying to break it. The serpent expanded its wings to their full reach and knocked the hellhound over, giving the serpent some time to recover.

I looked toward the bathroom door, and to my surprise, the boy was still standing there. He put his finger to his lips, signaling me to be quiet. I acknowledged his gesture and remained immobile where I sat on the floor, looking on as the more-than-pissed-off dragon, weakened by the bite to the neck, got to the door. To its surprise, the boy opened it. As he did this, hell's fires shot out and surrounded the serpent dragon, rapidly healing it. The serpent then grinned again, opened its mouth, and spit fire at the hellhound's back.

Surprised, the hellhound went in for the kill. It jumped back onto the dragon, and the dragon's claws dug deeply into the hound's body so that it wasn't able to move. The serpent's tail struck it multiple times in the chest, dealing deadly blows. The serpent got stronger as the fires surrounded its body. It dug its claws deeper into the hellhound's flesh, tearing away massive chunks of lost souls. The serpent picked up the hellhound, and as it did this, the hellhound, looking in all directions, saw me lying there motionless, my eyes focused on the fight.

It locked eyes with me, the fire from its eyes swirling and dancing around for a moment and then shooting directly into my eyes, cooking me from the inside out. It hurt like crazy, and the creature that was now in what had been my bathroom looked even more ferocious and furious.

The serpent walked over to my body, picked me up, and flung me, helpless, across the room. I hit the bedroom door, which to my surprise didn't hurt at all. I looked into the eyes of the serpent. Its scaly skin was dark with red stripes leading down to the tail. The red looked like molten lava and was sweltering. This creature looked ancient.

I felt as if I were dying. My heart started to beat rapidly, and my eyes burned like crazy. I tried to get up, but the injuries I'd sustained kept my body in a vegetable state. The fire in my eyes was making me feel cold to the bone. My biggest fear in this life was dying in my sleep and never waking up.

Now, the hellhound started to take control of my body. I could see its fire all around me. This beast had taken over my body and couldn't control its anger toward the inevitable serpent.

"You will come out of his body," the serpent commanded. The hellhound's howl sounding within my head made my ears ring and hurt, and I couldn't hear a thing. Everything around me faded into blackness.

I awoke with the alarm blaring and my ears ringing. I could see the fire whirling around and around in my eyes. Looking toward the bathroom and through its open doorway, I saw a bright light. I glanced hurriedly toward my daughter's bed to see whether the dog was still lying there. Nothing.

My mind racing with paranoia, I got up and walked into the hallway, and as I did, I heard a voice. It was faint, but it made my spine tingle and the hair on my arms rise. Slowly, I turned around and saw the boy standing next to the bathroom door. Inexplicably, the boy grabbed the bathroom door and slammed it extremely hard.

I jumped, feeling a cold draft of air on my neck. The boy's eyes had a worried look, and as I turned around to see what was breathing heavily on my neck, I felt my stomach turn and my knees buckle. The serpent stood there, its fiery, molten-lava eyes fixated on mine. I backed up slowly, not taking my eyes off the magnanimousness of the serpent. The ophidian slowly swayed its tail from side to side.

My voice quivering in fear, I asked, "What do you want?"

The ophidian replied, "You are housing a demon inside of you, and I want the demon out of your body. It is hiding from me. The sad thing for you is that it's hiding behind human flesh." The serpentlike creature then smiled, showing plenty of its teeth. "No matter. I will strip you of your flesh and make the demon suffer."

The serpent's voice and the smell of sulfur permeated the room, making me weak with fear. I was going to die and never see the light of day again. My heart started to race as the serpent walked toward me, burning huge footprints into the oak floor. I began to back away, and as I did, I felt the hand of the boy touching my shoulder. His touch was cold and felt awful as my quivering body trembled under the serpent's stare. Its tail began to stab at my body with burning jabs of hot intensity.

My legs were the first to be stabbed. It hurt like hell, and my legs were rendered useless. I felt the blood dripping down my body until a pool of it surrounded both of us. The serpent did not hesitate—it just stabbed and stabbed. It wanted to see me suffer. I was dying, and it was showing no mercy, but as my breathing slowed, it backed off. Where it had stabbed me, my body burned icily, like pure, cold death. I felt my life slipping from my body. Blood was all around me. I was dead for sure, and I knew I was doomed.

CHAPTER 11

THE BOY, MONSTERS, AND THE FIELD TRIP

I awoke with the sun shining through the window into my eyes. The world seemed larger, and as came fully to my senses, I discovered that I wasn't who I thought I was. I was some kid.

I got up and walked toward the door, on which was emblazoned a name: Julian Napoleon Richter. Here I was, a cop, not only really young but possessing the knowledge of an adult.

Through the still-closed door, I could hear the muffled voice of a woman in the other room, yelling, "Get up! Get ready for school, and make sure you make your bed. Grab your backpack and duffel bag for your field trip."

I looked toward the window seat, and waiting for me there were a backpack and a duffel bag stuffed with clothes. I grabbed both and started to stuff in all the necessities for a trip, like toothpaste and all those little things for the morning. The bathroom adjoined my bedroom, and I felt good—young and full of energy—as I looked into the bathroom mirror. I put on sneakers, blue Wranglers, and a white button-up shirt.

As I looked into the mirror, I noticed my bright, reddish-brown eyes, my straight hair, and the freckles running all along my face.

"What, am I the boy?"

The woman, again sounding muffled as she left the other room, was instructing me to gather all my stuff and meet her at the car. I heard the car alarm disarm as she unlocked the door from inside the house with the keyless entry remote. The house was vibrant with color, and the walls were all high as I looked up to the level ceiling. It was a new home by the smell and look of the carpet, and the walls had bullnose corners. The drywall had a variance of color that gave the home a more fascinating look. The pictures all over the walls were of the family living here. I was surprised I didn't know the family from my work in the community.

I walked to the door and looked down at the floor mat. The Richter Family, it read, obviously customized for the family living here. As I opened the outer door, I found another floor mat. Welcome, it proclaimed.

The car was brand new, a muscle car. The trunk of the car opened magically—that remote again—and as I glanced up, I could see the lady at the window gazing out at me and smiling. I put my duffel bag in first as it was the heaviest. The backpack was next. Closing the trunk, I went to the passenger side, slipped into the front seat, and sat waiting for the woman, who I guessed was my mother, to come down to the car.

I waited for quite some time, amusing myself by peering around the neighborhood. Then I noticed a boy out in the distance causing problems. When I saw the boy, I realized that he looked like the man in my dream, the badass guy who was always up to no good. But he was much younger than I remembered.

"What the hell is going on?" I kept asking myself. I knew I was dreaming, but I could not wake myself up. I watched on as the boy in the distance grabbed an apple pie from a windowsill and started to eat it. When he'd had enough, he simply disposed of the rest of the pie. His mother came out and, finding her apple pie gone, started to cry. She called out to her son, and he came running to the house. His mother began to question him about the pie.

"Kaleo, where is the pie?" she asked.

"Mommy, I didn't eat the pie," the boy replied.

She looked at him carefully, noticing that as he lied to her, his head moved to the right.

"Kaleo!" she said with a stern voice, staring at her son as the tears rolled down her face. He was an excellent liar, but mothers always know when their children are lying. One way or another, they can always tell.

Still crying, she went over to her son and admonished him to always tell the truth and be a good boy. She asked again whether he had taken the pie, and he again denied it.

"Stop lying!" she told him.

He looked at her angrily and backed up, but I could hear his muffled response.

"You fucking bitch! Leave me alone! I told you already that I didn't eat the pie. What the fuck is wrong with you?"

He turned to run away but stopped in his tracks when he was met by a huge beast. The beast was unlike anything of this world. His mother also noticed the beast and fell down to her knees, shaking in utter fear. She immediately started praying for her son, and her heart sank, knowing her son was in serious trouble.

Her son looked up at the massive beast. It had razor-sharp claws and looked like the devil. The beast grabbed the boy by the head, picking him up with ease. The boy screamed in pain and agony as the beast dug its claws in deep. The ground underneath the boy started to turn into a fiery pit.

The boy started to scream, "Mommy, help me! Mommy, please help me!"

His mother sobbed as she prayed on, asking for forgiveness. From where I sat, I could see black hands coming from the pit underneath the boy. He screamed as the hands started dragging him down into the depths of hell. I gasped as the boy said, "I will stop lying to my mom. I promise! Just let me go!"

The beast relentlessly gripped the boy's head harder, and he started to convulse as if having a seizure. Then he passed out. His mother ran toward the beast and jumped into the pit, grabbing her son and praying as they were both being pulled into hell.

The lady held her son tightly, and the beast hesitated. Raising its other hand, it struck the mother with its claws. She flew out of the pit and landed hard on the ground. For a split second, a bright aura hovered over her. Her wounds were deep and fatal. The aura's bright-white, pure light descended upon the mother. The atmosphere turned green and healed her wounds instantly. The cuts just vanished.

Confused, the beast looked all around but did not find the source of light that had healed the mother. The beast's eyes then found me in the car. I didn't move as the smell of sulfur crept up my nose. The creature released its grip on the boy's head and started making its way toward the car I was sitting in. But the aura was swift—with no hesitation, it went into the fiery pit and seized the boy, in seconds raising him from the pit.

I looked on in amazement as the beast came toward the car. Meanwhile, the boy was being healed by the aura, which again turned green. The boy's wounds disappeared instantly, and the boy remained unconscious. It now seemed the aura was in fact a man with brown hair and bluish-green eyes. He put the boy down near his mother. They were both unconscious.

The aura moved quickly as the beast raised its muscular arms to rip apart the car. In the span of a few seconds, the aura's power came upon the beast as a flash of golden light, and the apparition of a golden sword sliced through the beast's abdomen.

The devilish creature's eyes were a dark red, and its face was extremely muscular. I watched in amazement as the creature looked down at the sword and grabbed the tip of the blade with his claws, looking shocked as he spit out what looked like bug guts onto the windshield. The sword burst from the beast's abdomen, and the devilish creature turned around with a hellacious growl and positioned his body to attack.

"You're not supposed to be here," the creature said. "Why have you come?"

The light from the aura was brighter than any light I'd ever gazed upon, and although I could not tell whether the beast had suffered a fatal blow, it sounded as if it was dying. In a fury, the beast released a series of pulverizing attacks on the aura.

"Answer me!"

The beast slashed and clawed, but with ease, the aura moved the beast away from the car. The creature began to pursue the bright force, and as the beast came upon the pit, the aura hovered not more than three feet above it. The beast was furious at the brightness of the atmosphere and the luminance of the light coming from within it. The creature continued to slash and fight, but it had no success in extinguishing the purity of the aura. The blackened, sooty hands were pulling and dragging the beast down into the pit as the aura used the golden sword to deliver another mighty blow, piercing the beast's shoulder. With a deafening roar, the animal was dragged into the fiery pit.

The aura hovered over the hole for a few seconds, and the pit sealed itself. The boy and his mother were now coming to, and when they looked at each other, the boy gave his mom a big hug and cried in her arms. His mother looked at the ground and gasped as she saw for a split second an image of a demonic creature's eye gazing at them from underneath the ground. It was red. It was a symbol of what would come in the future if the boy ever did anything wrong.

At that point, my mother came up to the car, startling me. She was disgusted with the residue of bug guts on the windshield.

"Damn bugs," she said. "They're always so hard to wash off once they dry." Turning to me, she asked, "Honey, did you get all your stuff ready for the field trip?"

"Yes," I said.

She smiled, stuck the key into the ignition, and started the car, and off we drove. On our way to the school, she hummed along with the radio, beginning to sway from side to side as she got more and more into the song.

The boy, the beast, and the aura were sinking into the depths of my mind. I tried to recall the events in the order in which they'd occurred to try to find something of meaning.

I asked myself, "What? How? Why did this happen? What was the reason for me to witness the boy's punishment as a child and the healing of the mother's wounds in midair?"

I looked out the window but had to struggle as my body was now a child's. It was much harder to be a kid, although this kid was slim but muscular. The arms seemed well developed, and I felt as if he were as fit as raging bull. He wasn't very tall for his age, but what he lacked in height, he possessed in strength.

We came up to the James K. Polk junior high and high schools. I got out of the car, grabbed my stuff for the field trip, and kissed my mother good-bye.

"I will see you in two weeks," she said. "Have fun, and please try not to get into trouble."

I nodded and started walking, but I was shocked when I entered the school grounds. In the back of my head, I could hear words repeating.

"I want your soul. You cannot escape me. I want your soul. You cannot escape me," the children all said as they were sitting in the sandbox and looking at me with those horrible eyes.

My spine tingled as I saw those god-awful sharp teeth, and the children's eyes were on fire with a tornado spiral spinning around and around. Their eyes dripped blood and grease as the fire burned into their flesh, cooking them from the inside out. The children all had dark smoke rings burned around their eyes, and as I looked at them, they eerily repeated, "I want your soul. You cannot escape me."

These heathens were not children at all but the little demon-like creatures who would swallow your soul into the depths of the dark abyss if given the opportunity. I was wary of the children, and I shakily walked by them, trying not to give them the attention all children need to survive, figuring that if I ignored them, they would leave me alone.

I started to walk around, examining my surroundings and trying to focus on the main concept of the dream. I could see a grassy field and the sandbox for the day care center, where the children sat repeating, "I want your soul. You cannot escape me."

I had made the mistake of not looking at my surroundings in the other dreams and had found myself face-to-face with a hellhound. I'd turn around, and suddenly the massive dog would jump right into my body, causing my eyes to adopt the same swirling, tornado-like fire that would start instantly cooking me from the inside out.

I could have sworn that when I awoke that morning from the dream, my eyes were burning the same bright red as the eyes of the heathens now tormenting me. I knew that I'd had dream after dream.

"Why can't I wake up?" I kept asking myself.

I walked around, looking at the structures in front of me, and noticed the massive walls of the campus. The school had been designed for a large population of students ten to eighteen years of age. I suddenly realized that I must be reliving the boy's life. But why? Why here, of all places, and why now? Was this the school field trip the boy had attended? If so, I now knew his name!

I turned around, startled by the roar of many students running in the direction of four waiting school buses. The girls talked gibberish as the boys walked by with their stupid sighs of adoration and puppy love.

"Give me a break," I thought to myself. "This is not a dream. This is hell."

I heard a loud noise behind me, and as I turned around, fear struck at my heart. "Oh, shit. The dog." Panic started to rise in my chest, and I felt flushed and red in the cheeks. "Not again!"

The fire from the dog's eyes tearing into my body would always hurt, and I'd feel as if I were losing my soul as the fire burned at my very existence from inside my body. I'd feel as if I were possessed, and I would come out of the dream manic and scared. At this point, I started to suffer an anxiety attack, my heart racing, as I tried to accept the inevitable.

But to my relief, I turned around to find not the hellhound but a large gentleman looking down at me. He called my name.

I was stunned. "What?"

"Damn it, Julian, get on the bus. We've got many miles ahead of us, and you're dillydallying like a little girl."

"What the fuck?" I thought to myself.

One of the boys came up to the man and said, "Mr. McGee, when are we leaving?"

"Right now," he bellowed.

Mr. McGee had to be the gym coach—he was huge. He again started to get on my ass for not moving fast enough.

"Damn it, boy, get on the bus!" the large, overgrown, steroidal teacher shouted.

Confused, I did as I was told and ran over to one of the buses, climbing aboard. This one girl kept staring at me. Her hair was long and dark and looked almost like oil. Nasty. I looked over at the playground where the children from the day care were playing in the sandbox and was amazed to see a large black dog devouring the children. It tore at their flesh and ate them. Blood splattered all over the sand. The animal swallowed most of them whole, and as it did this, it was evident that their souls were being eaten whole and taken into a new form of hell.

The children's faces, all bearing expressions of torment and sheer terror, made imprints on the dog's massive shoulders. I turned away to notice the girl with the black hair walking over to me down the aisle of the bus, and I realized that she had those same fiery, lit-up eyes from my early dreams. She came closer and closer. When she got to about ten feet in front of me, my heart began to pound. The little girl was my daughter.

I gasped. She looked dead, dark, and angry. She came up close to me and reached out to touch my hand with her scaly fingers.

I couldn't breathe, and my heart felt as if it were about to pop out of my chest. She looked over at me and smiled. I could see the black blood in her mouth drip down the crevices of her teeth. I felt sick and wanted to get the hell off the bus. But she passed by me and said nothing. I looked out the window again and saw that the dog had finished devouring the children. The children's chants of "I want your soul—you cannot escape me" eerily echoed throughout the massive dog's body. The children's mouths moved as the dog walked closer to the bus.

"Julian? Julian! *Julian!*" Mr. McGee repeated. Startled, I looked over at the gym teacher and noticed that he was yelling at me.

"Huh?" I asked.

He looked over and told me to start paying attention, or I would not be going to Camp Devils Lake.

"What?"

"Stop acting like a wise guy," Mr. McGee said, "and state whether you are present or not."

"Present," I shouted enthusiastically to ensure he knew I was on the bus. The other kids around me chuckled. Mr. McGee threw me a disgusted look and went on with the attendance.

I looked out the window and noticed that the dog was gone, and the school was starting to disappear behind us on the long stretch of road. We drove and drove, and when we finally arrived at the mountain, it was seven in the evening. My class went to our assigned quarters, where we unpacked our clothes and put them in the drawers. I dropped my lanyard and went to pick it up, but as I bent down, I locked eyes with the same little girl that had been on my bus. She was staring at me; her eyes were trained on mine and were very dark. It made my backbone feel frozen.

She came over to me, touched my lips with her scaly, Komodo dragon–like fingers, and then walked away slowly. I could see the blood on her dress and was in utter shock. My heart was again ripped to pieces at the thought of not having been able to help my daughter as she screamed for me and her murderer took her life.

This was not a dream but an attack on the inner depths of my soul, and the entity and the devil-like creature were doing it in such a way that I wanted to shut down and just die. I kept reminding myself of this, and it drove me to want to figure out who Julian was and what strange, powerful, evil forces we were tampering with here at Camp Devils Lake.

I looked around and noticed that the quarters were right next to each other, and I could see those of the high school students perfectly.

"There are many more middle school students than high school students," I thought to myself. The younger students would be sharing quarters while the older students would get their own quarters. The teachers were taking lists of names of students who were in each set of bunk beds. The future crime scene I had just investigated looked eerily normal at this point, and it was interesting to see the students and teachers on the trip interacting. The kids joked and laughed about the new social media and the fact that when they got closer to the mountain, some were not able to use their cell phones depending on which service provider they had—they worked up to a certain point, but then the service dropped. One boy was complaining about how he'd had service at the bottom and the middle of the mountain but that up here, everyone had to use the landlines. The drama queen of the group was a girl who complained her life sucked without her mobile device.

I chuckled and started to make my way to the cafeteria, where we met up with the camp director. "Mr. Satan himself—in the flesh!" he joked. I rolled my eyes and walked away, trying not to pay attention to the camp director. The night sky was dark, but with all the stars lighting up the mountain, it did not seem so dark. It had taken about a half hour for me to unpack. Once I had finished, I decided to go down to the lake with some of the other kids, and as walked out of the quarters, my ears were instantly hit with the sounds of the forest.

I could hear the breeze hit the trees and the sounds of tree branches cracking in the distance from the creatures of the night. I even heard the cawing of crows, the howling of wolves, and the autumn leaves brushing the ground. The air was cold and crisp, and it felt good to be outside as I walked with my peers to the lake. We could already see a large campfire blazing in the distance. It was incredible—the flames were high off the ground.

I became startled as I heard the screams of a man in the distance. I looked in the direction the screams were coming from and realized it was the camp director. I could see the real image of the entity ripping at the camp director's soul. The entity was ruthless in its attack, showing its true power with no signs of mercy. It was striking fear into the hearts of both the children and the adults at the camp. They were horrified and shocked. The camp director was possessed and was now suffering terribly. But how did this happen, and why was this happening? Ideas and thoughts about God swirled through my head. If he were here right now, would he put a stop to the torment and suffering? I started to think that God did not care about good or evil—maybe he was indifferent, just standing by and watching, letting the course of life determine a man's future.

The camp director fell twice, got up again, and then said in a loud, eerie voice, "He comes to feast upon all your souls!" With that, the man died, falling to the floor as the entity devoured his soul, and I thought God was a God of presence, or rather existence. The entity was using the man as a smoke screen to strike fear into the people here, an illusion to change the perception and mood of the camp. Wasn't this how the government controlled people who were going to lash out in public? We as police officers also put up smoke screens, utilizing the media to enhance the sense of a lack of control in the environment, using such things as the mosquito scare and the West Nile virus to calm the public and keep people at home whenever widespread panic or anger rose. Similarly, the entity wanted these people to stay here at Camp Devils Lake, stating loud and clear, "I will be who I wish to be in this world, and neither God nor the devil, neither good nor evil, will stop me."

The camp director had fought until his last breath. He had holes and gash marks on his face from which blood spewed everywhere. At the end, the poor camp director lay in a pool of his own blood. The students gathered around, everyone in shock as we stared at his limp body, twisted and mangled. He didn't move—he just lay there motionless. It took a lot of force to mutilate a body that way.

As we stood there terrified, I covertly inspected the camp director as thoroughly as I could. What most sparked my interest was that his eyes burned a fire-like red. They were wide open and ideally positioned for the entity to see everyone. The entity had planted the smoke screen with the camp director but corrected it through an eerie scene with the burning eyes. It caught the attention of every man, woman, and child present.

What did the entity want? Why was it taking the time to show me what had happened here at Camp Devils Lake? Time always showed the actual course of action. I would have to wait to find out.

CHAPTER 12

THE PATH YOU CHOOSE

Standing there before the remains of the camp director, I was suddenly startled by an overwhelming sensation of the boy's presence in my mind.

"Rodger!" I kept hearing over and over again. It was Julian, trying to speak to me.

Inside my head, I responded, "OK, what do you want Julian?"

The answer came back, "Rodger, you need to go to the radio tower and investigate the scene of the crime."

"Oh, why did I ask?" I muttered sarcastically.

"Rodger, it's important that you look into the camp director's past. He believed in the occult, but I don't know what he was trying to do here at the camp."

In my thoughts, I asked, "How do you know?"

He said, "The entity was already dead, but it's drawing its power from the mountain. It's bringing back the lost children of the mountain. It wants the earth for itself. Rodger, it keeps saying that Urantia is its to control!"

"What is Urantia?" I asked. I'd never heard that name before.

In my mind, Julian shrugged his shoulders and said, "It's another name for earth."

It hurt like crazy to hear Julian speak. It was almost as if I had a loudspeaker in my head.

"Rodger, I am three frequencies above your current level of living. It is going to be louder up here."

"OK, Julian. I will investigate the cause of the camp director's death. What else do I need to know about the entity?"

"It cannot and will not die or stop its reign of terror!"

My heart sank as I tried to swallow that piece of bad news.

"So what now? How do I get rid of the entity?"

"Rodger! You cannot get rid of the entity altogether, but you can keep it on the mountain. The problem is that the entity has already started to spread fear to the people. Its presence in the hospital, its killing of the priest and the mayor, was broadcast on live television. Rodger, all it takes is for the fear to corrupt the public, and the entity will reign supreme in the countless lives it will take. It extracted mine, but I was not afraid. It did it while possessing the man in the car. It manipulated the man and made him kill me. That was its way of bringing its presence into the public eye.

"The driver stopped the car at the bottom of the mountain and turned his body around to find me hiding in the backseat. His eyes were on fire, and as I looked into them, the swirling of the fire made my body feel I was being hypnotized and possessed. I felt no pain when the fire jolted from his eyes into mine. I could see the entity's black demonic face as I was killed, sense its sinister laugh and haunting darkness as it tried to devour my soul. I plummeted into the depths of darkness, falling deeper and deeper until I came upon the forest. I had fallen onto a roadway in the woods. I could see fire in the distance, but it was extremely far from where I was—and the air smelled awful, Rodger. It was hard to breathe. It stunk like a science experiment we did in class. The smell of sulfur.

"I could see a river of blood, and its smell and toxicity were deadly. The people thrown into the river would scream out as if acid was disintegrating their bodies. Their flesh dissolved in the lake, and my mind couldn't handle their agonizing cries of pain. I looked away onto the forest floor, which was coated in *mala mujer* plants—that means 'bad woman' in English—which are beautiful yet deadly. We learned about these plants in school because they are indigenous to the mountain at Camp Devils Lake. The milky-white fluid dripped from its thorns as I walked through the forest, which was made up of huge, dark trees, and I could see eyes hovering above me in the distance, watching my every move—huge yellow eyes, watching and never blinking. I could hear the sinister hoot of the entity, and at first, it made me jump. Rodger, I could feel the presence of the shadow people, and their intentions were deathly. I looked down at my feet and noticed they were all bone. I started to panic, but I felt no pain.

"The entity's sinister laugh made my bones feel cold. The road on which I traveled was covered with intertwining mala mujer plants. Millions of them. I had been walking on them and hadn't even realized that the plant's milk had dissolved the flesh from my bones. I suddenly felt pain shoot up my legs—but how, and why? I hadn't felt the pain before, so why now?

"I could hear the entity as it lurked in the darkness, watching me and following in the distance. I came to a fork in the road, marked with two signs. One was written in a foreign language I didn't understand. The other sign said, 'This road leads to...'—and then the other sign turned into a language that I *could* understand: 'The path you choose will...'

"'Where? Which road should I take?' I screamed out to God. 'Which way?' I noticed that the darkness, the trees, and the eyes hovering over me cringed at the word. I repeated it slyly: 'God!' The entity bellowed a hellacious growl of distaste but stayed where it was. It was keeping its distance, but why? I looked at the signs and thought, 'What am I to do? Which route do I take?'

"I looked down at my feet and realized they were badly burned and black as charcoal. And then I knew—I was dead! Rodger, it took my life and burned my body. Its intention was to kill everyone on the field trip, cause fear in the community, and raise public concern about the mountain's evil powers. Rodger, imagine and envision my experience.

"I decided to take the route with the mala mujer plants jabbing at my very soul and existence. The thorns and the milk from the plants landed on my skin and burned right through it as I transected the thickest part of the forest. The other road had been smooth and clear of any danger, but rather than turning back, I continued to travel the road I was already on. It was the road with the most difficulty.

"I could hear the entity laugh as I struggled through the black, deadly forest. The mala mujer plants were as sharp as barbed wire as they jabbed and stuck to the bones of my feet. As I walked, I was made to endure the pain of seeing all my friends and teachers being tortured in the trees as the demonic creatures indulged themselves, shredding the flesh from their soulless bodies, and the screams of all my friends tore at the inner depths of my soul. I felt no physical pain, no fear, but the emotional pain was severe.

"As I got to the end of the forest, I was met by a woman, but this woman was not like you or me. She was naked and hideously dark, and she looked at me with enormous black, alien-looking, demonic eyes. In an instant, an intense feeling of fear came to my mind. I thought of the other road.

"'What if...' raced through my thoughts.

"The woman spoke to me softly. 'Where is it?' she asked.

"I looked at her, feeling sensitive to her needs. 'What is it you're missing?' I asked her.

"In a sharp reply, she screamed, 'Where is the fucking door?'

"I looked all around that end of the forest. I couldn't see a door, but the brightest light was coming from down below, at the end of the massive wall of trees.

"I pointed and said, 'The light.'

"The woman screamed in anger, 'Where is the fucking door?' She walked around at the end of the forest and frantically continued to search.

"'Ma'am, there is no door here.'

"She turned around with fire in her eyes and laughed demonically.

"'Julian, I know who you are, little boy. Come to Mala Mujer and show me the door.'

"I walked up to her and felt the hairs on my back rise at the sight of those dangerous thorns leaking their milk onto her body. She must have been in agonizing pain, for the thorns were stabbing deeply, and as she moved, the demonic flesh was ripping, and the milk from the mala mujer plants leaked down her body onto the ground, turning a deep acidic red as it fell and formed a giant puddle. I tried to keep my distance from it. The pool seemed to seep down below the mala mujer plants, which were the cause of the vast river of blood.

"'Is this hell?' I asked.

"Mala Mujer replied, 'Yes. You have been brought to hell by my brother. Now show me the fucking door!'

"I looked at the massive wall of black trees and made a suggestion. Pointing to the highest point of the trees, I said, 'I think it's there.'

"Mala Mujer pushed me hard to the floor and said, 'Wait here, you little shit.'

"I fell hard onto the mala mujer plants. I tried to get up, but their thorns sank deep into my skin and face. It didn't hurt, but they again tore at my flesh.

"The sadistic laughing of the entity continued as I pulled my body up and ripped the thorns off my face, my clothes, and the side of my body on which I'd landed. I could see my blackened bones, the result of being burned alive. I knew I was no longer living. Mala Mujer was looking high into the trees as I picked myself up off the ground. My bones were black and juicy looking. Mala Mujer suddenly grew forty feet tall, her eyes at treetop level. As loudly as she could, she screamed, 'You lying little shit! Who the hell do you think you are?'

"I took several steps back, amazed by the enormous-looking woman. Her eyes were on fire, and as she moved, the milk from the plants dripped from her body onto the ground, the blood now dissolving the mala mujer plants as it seeped into the ground. I looked down again and could see the light coming through an opening in the trees. I made a run for it and jumped into the light. But the mala mujer grabbed hold and wrapped itself around my foot, and that's when I heard it. The entity in the darkness roared as it saw me jump into the light. It said triumphantly, 'That's it! The door. We are free to walk the earth!'

"The mala mujer plant was still holding on to my foot. Controlled by Mala Mujer, it grew at a rapid rate, pulling me up high into the sky. Her body was enormous, but her features were still the same. I noticed that when I'd jumped into the light, my skin and arms were all back to normal.

"'You little shit!' she yelled.

"Gripping my body with her hand, she swiftly stripped the flesh from my bones and held up my birthday suit in the distance, laughing sadistically. The entity excitedly joined in on the fun. Its face was dark and cold—it made me feel dead. Its claws were razor sharp, and the atmosphere turned cold. Even though I was already dead, the unbearable coldness of death rattled my burned bones.

"My eyes were still attached to my head, and I could see the ancient eyes of the demonic-looking entity. It had horns, claws, a tail, and a hideous face with deep, burning red eyes. It scared me, but then I remembered I was already dead. It could torture me, but I would feel no physical pain—just emotional pain.

"The entity, though, is very crafty, because it already knew this and started to attack me. Its first ploy was to torture one of my friends in front of me. It grabbed a boy from my class named Donald and began beating him with a baseball bat right in front of me. The entity is no ordinary being. It is ancient and knows all the ins and outs of torture. I started to cry inside. I felt bad for Donald. The entity laughed as Mala Mujer stuck the milk of the plant into Donald's mouth. He screamed as it burned going down, and then his body went limp and he died.

"'Again, again!' the entity said. Donald awoke and started crying. Mala Mujer looked at him and said, 'Do you want to know how I got my name, little boy?' Donald couldn't move—the entity had wrapped him in the mala mujer plant.

"'Let me go!' Donald pleaded.

"'Oh, I will, but first let me tell you the story of Mala Mujer. It was dark and stormy the night I died. I was deep in the mountain of Devils Lake, where my parents were ordered to have all the children come before Lucifer. I was a beautiful girl. My mother took it upon herself to try to end my life before I could stand before Lucifer. My mom was a beautiful woman and loved me dearly, but she couldn't bear losing me to the darkness of Lucifer's lair. When I got home that day, she had the mala mujer plant. She pulled the plant apart and wrapped it around my head. The milk from the mala mujer's flower dripped onto my beautiful face and caused me horrible pain. I was in shock and asked my mother what she had done. She said, "When you look upon Lucifer, he will cast you out as being hideous." But what she didn't know was—she was wrong.

"'Lucifer took me in and gave me a purpose in this life. I was to kill my parents for their wrongdoing, and I did it by pushing them both into the mala mujer plants in the backyard. I was chewed up and spit out by Lucifer to do his bidding, but now I am tired of doing his bidding and want to follow my brother's lead. He is the main reason for our surviving and having fun down here.'

"I couldn't do anything but watch. The entity was now laughing hysterically and pointing at Donald's body, now completely entangled in the mala mujer. The milk was dripping onto his body and causing him to scream out in pain. But Mala Mujer had not finished. She searched his innermost fears and caused a swarm of spiders to attack him.

"'Donald,' I said. Donald was screaming so loudly he couldn't hear me. I tried again. 'Donald!' I yelled, and the entity put his claws up. I realized that I was talking, but nothing was coming out. I had no skin or vocal cords. The entity continued to laugh hysterically. I looked down at the ground and said to myself, 'Here goes nothing.' I tried to maneuver my bones upward to escape the clutches of the mala mujer. But I just dangled there motionless. I had no limbs to help me move. It was a sick game of fear and emotional punishment, and I was going to have to watch. I could see Donald's body go limp, and I knew his death was imminent.

"The entity was disgusted with Mala Mujer. 'You killed the boy!' it said.

"'Yes, but his soul will be lost for all eternity,' Mala Mujer ranted. They both started to laugh and then turned toward me. I couldn't move. My eyes were the only things I *could* move. 'What's next?' I thought. The entity's powers were growing stronger. The air was colder now and was rattling my bones, and both Mala Mujer and the entity taunted me, moving their bodies as if they were me. The entity, hovering, looked me in the eyes and then laughed as I turned mine away. Its smile, with its razor-sharp teeth and inky black fluid between them, was satanic.

"'You can see and hear because I want you to,' it said. 'You are dead and in hell. You have shown me the way into your world. I will thank you now, Julian, but be prepared, because like little Donald over there, you are going to die in a manner ten times worse.'

"I kept trying to take everything in and understand my current situation. 'How do I escape?' I thought. 'How?'

"The entity and Mala Mujer were both contemplating how to kill me. While my body dangled, I couldn't do anything but watch. I envisioned myself with my skin and limbs, thinking it might help me move.

"'How do you want to kill the boy to make sure his soul is forever tormented in nothingness?' the entity asked.

"I extended all my six senses, seeking sensations. I looked all around and then at my body and realized I had skin. 'How?' I asked myself. 'If I can envision my skin and limbs back on my body, I must be able to envision other items and have them appear.' I started to think of holding a long samurai sword in my hand, intending to use its sharp blade to cut off the mala mujer plant that was still holding my leg, its grip seeming to get tighter and tighter.

"The sword came slowly at first, but then it appeared fully formed in my hands. It was long and white and had a super-sharp blade, and I chopped at the mala mujer plant. It loosened, and I started to fall fast, hitting the ground with a hard thud, the barbs of the poisonous plant still digging deeply into my skin. It didn't hurt, but it was extremely hard to get up—they ripped off my skin. But I just envisioned my skin whole again, and presto—new skin.

"I got up and made a run for the light, jumping into it and reaching a brighter light at the end of the tunnel. It was so bright that for a solid thirty seconds, I could not see anything. I could hear Mala Mujer and the entity questioning where I had gone. 'Where is the little bag of bones?' Mala Mujer asked. I started to fear their wrath and jumped when they started coming after me. I knew they would follow me, but I vowed never to go back to where the dark forest of hell, the Mala Mujer, and the entity had killed all of my friends. They now only live on through my memories, Rodger.

"As I reached the end of the tunnel, I envisioned myself on a cloud to carry me high into the sky. I was flying high above Camp Devils Lake. I could see you and Angela fighting your way into the radio tower. The snakes and the clouds in the sky were a deep, dark purple. Rodger, you didn't notice the murkiness of the atmosphere when you got to the mountain because you were too busy worrying about why Angela was with you. The clouds were a deep, dark purple, Rodger. I let the beast out onto the earth.

"The entity and Mala Mujer both started calling their brothers and sisters to come upon the earth. 'We are home!' they all screamed. I could hear them all chanting as they began to scatter across Camp Devils Lake.

"Rodger, you've been living my life in the past, but right now, Rodger, you need to wake up! Rodger, wake up! The entity is taking your wife to the mountain!"

The boy started to shake my body, screaming, "Wake up! Wake up! Wake up!" I could feel his cold, dead hands on my shoulders, and instantly I felt the cold, hard concrete of the staircase. My nose burned as I took in the smell of sulfur, and I screamed out in pain as I tried to move. The entity was stomping on my back, and my head and face hit the floor really hard as it pushed me back down. Its dark, red eyes bored into mine as it picked up Irene.

"No!" I screamed out. "Leave her here. Take me instead."

The entity laughed cynically and said, "That would be too easy, Rodger. I want to see you suffer."

The dim light in the staircase enhanced the glow of the entity's eyes and instantly terrified me. I focused on trying to see Irene, but the darkness had devoured her body. I could no longer see her.

The entity looked at me and said, "Meet me at the mountain. You will like what we have done to the city. It needed a new look. When you get back some of your strength, you can try to save your wife. Oh, and Rodger, listen carefully."

"Daddy! Help Mommy. Help her, Father." The son of a bitch was using my daughter's voice to taunt me.

"Fuck you!" I said as I tried to get up.

"Rodger, you're weak and need to save energy."

Its eyes burned brighter and brighter. I could see Irene and its black demonic body carved and cut. It had the mala mujer plant all over itself. I gathered my strength and pushed myself to my knees.

"Good, Rodger," the entity said. "Now help your friends and the people of the hospital. You'll find they are already under my control."

The entity had torn a hole in space, into which it now jumped, carrying Irene, and I was left alone in the dark coldness of the hospital staircase. I tried to gather enough energy to move, but my body and head hurt so much that it was impossible at the moment. I just fell face first onto the cold concrete of the staircase. As I lost consciousness, my mind desperately cried out, "Irene!"

CHAPTER 13

BAD LUCK

My body felt like a rock sinking to the bottom of a pool. Gravity was now my enemy. I'd just fallen down a flight of stairs and dreamed about the boy and the camp at Devils Lake, his journey into hell, and his experience with Mala Mujer and the entity. I tried pushing my body up again, using all my might to turn and sit on my butt.

As I thought of the boy and the camp director, the idea of going back to Camp Devils Lake made me cringe. I stopped and thought about the dream I'd just had. I realized the aura had healed the mother by turning green. As an experiment, I envisioned a green bubble around my body to try to heal it. Just then, Julian's face came out of the wall and scared the hell out of me, so much so that I lost my concentration. The boy encouraged me.

"Envision the green color around your body, but have faith. It will heal you. I can see the green aura around your body. Rodger, where is Irene?" Julian asked.

My heartbeat was starting to come back to normal. "The entity has taken her to the mountain."

"I fear she is in grave danger, Rodger. You will need to go to Camp Devils Lake to save her, but first you will need to have faith and heal yourself. Believe in the power, have faith, and your body will heal."

I thought to myself, "Get real, kid. This is the real world, and life sucks."

"Rodger, stop thinking to yourself."

I looked at Julian questioningly. He could hear my thoughts as I was thinking them. Julian started to explain the power of the green aura and the reason to have faith. There I was, in the dark and talking to a dead kid. Had I gone insane?

"Rodger, I can still hear you. Do you want to save Irene?"

So I started thinking about healing my body. It was extremely hard to believe in the power of the green light.

Julian kept saying, "You lost it." He came face-to-face with me and told me it was important that I heal my body. He guided me as I began trying to focus on the power.

"Relax your mind, and close your eyes, Rodger. Gather your strength, and believe in the power you are summoning from beyond your comprehension."

It was like meditating, but a stronger connection linked me to the spiritual connection of the afterlife. I felt the power of faith and the belief in God release all my pain. It felt good to let go of everything. Thoughts of my daughter's killer and the pain caused by her death lifted, making my heart feel lighter.

Julian was surprised. He told me that all the colors were surrounding my body, healing my soul, my mind, and my body right to the inner core of my existence. I felt the third eye and opened my eyes. I was hovering above the ground.

In fear, I looked at Julian. He was in shock, trying to understand what had just happened.

"Rodger, you found your faith and the actual power of the belief you have in your spiritual awareness. It's enhancing the feeling of how you are going to heal your body, the single purpose of finding your faith in God and gaining the strength of a single mustard seed to move mountains in your way.

"Rodger, you are healed. Rodger! How do you feel?" Julian asked.

I told him I felt great. The world no longer seemed normal to me. I felt I was on a whole other level of spirituality. The feeling was intense.

"Julian?" I asked. "How is all of this possible?"

"You had faith and chose to believe in your version of God. I think that is the reason you were able to heal your wounds along with most of the dark inner feelings of grief and hatred about your daughter's killer and her death. Believe in what you have gained access to, and you will find a way to defeat the entity's power. Rodger, you are ready to go rescue your wife and save your family."

The whole hospital was still in total darkness, but with the energy flowing through my body and my newfound strength, I knew I was ready to investigate the cause of the camp director's death and ask Julian a whole bunch of questions about his own death. The boy had come to me. He wanted me to help him and let his soul rest as I finished my investigation. I would help him. I would rescue Irene. I would not be defeated.

I landed on my feet and realized that my body didn't hurt as it had before. It felt new and revitalized. Physically, I felt much stronger, but I was also more mentally focused. I looked around and noticed that Julian had disappeared. He must have exhausted his energy and been forced to reenergize on the other side. The room I was in was frigid, and I could smell sulfur in the air. It made me gag. I felt as if I were in hell, but I knew it wasn't because of what Julian had told me about his experience.

I made my way up the stairs and came to the door through which I had fallen. How had Irene gotten down there with me? She was supposed to have stayed in the room with Angela. What had happened?

I opened the door and let my eyes adjust to the darkness. As I walked into the main lobby, I felt a crunching underneath my feet. It felt awful. I fumbled around the hall and came to the circulation desk. I walked around its perimeter and found an opening in its center. The room was cold, and the floor was alive and moving beneath my feet. I looked in the desk for an emergency supply kit, opening all the drawers before finding a large flashlight.

I turned it on and positioned the beam downward. I could see tarantulas, Brazilian wandering spiders, and centipedes crawling all over the floor and walls. Repulsed, I started stomping my feet to get the centipedes and spiders off my pant legs.

"Rodger, pull yourself together," I told myself. I pointed the flashlight toward the hospital exit and could see the glass doors. The hospital's power was completely down.

I continued to stomp my feet as I focused back on the circulation desk and spotted a fire extinguisher. A bright idea came to me, a way to slow down the spiders and centipedes. I walked over to the fire extinguisher and pulled the pin. Pointing the hose down toward the floor, I started to spray, sweeping the foam everywhere.

As I made my way toward the glass doors, the crunching of the spiders under my feet felt gross. I could see all the men, women, and children lying dead on the floor, the spiders and centipedes crawling all over their bodies, in and out of their mouths. I saw one of the centipedes wriggle out of a woman's ear.

I gulped as I finally made it to the glass door. I pulled at it and found it locked. "Damn!" I said. Casting about for something to break the window with, I realized I still had my gun. Grabbing it quickly, I put two bullets into the glass. The windows were thick, and the bullets didn't penetrate all the way through, so I took the fire extinguisher and pounded the glass as hard as I could. Finally, the window shattered.

As I leaped through the broken doors, I felt cool, moist air hit my face. I looked up into the sky and saw that the clouds were a dark purple color.

"The end of the world," I thought sarcastically.

I could see a ton of cars stalled all around the hospital. What had happened? I thought about Irene. Where had the son of a bitch taken her? I walked around the parking lot, looking at all the bodies and finding no one alive. They had all been killed by the mala mujer plants. I gasped at the sight of even the children wrapped in the barbs. My heart fell deep into the depths of my soul, searching for some hope.

Gathering my strength, I looked toward the mountain.

"Here we go, you son of a bitch!" I yelled out loud. "It's time I put you and your brothers and sisters in your fucking place. You are going back to hell—the same hell you were cooked up in."

Back to the final abomination in the world of the entity and the control it had over its brothers and sisters, back to the influence of the only one powerful enough to ensure its home on earth and unstoppable reign of terror—the entity of Camp Devils Lake. Its evilness. Its lake. Its supremacy over the people of earth. But in my dream, the devil had attacked his creation, and the entity had hid itself in my body.

"Do not let the entity taunt you into going head-to-head with it, for the entity will crush you," I told myself. The entity was not to be respected or feared, but the power it possessed must command respect and fear, because we were at its mercy—except when we cloaked ourselves in the power of our belief in a supreme being that helps every living thing on this earth. The entity as well, questionably good or evil.

The all-forgiving and all-knowing is known by many names and ideals to ensure the well-being of the spirit and the afterlife. One predominant religion is gathering into consideration the whole world's beliefs and ancestry. The religion will help in addressing all the world's problems in government, law, preference, and war with one great cause—the evolution of society and the gathering of nations, together addressing issues as a whole, setting aside differences and looking toward the future.

What does the entity want with the earth? The entity has time to ensure its supremacy, but time diminishes the effectiveness of any one rule. The history of man is riddled with the state of religion and kings and their demise from military and power, but time has always caused the death and evolution of some other people's idea of a perfect society. The entity was once a living being who became corrupted by the overwhelming power of the devil himself.

"Irene, I am coming," I thought. "The entity will probably kill me, but I will succeed in finding a way to trap it on the mountain."

The keys to the car were in my hand now, and I was looking toward Camp Devils Lake. I knew what I had to do. I had to save my one true love, Irene, and die to save myself from the darkness swallowing my soul. I had to accept my daughter's death and face her killer to forgive and forget my problems. I had to be at peace with my spirituality and past.

Without waiting another moment, I put the key in the ignition and started the car. The engine turned over as the radio blasted, "He comes to feast upon your soul!" It was the entity's dark, demonic voice. I pushed the power button on the radio immediately to turn it off, but to my amazement, the radio continued to play.

"Today on *Entity Talks*, we are going to address the world's terrorists," it said.

"Oh, my," I said slowly. "What is he doing now?"

I drove up to the police station and noticed that everyone walking around the building had the mark of the entity—their eyes were all burning a fire-like red. I parked the car at the end of the street. The whole dynamic of the street was a one-way road going north toward the mountain.

The people in the city were all walking around, screaming and crying out for help. The children across the street were playing in the sandbox with the demonic children.

"Look at my teeth," the children kept repeating.

"Rodger, are you dreaming again?" I asked myself. But I knew this was not a dream. The people at the hospital were all deceased, all dead. The earth had changed—it now reflected the image of hell. The entity was now in total control. Its presence and image were known to everyone on earth, but the roots of its power were on the mountain at Devils Lake. The homeless all ran from the deathly hellhounds that were slashing and biting into their flesh. The homeless had always been a problem in the world, but they never bothered anyone and just moved on when told to move along. The chaos was all around me, attacking me from all angles.

I made my way to the station and walked through the wooden doors labeled POLICE.

"Rodger! Come into my office—now!"

I looked toward the room I'd been summoned to and realized it was the chief's office. I rolled my eyes and walked in, and my heart skipped a beat as I saw the monstrosity staring at me from behind the desk. It was the entity!

It was in a business suit and sat looking at me with its evil eyes.

"Rodger, come in and have a seat. We need to discuss business," it said. "Rodger, please do not be rude. I am growing impatient. Rodger!" the entity screamed. "Sit down!"

I walked over to the couch and stood there, not looking at the entity but gazing at the framed pictures on the wall. The entity, royally pissed off, gripped its fist tightly and shattered the glass inside the frames.

"Look at me, you little shit! Or do you want Irene to die?"

I turned slowly toward the entity and asked, "What did you do with the camp director?"

The entity looked confused as it glared at me with deep hatred. It said, "I killed him. He was a real shell on the outside but a sadistic criminal in the inside. He was as evil as I am. You're good at your job, Rodger, but when a man is crying out for hell on earth, he has been granted it through me. The camp director was a monstrosity to humanity. He was good at his job as well. He was a murderer. He believed in the same darkness the politician did and gained his powers from the devil. Ah! Rodger, you have been talking to the boy. He must have told you by now. Rodger! Did he tell you?"

"What do you mean?" I asked.

The entity smiled darkly. I could see its sharp, jagged teeth.

"You have not had time to uncover the truth about yourself. I will allow you to do your job, but Rodger, when you figure it out, please understand that I have done you a favor—I wanted the heart and soul of your life! Remember," the entity stated. "Remember, Rodger, what you had to endure. The son of a bitch took your little girl. You became enraged with anger and anticipation, and you jeopardized your career as an officer. The investigation was set up. Your friends at the police station told you the investigation ended in a standoff between the police and the man in question. Sound familiar, Rodger? I hate to break it to you, but you were deceived. Tricked by a good friend. He said they shot and killed the son of a bitch, but when they retrieved his body, they did not do DNA tests to confirm he was the suspect. The scars on his hand had already been there, but it was a good cover-up to make you think the confirmation of the man being the suspect in question and the murderer of your beautiful baby girl, Reyna, was legitimate."

The entity was good. It was using my style of thinking and my daughter's memory to affect me, and its words made my heart sob with pain and agony. Tears welled in my eyes as I gathered in all the information the entity was feeding me. They overflowed as it continued. It was no longer in a business suit—it now appeared to me as my daughter.

My knees started to weaken. It was so hard to look at her blank, dead eyes and her white dress stained with blood. The entity, enjoying my pain, continued. It was in total control. The smell of the room turned to sulfur and reeked like ash.

"Daddy, why? Why didn't you help me? You were my hero. My knight in shining armor. You were supposed to save me, Daddy!"

I reached my hand out to calm her, but the entity reappeared at that moment, shouting, "Enough!" and laughing sadistically. I snapped out of it. I felt the demonic power and made my way toward the door. The entity lifted two fingers and shut the door easily.

"Rodger, we are not finished. You leave when I let you."

I turned back toward the entity. "Listen, you son of a bitch--"

"I'm listening, Daddy." The entity had transformed into Reyna again and was sitting there, smiling at me. I could not believe my eyes. It was toying with me, tearing me apart from the inside.

"You are going to be defeated. I will find a way to defeat you!" I said.

Smiling, the entity said, "You can try, Rodger, but I will have fun until you figure out a way to defeat me. Keep searching!" It smiled indulgently and changed into my daughter again. It was using her body, which made me feel I was losing my sense of reality.

"Rodger, listen." The entity had transformed itself back into the monstrosity in the business suit. "I want you to finish your investigation. I will let you live long enough to see you pull the trigger. I mean, blow your own head off. Still, you will need to figure out who the camp director is and where he was living while conjuring up a spell to release me. You will also need to investigate the boy's death.

"Rodger, I searched your whole mind just now and fully understand how you work. Here is an opportunity to leave here alive. Please take my offer. Investigate and do your job the way you were trained to. Look at every detail, every aspect as you use your skills as an officer. It will ultimately help you uncover the cold, hard truth. When the time comes, you will kill yourself, as I said, by pulling the trigger. But please understand, Rodger, that I do everything for a reason. You and your wife, Irene, were given the opportunity to live your lives with Reyna, and you refused my offer, telling me to go to hell. I laughed because when you refused, I was already bringing hell to earth, and there is nothing you or anyone else can do to stop me, or my wrath, or my brothers and sisters. Rodger, the next time we meet, you will not live to see another day. I guarantee it. You will die internally but slowly."

Its wicked tongue sliced the air and twanged my ears as it spoke.

"Rodger, you have no power here, but how were you able to heal your wounds? This is a surprise to me. How were you able to heal the wounds you got when you fell down the stairs? You were seriously hurt. Rodger, answer me!" the entity yelled. "How did you do it?"

I looked into its eyes with pure hatred and said, "I healed myself using the powers of the spiritual world and gained access to newfound strength. If I were you, I would fear me now more than ever."

Disgusted, the entity spit a venomous fluid from its mouth onto the floor. "Well, Rodger, I will see how you fare against my brothers and sisters. You will find them highly dangerous to your life. You will also not be able to escape their powers. I do hope your newfound power will help you."

Moving quickly, I opened the cabinet near the door and pulled out a shotgun, pointing it toward the entity's body and releasing two rounds into its chest. The entity laughed sadistically and a second later had turned into my daughter and was again talking to me in Reyna's voice.

"Daddy, why did you shoot me? You hurt me. Why is it getting dark in here?"

The entity reappeared. It looked at its demonic hand and made its claws super sharp. Pushing back the desk aggressively toward the wall, it came face-to-face with me. I could smell the sulfur radiating from its demonic body as it picked me up with one hand. I pushed the shotgun into its chest again and pulled the trigger. It smiled and said, "You're out."

I tried again and realized I *was* out. So I punched him hard in the face. It licked the blood with its long reptilian tongue as it dripped off its cheek.

"Rodger. Good. Use the aggression and anger toward me. I am not the one you should be mad at, but let me show you out of my office."

It opened the door and walked with me, holding me up easily with its hand. I was powerless. As we walked out, we were greeted by its demonic brothers and sisters. They were all very dark and extremely powerful. Their smell was horrible and made me gag. The entity slammed me hard onto the floor and then proceeded to talk. I felt weak and helpless. I could not move because gravity was pushing down so hard on my body. Out of respect for its brothers and sisters, the entity greeted all of them.

"Hello, brothers and sisters. How are all of you doing today?"

They all said they were happy to be back on Urantia to wreak havoc on what is now known as earth. I could tell these demonic forces were all ready to go out into the world and cause mass destruction.

"Brother, what of the human? He has not been possessed?" A male voice questioned the entity. This made the entity smile, and it started to laugh sadistically. "Mwa-ha-ha-ha! It's all right, my brother. This man's name is Rodger. He plans on killing all of us in the next couple of days."

The entity paused dramatically, and the dark, demonic creatures all laughed in unison.

The entity continued, "Rodger here is looking for his wife, Irene, whom we have deep within the woods of Devils Lake. If you come across Rodger, please feel free to rip him apart emotionally, physically, and mentally. He is no match for our power and will soon lose his life in a battle of good versus all of us pure, dark evil. Rodger does not like to feel pain. He is right before us now, threatening our very existence."

One of the demonic creatures was extremely pissed off at this. He walked over and snarled into my face, and before he left, he showed me his claws and slashed my chest open. The nails dug deeply into my chest and felt like a burning fire, and as he maneuvered his claws toward his brother on my left side, I cried out in agonizing pain. The entity closed its eyes and swayed its head in a circular motion.

"Brother, he needs to live long enough to finish his investigation. It is important, so please, let us not kill him just yet." The entity hesitated when its brother did not leave my side.

I found the presence of the being terrifying because he was so huge. His face had two huge fangs protruding over his chin like a saber-toothed tiger's, but his face was softer than the faces of his brothers and sisters. Glancing up, I noticed that the entity was staring at me, the intent to kill plain in its eyes. I felt the whole world beneath me start to crumble. But then I remembered my dream, and I envisioned a white sword with a golden shield in my hands to protect myself from the damned children of the mountain.

"Vesuvius, when you stabbed the man, did you know he was able to heal himself?"

The entity seemed to be in shock. The wounds on my chest had bled out at first, and the blood was all over my shirt and pants, but now the wounds had healed. The entity took a step toward its brother and roared, "Do it again!"

The entity was pissed off, and I knew he would get revenge. I tried to get up, fighting the gravity pushing down on my body, crushing me and making me feel unable to move.

The entity said, "Good, Rodger. Get up."

I did, and this time I looked at my hands. They were on fire. What did this mean? I looked at the shield and sword now appearing in my hands.

The entity yelled out to Vesuvius, "Move!"

In a flash, I slashed at the enormous creature, cutting deeply into his chest and feeling the roughness of the bones as they crumbled beneath the sword's might. The white light coming from the sword made Vesuvius cry out in pain. Vesuvius looked down into my eyes and laughed hysterically.

"Rodger, how did you..." Confused, the creature fell to his knees. Now the snake woman came forward, elongated her tail, and grabbed hold of my arm that clasped the sword. She pulled me back to her and punched me hard in the face. The entity excitedly watched as I was passed around the huge room from one demon to another, being hit and cut in turn by their claws. The entity was the last to attack as I was pushed back to my starting point. The entity picked me up again with one arm and told me to look at Vesuvius. I looked into Vesuvius's eyes. His wounds were healed, and he was now extremely pissed off.

"Rodger, the next time we meet, I will take great pleasure in tearing you apart."

I could not move. Conjuring a sword and a shield to protect myself had drained me of energy, and I found there was no hope. There were too many of the lost children in the room, all working together to try to kill me. I felt my heart drop as the entity changed into my daughter again. It walked toward me and started to talk. Softly.

"Daddy, it's dark in here. Help me, Daddy. Why haven't you helped me? Daddy, I love you. I want you to give in to the darkness of the entity so we can be a family again. Daddy, Mommy is down here with me, and she too is waiting for you. Come now, Daddy."

The voice now changed into a dark, demonic, evil voice. It was now or never. I was next to the entrance door, so I gathered all my energy and darted toward it. My little girl was now calmly walking in that direction. She had a grin on her face. I thought for a moment. Were they letting me leave? They didn't move. Vesuvius looked at his brother and did nothing. He was waiting for his brother's orders.

I got out of the police station and noticed that the sky was dark. Reyna stood there for a moment, and then she changed into the entity, and it slammed the door. Lightning flashed, and a fierce wind pounded my weak body as I staggered to maintain my balance. I couldn't comprehend what had just happened, but it had hurt each time I got hit in the face by the entity's brothers and sisters. I could see and feel all the children's deep, dark secrets and the hatred they had for Lucifer and their parents. I stopped thinking about the lost children's past lives and staggered down the street to my car.

The wind made it extremely hard to run. My feet still felt as if the earth's gravity were unbearably heavy on my muscles in my back and my legs. I finally made it to my car and hit the unlock button on the remote. I struggled to get the door open. The wind whistled and howled as the air rushed into the car. I dived in and suddenly heard the cawing of many crows.

Dismayed, I put the key into the ignition, started the car, and drove to my house for supplies before heading up the mountain. The next road was to hell, and I knew it was the only road I could travel. The entity knew I was going to try to defeat it and its family. The entity had boldly invited me to try. It did not care about me or my life, and it did not care about the world. It wanted to control the earth and its people. It wanted domination over the earth and hell.

Where was their creator lurking? Was he happy his children were doing what he'd set out to do? These questions and more started to attack my innermost fears. The destruction had started long ago, but how was all this chaos to be stopped? Who could end it?

Just then, the boy appeared in my car.

"Rodger, you look like someone's beaten you to a pulp. Why don't you heal yourself like you did in the hospital?"

I thought about it for a minute and immediately started to feel a little better.

"Good, you are almost done healing. Rodger, what happened to you?"

I turned around and asked Julian the same thing. He was shocked. He looked at his own body and said, "It's hard to appear on the earth and stay for extended periods of time." Julian looked puzzled as he asked me seriously, "Rodger, you know I did not mean to leave when I did, don't you?"

I looked at him and said, "Whatever, kid. What happened to you the night of your death? Why is it I have to investigate the camp director?"

"Rodger!" Julian screamed. "Look out!"
A huge tree had started to fall. I immediately stood on the gas pedal and made it past the falling tree by just a hair's breadth. Julian was shaken at first but then looked on toward the mountain. The wind pushed the car hard, swaying it enough that I could feel it while I was driving.

I thought to myself, "This has got to be another weird dream."

I started to question my mental state and whether I should be investigating the cause of this boy's and the camp director's death. I'd been trying to put the puzzle together when the entity was feeding me its story. It had mentioned that the camp director had been a vile man with a record of killing people. It seemed also to be hunting the man who had murdered my daughter, who was still at large. It had also mentioned…

Deception. Hearing that word had hit me so damn hard. The police department had set it up to make sure I was no longer worried about the case. I was going to lose my job as an officer if I'd kept it up, but even so, they deceptively set up the man's death using a cadaver. The people who I thought were friends had actually perpetrated a cover-up just to make me feel better. The entity had not mentioned the night they brought the man into the coroner's office. I had let the motherfucker have it, and it had felt good to let go. I'd shot every round in my gun into the man's cold, dead body. I had cussed out and punched the man as hard as I could. The Office of Medical Investigation investigates any death occurring in this state that is sudden, violent, untimely, or unexpected, or where a person is found dead and the cause of death is unknown. The OMI determines the cause and manner of death in these cases and provides a formal death certificate. The man did not deserve to be buried. He should have been burned alive and forgotten.

My heart lurched when the boy put his hand on my wrist. It felt cold and dead. I could feel the kid's emotions and pulled my hand up toward the steering wheel. Turning to him, I asked, "What happened to you the night you died?"

The boy started to tell me about all the eyes hovering in the trees, how all the animals had begun to die, and the mere fact that all his friends were killed, looking dead, their eyes all burning a fire-like red. His description of the girl who was about to die was so detailed that I gagged. The idea of being cooked from the inside out made me sick. How was all of this possible? Was I going insane? Was there a way out of all this mess? What if I was not able to succeed? Who would take on the entity?

Just then, the radio started to play, even though I had turned it off earlier. It was the entity—it was trying to get my attention.

"Rodger, stop. Rodger, stop. Rodger, stop," the boy said calmly. I braked, realizing I was going way too fast. I had not been paying attention, becoming more and more interested in Julian's story. What in the world was I going to do? I started to question my abilities of reasoning and understanding reality. The reality of the whole situation was now very different and not of this world.

"Rodger, please drive safely," Julian said, "and pay attention to the road."

I was caught up in the whole great beyond, and my mind was miles away from the current situation. I looked at Julian. Smiling, I realized I must be going insane. The radio, the boy—I snapped and started to laugh hysterically.

Life sucks. Growing up, dealing with bills and paperwork. The dead and beyond. What more than the tragic end to my daughter's life, the constant reminder from the entity, and the soft glow of Irene's eyes? My heart felt as if it were going to explode.

"Julian?" I said.

"What?"

"How did you die? What was so special about you?"

"I don't know, Rodger. I was just watching everything happen. I died because the entity was able to possess the driver of the car. I had never seen him before. He was in a hurry driving down the mountain. He started to panic as the radio began to switch stations while he was driving. The entity said, 'You cannot escape me, boy!' As the driver tried to cope with his shock, the giant ball of fire formed a gigantic dog that ran after us, but it fell hard to the ground when it ripped the bumper off the car. Why, Rodger?"

"What happened to the dog when you got to the bottom of the mountain?" I asked. In answer, Julian said that at first it was shaken up, explaining that as they got farther away from the mountain, the dog had disappeared. Questions started to swirl in my head, and I began to notice that the mountain was looking deadly, that the once-beautiful scenery was disappearing. The mountain had become a dark and eerie place.

I turned down Nero Street and traveled up a block before coming to my house. I parked the car in the driveway, got out, and walked around to the backyard, where I ducked down the stairs into the cellar. Grabbing riot and tactical gear, I put it on. I knew this was for Irene, the mountain, and the entity's brothers and sisters. On my feet were Belleville Tactical Research Khyber boots. The more gear, the better, right?

"Wrong!" I thought to myself. "Rodger, you will need to be mobile, agile, and tactical. Do you really need all the fancy crap for the entity? Why not just go in low and tight?"

I decided to keep minimal ammunition and have no extra bags or dump pouches. I already had two holsters.

"Think, Rodger. What do you think you'll use?" I asked myself. "Special Forces and Marines go in with seven magazines of ammo and carry light in combat situations."

So I decided to go in light and easy. I packed the Gerber Tanto knives in my vest just in case I needed them in a situation with the lost children of the mountain. I also strapped on a custom-built rifle from the SWAT team, the gun type known as the Competitor. This gun was special because it was custom made with a midlength free-floating quad rail. I felt I had all the ammunition I needed for the mountain.

I grabbed a long flashlight and attached it to the waistline strap on my belt. Emerging once again from the cellar, I took a deep breath and said, "Here goes nothing." I walked back to the car where Julian sat waiting. He gasped as he saw me walk up to the vehicle—I was ready for combat, prepared to face the many challenges ahead at Camp Devils Lake. I got in the car and put the key in the ignition. I knew I was in for the fight of my life, and I welcomed the challenge. I was ready to go fight the supernatural.

I backed the car out of the driveway and headed out. As I drove up the mountain, I noticed that the clouds were a deep, dark purple with a red haze and that the creatures of the night turned their attention toward the car as we passed. No sun was visible in the sky, just the dark, purple clouds and the red haze.

Looking around as I drove up the mountain, I noticed many different species of birds perched up in the trees, but they all looked creepy and scary. I could see vultures, ravens, crows, and owls. The owls were huge, the size of people, and had huge yellow eyes. The drive up the mountain seemed to take an eternity and felt as if doom waited at the end of the road. The trees were all dead, which, as before, enhanced the intense feeling in the air. They were black and entangled in the barbed wire mala mujer plants all around them. This spelled death. These plants usually did not grow above three feet, but these seemed to be on steroids—they were suffocating what little life was left in all of the trees on the mountain.

The road started to become narrow again as I continued the ascent. I noticed that a barricade had been set up ahead. A sign right in the middle of it read, "Keep out! Beware the mountain! Beware the entity!" It looked like red spray paint. As I got closer to the barricade, I slowed to a stop and put the car in park. Glancing over to the passenger seat, I saw that Julian had vanished.

"Julian," I called. "Where did you go?"

I got no reply. I knew now that I was on my own. Opening my car door, I immediately couldn't breathe. The air contained sulfur, which burned my skin and my eyes. I gagged and threw up, continually trying to draw breath. I waited there for three full minutes before my body got used to the smell and my eyes stopped tearing, and then I started to walk around, feeling the warmth of the air on my skin. It almost felt as if I were in hell. The feeling was constant and did not feel natural, as if radiation were continuously hitting my body.

I walked over to the barricade and took a closer look at the sign—it had been written in blood. I could see its freshness. The townspeople must have put the barrier up here recently, probably about an hour ago, but where were all the people, and why were there a bunch of tractors behind the barricade?

I walked around the barrier and gasped. Seventeen bodies were laid out on the ground, chanting, "I want your soul, and you cannot escape me!" I examined the bodies and realized they were all dying slowly. All were suffering, their eyes burning with fire and swirling red. I remembered that this was exactly how my eyes had looked when I came out of my dream, but in each body, the two eyes were swirling tornado-like in opposite directions. It was cooking them from the inside out—I could see gray grease coming out of their eyelids.

I looked down at the ground and realized it was covered in mala mujer plants. To my amazement, they covered the whole forest floor. I took one step and then another, and the milk from the plants dropped onto the forest floor, turning red as blood and smelling awful. Yes, awful—worse than the sulfur smell. It smelled like death, and I could see the blood fall and flow down toward the lake.

As I looked in the direction of the flowing blood, I gasped in sheer terror. The lake was a boiling bath of blood, and Mala Mujer sat at the side of the lake. She was gathering men, women, and children from the town and throwing them into the lake. I couldn't hear their screams at first, but as I walked toward them, I could hear the children screaming at the tops of their lungs. "Help! Help me! Please!" Mala Mujer laughed sadistically, mockingly repeating, "'Help! Help me! Please!' You drown slowly and die as the blood of hell deteriorates your skin."

They were all entangled in mala mujer plants. Mala Mujer was twenty feet tall and continued her raging torment. I walked toward the lake and realized I was now near the quarters and the main buildings of the camp at Devils Lake. I walked up to the building and noticed the cabin walls were all moist with mala mujer milk. The white fluid dripped onto the floor and made a hissing sound, almost like water touching a hot pan.

I walked up the stairs and into the building, finding myself in the central office. In my dream, the camp director had been talking with the students in the adjoining cafeteria. The central office was full of cubicles and desks, but it was dark. I hit the switch to turn on the lights. I didn't know where the camp director's office was located, but I knew it had to be an actual office. I walked around the cubicles, noticing that there were no signs of anyone working at the camp.

"Huh," I said to myself. "What happened to all the people here?"

I continued to investigate all the desks and computers. All were very old-fashioned CRT monitors with ancient desktops. The desks were all considerably dusty. Following the long stretch of cubicles, I came to an office. On the door was a name plaque. I gasped as I read it. Golgotha Zion! This was a Hebrew name: Golgotha means "skull," and Zion is the largest hill in Jerusalem.

Below the name on the plaque was the person's title: Camp Director. I turned the doorknob, but it was locked. The door was made of oak and was solid with no glass. "Damn," I said, and in a split second, I'd slammed my shoulder into the wooden door hard enough to break it open. I stepped back and massaged my shoulder for a moment. That stung. The durable wooden door had been built to last.

I pushed open the door, walked into the office, and gazed around the room. All the furniture—the desk, the bookshelves— everything had dust and cobwebs all over it.

"What the hell?" I said.

The room looked as if no one had been in there in ages. The camp director was dead, and I knew the entity had taken care of him, but what the hell had happened here? I tried remembering the dream of being in the camp but did not remember seeing this portion of the camp. It had been dark when I passed by, and no one else besides the camp director had been here the first night the boy had walked down to the lake. The quarters weren't too far from the cafeteria and office area.

The first time I had driven out here was after I'd been eating in the local café, the time I'd noticed that my investigation had many things in common with what was described in the morning paper. I didn't remember this area from when I drove up here that first time, either.

"Huh," I thought, and for a quick moment, I let out some frustration. I had been inside the radio tower when the crows started to attack and in the quarters when I'd come across the wolf. In the dream, I had been inside the quarters, looking at all the children running around unpacking and getting ready to go down to the lake. I'd also come across the camp director in the cafeteria as he joked around with the kids from the school. But this area was new to me and was causing me a bit of frustration.

I walked around the office and noticed another door hidden behind a bookcase. Curious, I pushed on the bookcase as hard as I could, finally managing to move it clear. I thought for a moment. Why the hell was the bookshelf put in front of the door? I went to open the door and was instantly disappointed. The damn door was locked.

I again proceeded to try to knock the door down but had no luck. I walloped the door with my shoulder once, twice, and a third time, but the door would not budge. I took a step back and cussed up a storm, as my shoulder now ached.

"What the fuck."

I pulled my gun out and shot three times into the wood near the knob of the door. The wood shattered and splintered as the bullets blasted their way through. I knew it was a crime scene and I would have a million questions to answer about using my gun, but I realized that all the people at the police station were possessed and under the entity's control.

"So who the hell cares?" I thought.

I pushed on the door, and to my surprise, it moved about an inch before stopping. I pushed hard on the door to open it more and was instantly attacked by a swarm of flies escaping out of the inner room. A smell hit my nose so damn hard that I threw up. Something was rotten.

There was no light in the room, so I knew it was going to take a while for my eyes to adjust to the room's level of darkness. I took a step back and gagged some more, and then took in a breath of fresher air. The smell of death wafted out of the inner room and into the office. It really reeked. I pulled my flashlight from my belt and turned it on, shining its beam into the room.

I gasped. It was an extraordinary crime scene. The smell of death in the room caused me to move back in fear and disgust. I found multiple bodies laid out on the floor at my feet. They appeared to have been there for months. I hunkered down to get a closer look. All were bodies of the people who'd worked at the camp.

"What in the world happened here?" I wondered. I noticed that each body had a name tag—under the blue "Hello, my name is…" caption were written their names. The first name I read was Wendy, then Gloria, Max, Bill, Todd, Catalina, George, Andy, and Jeff—all camp personnel. I counted the bodies as I memorized all their names. The smell made my gag reflex work overtime. I kept dry heaving, about to puke my guts out.

Looking for the cause of death, I saw that these bodies had nothing wrong with their faces or their eyes. It seemed the entity had not killed all of these people. But I questioned the motive for this crime. This was not like any other serial killer's motive—this was more of a slaughter. The bodies were laid out in rows, and each death had been different. George had a huge mark on his forehead, as if an ax had hit him in the head, puncturing his skull and hitting his brain. This is known as a traumatic brain injury resulting from an impact to the head. A blow to the head disrupts the normal brain function, resulting in an injury to the brain that may affect a person's cognitive abilities. In this case, though, I knew that death had been instant.

The rotting skin on all the corpses made it a bit hard to determine the cause of mortality. "The entity must want me to investigate the reasons for each of these people's deaths," I thought. I stepped out of the inner room and went to the desk. Grabbing a pen and paper, I wrote down all their names in the journal. I realized now that life was not like a storybook and perfect—it was a dangerous reality. By my definition, this crime scene was reality. It was a fact that life had been forcibly taken from them. This meant it had not been their time to die.

Life, this so-called reality, had been taken into the hands of a serial killer, and it seemed he was scared of being revealed as a fraud. This was his motive. Why else would he have killed these people? He was trying to escape and found the mountain a perfect hideout. He knew no one would come up here looking for him, but what he did not know was that I would have searched every nook and cranny of the mountain had I known he would run here. The man knew he would not be found. These bodies had already been here for years and had lain decaying in the office.

These people were all on the wall of missing people at the police station. And the entire time, they had all been dead. Superstitious people had blamed the mountain. We tried calling the camp director numerous times to speak with him and always got no reply. The department investigators had come up here and found that no one knew anything. It was interesting for me to know this now, because every time we had driven out to the mountain and asked to speak with the camp director, they'd said he was on a hike with some tourists. The police department always spoke with someone different. It had to have been a different one of the nine staff members each time. This surprised me—none of the investigators ever questioned the people's disappearances and the camp director.

There had been a staff list of all the people who worked at the camp, and only ten names were on the list. I walked over to the room in the office where the bodies were laid out and recounted them. I had counted correctly. Where was the tenth body? The camp director was missing—or was he?

I shifted the flashlight's beam toward the other end of the room and spied another small desk. As I walked over to it, I just about tripped over another body. This person did not have a name tag, but he looked like the camp director. His mouth was wide open, and he appeared to have been strangled. The lines on his neck were unmistakable. He had died a most extreme death. He'd been strangled and then stabbed multiple times in the kidneys. Bloodstains on his shirt and pants showed where the killer had continuously stabbed.

I started to feel sorry for all these people. All had been killed by either a knife, an ax, a gun, or someone's bare hands. Wendy appeared to have died falling in the woods—her body had dirt and scrapes and cuts all over it. She must have been running from the killer when she died.

I gathered all the information I could from the bodies and wrote down my perspective about their cause of death. Turning to the door of the small room, I walked back into the camp director's office and out into the huge room of cubicles. The door slammed hard behind me before I could catch it. The slam made my heart jump.

I walked out into the main room with a bit of enthusiasm. But then the room got cold. I could see my breath as I walked toward the building's exit. When I reached it, I could see children crawling in the mala mujer plants as they tried to leave the reality of death. All were being stabbed in the hands, and their legs were starting to show bone as the barbed wire–like mala mujer ripped their skin off. It was hard to watch and really hard to stomach.

I looked over at Devils Lake and was surprised that no clean water was visible in the entire long stretch of lake. It was a boiling bloodbath of all the townspeople screaming in pain and agony. In the distance, I could hear their cries—"Please help me!"

I could still feel the smoldering-hot environment on my skin as I started to walk toward the lake. I knew enough now about the serial killer who'd killed off the staff here at Camp Devils Lake. I knew that the killer's intent was to try to lure all the kids of the school and take them out one by one, but if he believed in the occult, he probably wanted extra help from the lost children of the mountain. It seems evil will seek out more evil, and as time goes on, it will reveal the monsters they have become.

I walked out toward the part of the camp where they chopped the firewood. An ax was embedded in the side of some stacked wood, and I noticed immediately that it hadn't been used in a long time. The ax had bloodstains on the sharp end. It was likely the same ax that had been used to kill George. The giant blow to the head must have killed him instantly, and the camp director knew he would have to get rid of the body fast. He must have followed George out here and waited for the right moment.

I looked at the ground and noticed many footprints. The shoe sizes were small. I thought of the school and the children walking around the camp grounds. These footprints seemed to belong to much younger children, though, like elementary school kids here on a trip to the camp. This seemed like an endless circle of death. This would explain the unusual disappearances of many of the children from the town. The mayor and the townspeople would have never come up here to look for their children, never even considering the possibility they were on the mountain.

I walked over to a nearby shed and saw long marks on the ground leading up to it. I knew what I would find, and I could feel my guts constrict as I pushed on the latch of the door. As I opened it, I was met by death yet again. The shed contained the bodies of many small children, all packed tightly against the wall. It was a serial killer's delight. The writing on the door made my heart sink. I took a step back and read them slowly. "I wanted the heart and soul of your life."

It was the children the killer was after. I understood now what the entity had been talking about. The monster who had killed my baby girl had been living up here all this time. He was kidnapping innocent children and bringing them up to the mountain to kill them. He killed them with a knife near the same place my daughter was stabbed. I felt all the anger and frustration build up into my chest as tears began to trickle down my face. I knew the man was the killer of my baby girl. He'd left the same mark on the floor the night he—

I stopped and felt my heart sink again. I thought of Irene, and I knew I had to fight the lost children in order to get her back. I looked toward Mala Mujer, and I knew she would have to be the first to die. I could not bear to see all the townspeople, the fire in their eyes cooking them from the inside out and the mala mujer plants ripping at their flesh, as they all continued to try to get away. I closed the door to the shed and prepared myself for the hike to Mala Mujer.

CHAPTER 14

MALA MUJER

I made my way farther up the mountain and felt the mala mujer plants crunch beneath my feet. As the plants broke, milk from the broken twigs splattered all over my shoes. The mountain had changed—it had become a living, working deathtrap. The mala mujer plants jabbed at my shoes with each step I took. But these shoes were top of the line, and I knew they were virtually indestructible.

The trees were all huge, dark, and deadly, all of them encased in mala mujer plants and their sharp barbs. The altered conditions signaled a new form of torment and suffering in *this* dimension, not just in the afterlife. The air still contained sulfur, and the heat of the mountain was sweltering. The skin on my arms started to blister because of the extreme heat and lack of oxygen, which, while still present in the air, wasn't enough to keep me breathing and walking. I had to hike a bit and then stop and breathe, and because I was at a higher elevation, this really slowed me down and made me feel weak.

I continued little by little toward the primary source of the mountain's dark and evil powers of the lost children. These children were lost many years ago, and they were now trying to create a new world by taking over the current one. And these lost, soulless children were going to succeed if I didn't find a way to stop them.

I walked deeper into the thick forest and was startled when a boy wrapped in the mala mujer plant reached out with his bloody hand and grabbed my shoe. I jumped and backed away, instinctively training my gun at the boy's head. Carefully, I repositioned the gun away from the boy and, extracting one of the knives from my combat gear, started to cut the plant. Milk from the barbed wire twigs hit my hands and burned like hell.

"Fuck!" I screamed out in pain. "Son of a bitch! Ouch!"

Grabbing the boy, I pulled him slowly up off the ground. His face and body were severely cut, the sharp thorns of the plant lacerating his arms and legs. I felt nothing but sorrow and grief for him. He was no doubt going to die.

"What happened to you?" I asked.

"The entity has taken over the whole town," the boy replied. "It attacked a reporter and ran amok, striking fear into the townspeople. It made everyone watch as it slaughtered the reporter. What is your name?" he then asked me.

"Rodger," I replied. "What's your name?"

"I'm Elohai Abraham."

I stepped back and squinted down at the boy. In my whole life, I'd never come across a name like his. It was a cool name, and the boy didn't hesitate in saying it, either. I shrugged and asked whether he knew of any way to beat the entity. I did realize he was a kid, after all, but he replied, "You will have to beat the lost children one by one, and when you come to the entity's lair, you will not be able to defeat it, but you can trick it. It is very smart and ancient. It will not be easily deceived, but with time, you will understand how it can be tricked. You will have to look into your heart and soul to deceive the entity. It is a being far stronger than you will ever be."

I noticed that this child did not have the fiery red eyes that all the others did. He was different. His wounds had now healed. The boy stood up and walked on the mala mujer plants, and to top it off, he was barefoot. But this did nothing to the boy—he ended up with not a scratch on his body.

He knew I was in shock. *I* knew I was in shock. I could not figure out how he'd done this.

He was smiling at me. "Rodger," he said, "you make me laugh."

I gasped as I looked at Elohai. He walked around with ease and then started to explain. "I endure what you have, will, and have not, Rodger," he said, walking up to me and touching my hand.

His touch was gentle, soft, and caring. I instantly felt energized. I could see the brightest light in my head and could feel it in my heart and soul. It was the purest and brightest light, and I felt oxygen surge back into my lungs, allowing me to breathe easily again. Elohai stepped away and said nothing. He just smiled and walked away into the thick, deadly forest.

Frozen, I watched as he walked away, standing there for a moment in shock. Who was he? I looked at my hands and realized they were now completely healed. How? I questioned everything about this event. I could still see the same bright light burning in the distance in the thickness of the forest. I looked at the lake and saw men, women, and children drowning in the pool of boiling blood. Their screams tormented my heart and shook my soul.

I walked through the forest toward the middle of the mountain, where the lake was most open and visible, and suddenly came upon Mala Mujer. She was huge, dark in color, and entirely nude. I gasped as she hurried the children with their fire-like eyes into the lake of boiling blood. The once-beautiful lake smelled like death. The children all screamed as the blood from the lake started disintegrating their flesh. I gasped and put my hand to my mouth.

Mala Mujer heard me and cried, "Rodger, come here!"

I could hear her loud and clear over all the screams. I slowly started to walk over to where she was standing—ten feet away, six, and then I stood right before her. She was attractive and had deathly mala mujer vines wrapped all around her body.

"Good!" she roared. "Rodger, how do you like the air and the scenery?"

I took a step back and answered, "It's scorching up here, and what horrible air! This poisonous gas, sulfur dioxide, is harmful to my health and to all the plants and animals in the forest."

Mala Mujer looked at me questioningly with her badass eyes as she paced back and forth. She licked her lips seductively.

Angrily, she said, "Rodger! What are you going to do? You have nowhere to run and nowhere to hide. It seems you're going to have to kill me, but how are you going to do it? I see you have a big gun, but the gun is useless and won't work on me. How are you going to kill what is not of this earth? I know I have no weak points. How, Rodger? Please tell me."

I thought for a brief moment and noticed she herself was not going near the boiling pool of blood. If somehow I could lure her into the boiling pit, she would inevitably dissolve in the acidic bloodbath.

"I don't know how I'm going to kill you, but you must be destroyed, Mala Mujer."

She bowed her head and put her arms behind her back.

"It's just little old me, Rodger." She grunted as she said it.

"I must say, you've really suffocated the mountain with the mala mujer plant. It has devoured what little life was left here."

She smiled sadistically, displaying her teeth. They were decayed, rotten, and had centipedes crawling in and out of their holes. She was a beautiful creature, but her teeth were a major detraction from her seductiveness. She moved toward me, flaunting her beauty as she walked, but was suddenly distracted by a small boy who ran into her. With ease, Mala Mujer grabbed the boy, picked him up, and began cursing at him.

"Fucking little shit!" she bellowed. "You deserve to suffer, but not right now."

She made the mala mujer plant grow at a rapid rate and wrapped the boy in it. The barbs jabbed at his skin and cut deeply into his body. The boy screamed in pain as she pulled the vines tight. I aimed my gun and was going to shoot her, but then she looked at me angrily. Her eyes were on fire, burning with a deep, dark blue flame. This blue flame was the hottest point. She became extremely pissed and slammed the little boy against the ground several times. She was trying to hit me, but I backed away, avoiding the swings and any damage from the blows. As I dodged the attempt, she finally flung the child into the boiling lake of blood. I knew the child was either dead or unconscious. His limp body floated on the bloody lake for a brief moment and then was swallowed whole by the gruesome, boiling liquid. He would never be seen again.

I got an eerie feeling in my stomach. Mala Mujer was ruthless, powerful, and out to kill. She delighted in killing and had enjoyed the boy's screams of pain and agony. It was me and her now. She started to walk toward me, slowly swaying her hips, trying to get my attention.

"Rodger, do you think I'm pretty?"

I coughed and said yes. Smiling, she put her hands to her face and giggled.

"Do you want to see what I actually look like?" she asked under her breath as I squinted my eyes in wonder at her. She smiled again, and her hideous-looking teeth made me gag.

"Rodger!" she yelled. "Do you want to see what I look like?"

I squinted at her again. Somewhat confused, I asked, "What do you really look like?"

She gave me her rotten, decayed smile once again and put her arms down to her sides as her nails grew super long and sharp. Her body had started to change. The mala mujer plant was wrapped tightly around her head, and blood ran down her face. She looked hideous. Her neck and chest were severely burned, and her body was blistered from the amount of milk draining down her body.

The lake of blood was now covered in a thick blanket of fog as the metamorphosis into her true form commenced. She was hideously ugly. Her eyes were human now. She transformed from an adult to a child. I squinted again at the figure in front of me. Mala Mujer started to laugh sadistically.

"He-he-he-ha-ha-ha-ha! Rodger!" she yelled.

I felt my heart fall as I understood what was going on. This lost child was searching for someone to see her for who she'd once been instead of the monster she had become. I looked at her and felt complete and utter grief for her.

"How did this happen to you?" I asked.

She looked at me angrily and in a dark, demonic voice said, "My mother did this to me. She wanted the devil to look at how hideous I was and reject me so I wouldn't do his evil bidding. My mother was wrong. The devil embraced me as one of his own and transformed me into a beautiful woman."

"How? When you were already beautiful? He used you, Mala Mujer."

"No! No! No! You do not understand. He loves his children. I am his child. He made me into a beautiful immortal. Rodger, you are going to die slowly."

She lifted her hands, and the mala mujer plants wrapped themselves around my ankles and bound my hands. The barbs went deep into my skin and hurt like hell. I could feel the blood drip down my wrists onto my hands and from there to the ground.

Mala Mujer walked over and pushed me hard into one of the trees. I felt all the barbs penetrate my head, back, and legs. In pain, I screamed, "Ah, fuck!" I struggled to free myself, but I couldn't move.

"Is this the end?" I wondered.

Mala Mujer started to sway her hips back and forth again.

"Rodger, do you think I am beautiful now?"

I gagged as she licked my face. Her breath was atrocious—it smelled like death.

"Fuck, no!" I said.

She took a step back and slammed her foot on the ground. She was throwing a tantrum. She turned to me and started to chant.

"Smug Rodger, with your guns and gear, you're a dog. What God did caused me to live, and I now see it as pure evil. Boiling blood, boil as mine has for centuries, and seek revenge. Swallow their souls and devour their flesh. Leave nothing, nothing but death and destruction.

"Rodger, I have been wanting to do this for a long time now. How are you feeling? Do you feel the life slipping from your eyes?" She pulled my head toward hers and said, "Look how much blood you have lost."

I looked down at the ground and gasped at the pool of my blood at my feet. I started to feel weak. She pulled me off the tree and dropped me to the ground.

"You will not be able to continue if you bleed to death."

Mala Mujer was going to make sure I suffered. I fell heavily and now felt all the barbs and milk from the mala mujer plant burn my skin. Mala Mujer walked around me and started to pull the thorns one by one out of my back.

"Rodger, how are you feeling?"

I stuttered and said, "You're a bitch."

Delighted, Mala Mujer started to chant, "Earthquake in my wake as we summon the demons and the lost souls of the dead. One, two, and three, now you are free. Reyna, come out to me."

Had I heard her correctly? Was she summoning my dead daughter? I pushed myself to my knees and looked out into the distance. The lake bubbled and spewed as a skeleton started to walk out of the boiling lake. A white dress appeared on the skeleton, and the mouth kept opening and closing. I started to cry as the beautiful facial features of my baby girl start to appear. She walked out of the lake of blood, the bottom of her dress stained with the gore.

"Daddy!"

My soul crumbled as my heart sobbed in pain. I knew in my heart that she was dead and that this was just another trick to ensure I experienced pure pain.

"Rodger, here stands your daughter before you."

Reyna ran over to me and gave me a huge hug.

"Daddy, what's wrong?"

I looked at my beautiful baby girl and gave her a kiss. She was cold to the touch. I could not believe my eyes as she held me tightly. I gathered my strength and focused on healing my body. It took me a while to gather my energy, but I was able to heal myself the way I'd done before.

"How?" I asked. "How am I doing this?"

Reyna answered, "You are my daddy, that's how, silly! Daddy, can we play in the lake?"

She took hold of my hand and made a gesture toward the lake. I looked at Reyna in shock and squinted down at her. For a split second, she looked like Mala Mujer. I spun around and could not find Mala Mujer. I knew this was a trick, but where had she gone? I questioned the motive for being reunited with my daughter.

"Daddy, where's Mommy?"

I looked down at Reyna and answered, "She's on the mountain, baby. We'll go and find her soon."

"Daddy, I want to play in the lake."

"So do I, baby, so do I," I told her. She gave me a puzzled look and dropped her gaze to the ground.

"Daddy, do you love me?"

I smiled at Reyna and said, "Of course, baby. Why?"

She shrugged her shoulders and kept her eyes focused on the ground.

"What's wrong, baby?" It sounded almost as if she was crying, but when I went to comfort her, she caught me off guard and jumped into my arms. I held her tightly and started to walk toward the lake. I could feel my knees become weak at the thought of throwing her into the lake. I knew I had to defeat the lost children, but this was a chance at getting time back with my daughter.

Reyna looked into my eyes and asked when we would all be reunited. I told her again that we would be going to get Mommy soon. It hurt like crazy to lie to her. Mala Mujer had been right when she'd said that living equaled evil depending on the life lived, but this was insane. I was thinking about killing my own flesh and blood by throwing her into the boiling bloodbath. I looked deep into my heart and gathered energy from my soul. I thought of Elohai, the little boy who'd said, "You make me laugh, Rodger. I endure what you have, will, and have not." What he'd meant was, "I have already seen what you have gone through, what you will go through, and what you have not gone through." It seemed he was trying to tell me not to hesitate in my choices. He already knew the outcome.

This boosted my mentality and my ability to accept what I was about to do. I looked down at my daughter. She'd been so beautiful when she was alive, and now I seemed to be reunited with her. She had all the same smells, the same touch, and the same voice. My heart began to ache badly as I went along with the charade.

What is a charade? It is a game in which some of the players try to guess a word or phrase from the actions of another player who may not speak, or it is an empty or deceptive act. I knew how to play charades and understood this was a way for Mala Mujer to lure me into a trap and end my life. She thought she could use my daughter against me. Mala Mujer would love to see me sip from her deceptive glass of charades.

"She thinks this is how she is going to get me. Uh—no, no, no!" I thought in the back of my head. "Mala Mujer is greatly mistaken."

"Daddy, are you ready to play in the lake?"

I looked down at Reyna and smiled. "I will be ready in a bit, OK, baby? I just need to—"

"What, Daddy?" Her eyes met mine as she peered up at me. My heart began to pound. The entity and its brothers and sisters were being deceptively sinister in their plans to kill me.

"What, Daddy?" she repeated. "What do you need to do?"

She had a dumbfounded look on her face, which set her apart from my real daughter. I kept tearing up as she tormented me with my daughter's memory. She knew this was shredding the inner depths of my very existence. She was enjoying my pain, and the agony of the pain was what she prided herself in. It was a cheap trick to make me fall into her trap.

"But Daddy is going to have a little fun with Mala Mujer," I mused.

Turning to my daughter, I looked at her with my big brown eyes. She was about to get a rude awakening.

"Reyna?" I said to her.

"What?" she asked.

"How about we play in the lake, Reyna, baby? What color is the lake?"

She gave me a puzzled look and said, "Blue, silly."

Now I was puzzled.

Reyna asked, "What's wrong, Daddy?"

I looked into the lake and realized the boiling bloodbath was gone. This was the work of Mala Mujer, and she desperately wanted me to fall for her trick. I was now going to have to play her game and hopefully end up victorious somehow by not falling into the illusion.

"Reyna, baby, how about you lie down by this tree over here while I think a bit?"

I walked over to the tree and barely touched the tree with my hand. I could feel all the barbs from the mala mujer plant, but I maneuvered my hand so I could place my palm on the tree. To my surprise, this did not hurt—it did not prick my hand or my fingers.

This seemed to make Reyna uneasy. She fell to the ground and lay down, looking up toward the sky.

I thought to myself, "What is she thinking? She must be thinking that I'm either really stupid or that she has me right under her control."

Mala Mujer was very deceptive and would do anything to persuade me to go into the lake. I knew that if I did that, I would die. The boiling blood would appear once again, and my skin would melt off from the acidity of the boiling brew.

My thoughts were interrupted by Reyna. I looked down and noticed she was being wrapped in the mala mujer plants. I gasped as she screamed out in pain. My heart felt as if it were going to beat out of my chest, and her screams ripped at my soul. She was so full of life—the imitation of my daughter was being well played by Mala Mujer.

I put my hand out toward Reyna but then thought for a second. "I am right—this is a trick. I must hold back and let Mala Mujer play me."

Reyna was now intertwined in the plant, and I could hardly see her body anymore. Then Mala Mujer suddenly emerged from the tangled mala mujer plants.

"Damn!" I thought, berating myself. "I took too long."

Mala Mujer still looked like a child, but she was pissed off.

"Rodger! Look at me, Rodger!" she yelled. "I still want your soul," she now bellowed in a woman's voice. "Oh, Rodger, I have a surprise for you! Irene, Reyna, and Rodger all reunited here at Camp Devils Lake. Rodger, would you appreciate my reuniting you with your sweet, lonely wife and your beautiful, sweet, adorable child?" she asked.

I smiled. "I would love for you to reunite me with my family. I could tell them how hideously ugly you are and let them know how big of a killer you are, you bitch."

I pulled my gun up and unloaded all its ammunition into her body. The gun had a low kickback, and it felt damn good to unload the whole fucking thing. She screamed as the last bullet hit her in the head. The charade was over, and the mountain scenery, from the beautiful blue skies to the crystal-clear lake, all reverted back to her version of hell on earth.

I was going for another round when she roared in sheer anger, "Rodger, this is your last chance before I end your pathetic, minuscule little life. Do you want to be reunited with your wife and daughter?"

I looked at her with utter disgust and said, "Yes, I would like to be reunited with my *real* daughter and wife."

She took a step back, shocked. She was very confused that somehow I knew about her little game. She realized that I was playing her and buying time.

"Rodger, you are good." She smiled and walked over to me. "Here, Rodger, take this." She was trying to give me a piece of cloth. It was white and had red bloodstains on it.

"This is from Reyna's dress the night she died. Rodger, I am going to ask my brother to give me your wife so that you can be reunited. Then I will conjure up a spell to bring Reyna back. Rodger, why did you let me go on if you already knew I was not your daughter? Here is how you are going to die, Rodger. I will give you some brief moments with your wife and child, and then I will kill them off in front of you."

I was in shock when she said this because she was talking to me in a child's voice.

"Mala Mujer?" I said and looked at her. We were near the lake at that moment, and I pushed her hard as we walked. She stumbled, but to my surprise, she did not fall into the lake. The mala mujer plants wrapped around her body had grown out toward the lake and stopped her from falling in. With ease, she pushed herself back toward land and positioned herself face-to-face with me. She was pissed off.

"So, Rodger, you want to push me into the lake."

I simply lied, saying I'd accidentally tripped into her. She was very upset. She looked into my eyes with her demonic stare. I could see the darkness around her eyes and the purple tint in her pupils. Her stare was mind controlling. I couldn't move—she had me under her spell. She slapped me hard in the face, and I felt the sharp barbs of the mala mujer pierce my skin. It hurt like hell and made my ears ring as I stumbled backward. I could see the lake and feel the mala mujer plant crunching beneath my feet. I struggled to keep myself from falling, knowing that if I hit the ground, I would be in excruciating pain. The barbs from the plant would rip my skin off as I tried to get up.

I felt the unbearable pain, and the skin on my face swelled up as I gathered my strength to continue. My back, although I'd healed it, was still on fire, and it felt and smelled like hell. Although the boy had healed me to the point where I could breathe, all of my strength was drained from me when she hit me.

In a sort of flashback, I could see her being eaten alive by the devil. She looked hideous. I could see her mother putting the mala mujer plant around her head. Her mother broke the barbs in order for the milky liquid to burn her skin, but it melted her skin and made her face look hideous. The girl cried out in sheer pain as her mother delighted in her daughter's hideousness. She'd been a beautiful girl before her mother's desperate attempt to save her daughter from a gruesome fate. Mala Mujer's mother had felt trapped and confused. She'd wanted to show the devil how ugly her daughter was, but the devil saw the hatred Mala Mujer had in her heart and transformed her into this evil being.

"Boiling, boiling bloodbath…" Mala Mujer said. Her chant caught my attention as it started to excite the lake of blood. Out in the middle of it, I could see blood shoot straight up into the air like a geyser, an amazing phenomenon—the boiling blood must have shot up two hundred feet before crashing back down into the lake. Along with the blood, the bones and skeletons of people also shot up into the sky.

Mala Mujer was showing her true power now. In the next couple of minutes, she was going to try to kill me. Mala Mujer called to her brother and commanded, "Give me Irene. She will serve my purpose and fulfill his demise. Boiling blood, brew and brew, spew and spew, as we renew, renew. Reyna, come forth and talk with your father."

Bones rattled as she chanted and conjured up a spell to reunite me with my true daughter. At that moment, Irene walked toward me from the depths of the woods, badly shaken up. She looked into my eyes, and her tears began to fall.

"Rodger, they are all pure evil! I have been tortured and tormented with the loss of Reyna and the fact that you and I are no longer living together. Her death tore us apart and separated us from each other. I never did blame you for her death. I just could not live in the house anymore. It was the memory of seeing her dead, blank face and the pool of blood around her body. The blood would not come off the floor, and it was impossible for me to stay in the house alone," Irene said. "The entity said the man who killed Reyna was still alive. He was here at Camp Devils Lake, and he was going into the town and kidnaping all the town's children and murdering them!"

"Irene?" I said. As she raised her eyes to mine, I told her, "At the camp, the dead children were all in a woodshed. They all had branding on their bodies that said, 'I wanted the heart and soul of your world.' The man was a serial killer and needed to be stopped, and from what I gathered, the entity took care of this man. It didn't explain how, but it did. The tyrant who killed many children is now dead."

Irene and I were both startled as a thunderous crack rent the air. We jumped and turned our attention to Mala Mujer.

"Rodger, you talk to her as if you were both going to live. Ha-ha-ha-ha-ha! You are sorely mistaken. Irene, dear, do not think I have forgotten you, my beauty. You will soon be reunited with your sweet, precious Reyna."

I looked at Irene and told her we didn't need to go through with being reunited. We both understood she was dead and that there was no way we could ever see her again. Mala Mujer sat on top of a tree, looking down at us as we talked about Reyna. Her demonic eyes stared as she smiled at us from that distance.

It felt like the twilight zone. There I was, in the middle of the mountain's forest, face-to-face with Irene while Mala Mujer conjured some spell to bring back my dead daughter. I looked into Irene's eyes, and my heartbeat sped up. It felt good to see her, but judging by her slumped shoulders and the bags under her eyes, she was exhausted. The entity had pursued its game of making her feel lost to the world and lost to me, her husband. It had been persistent in its attempts to control her and her emotions, but Irene was strong and would not give in to the entity's efforts.

Mala Mujer screamed at the top of her lungs, and Irene instantly turned toward her. I too gradually turned to face her. She was looking at both of us sadistically.

"Rodger and Irene, do you want to be reunited with your daughter now?"

Glancing sideways at Irene, I told her under my breath that this was going to be a cheap trick to get us into the lake somehow but that we should play along. Irene nodded. Turning again toward Mala Mujer, she said, "We are ready to see Reyna…"

Her voice trailed as she said her name. It hurt her heart, and the anger and emotional chaos from the night we'd lost our baby girl came back full force. Mala Mujer lifted her arms up and repeatedly called out Reyna's name.

"Reyna, Reyna, Reyna, come forth and see your mommy and daddy. Reyna, Reyna, Reyna, expired no more, come forth and breathe again. Your mommy and daddy are waiting for you!"

Mala Mujer began to twitch with anger, and as she became frustrated with the summons, she yelled out, "Come out and play, you little bitch! Your mom and dad are waiting to see you!"

The sinister sound of her raised voice made the hair on my arms stand up. Irene gasped as she turned around and looked into my eyes. In the distance, a little girl was slowly walking toward us. She had a white glow around her body. I could tell this was different.

"Was Mala Mujer able to summon the dead from the afterlife, even from heaven?" I pondered as with my own two eyes I saw my daughter walking toward us. It seemed so impossible. This creature was extremely powerful if she was able to summon the dead from the afterlife. I was in awe.

Reyna came toward us and lifted up her hand. Irene put out her hand, and the tears started to roll down her cheeks.

Reyna opened her mouth and cried, "Mommy! Daddy!"

She was so happy to see us. Reyna gave Irene a huge hug and sobbed in her arms. Tearfully, she also reached for me, and I picked her up and squeezed her tight. I'd never felt so happy. It was too good to be true. I put Reyna down and forgot all about Mala Mujer. As I looked into Irene's eyes, I felt connected again. It was extremely hard to believe, but the little girl we had lost so many years ago had come back to life. She was living, breathing, and happy to see her mother and father.

Reyna looked into my eyes and gave me a strange look that I did not understand, but then she said, "Daddy, you have the glow as if you were already dead, but you are still living and breathing. You must have been touched by God. That's the reason you are still alive. It is extremely hard to breathe here, Daddy."

Reyna seemed to weaken suddenly, and she started to fall. I went to catch her, but I was too late. She hit the ground and immediately screamed in pain. "Ouch!" The mala mujer plant had cut deeply into her skin.

I turned to see Mala Mujer hovering over the lake with two mala mujer plants wrapped around her waist. Black liquid was coming out of her mouth, and milk from the mala mujer dripped from her waistline down into the lake. She stared into my eyes, and I could not move. Her stare was constant and deadly.

Irene tried to get my attention. "Rodger!" she yelled, but there was no stopping the deadly stare. Mala Mujer's eyes were a deep, dark purplish red and burned with anticipation as she commanded me to walk toward her. I started to walk in her direction. She was in full control of my body. My mind was in a dreamlike state. As I walked, I could not feel my legs.

"Is this it? Am I going to die?" I thought to myself.

Reyna by now had gotten up and was crying. I could hear her, but I was powerless to help her. Her cries were making my ears ring. Mala Mujer started to laugh a most sinister laugh.

"Rodger, come to me," Mala Mujer urged. "You have been reunited with your daughter, and now you can be at peace. It is time for you to die."

Reyna and Irene were both trying to prevent me from walking into the lake, repeatedly pushing me away from it. Mala Mujer's control was overpowering my reasoning skills and kept pushing me forward, and I started to walk toward a bright light. Magically, the dangerous forest floor disappeared, turning into a sandy hill. I took one step and then another toward the bright light.

Irene pushed with all her might, and Reyna held on to my leg. I could no longer distinguish who they were—they simply disappeared. The sandy hill seemed to get bigger, and the bright light seemed to get farther and farther away as I walked toward it. Within the light, I could see a person walking out toward me. It was Elohai. He was smiling as he emerged from the light onto the sandy hill.

I gasped and stopped walking. Irene, Reyna, and Mala Mujer all looked puzzled.

"What is going on?" Mala Mujer screamed. "How did he…"

She seemed baffled, but she continued to look deep into my eyes. She was intent on getting me to walk into the lake.

"Rodger," Elohai said. "How is it you are being possessed?"

I looked at Elohai in shock and asked, "Am I being possessed?"

He smiled and began to pace in a circle. "These creatures you are facing are very strong, and they are very manipulative of you and your family. It seems that when you touched Reyna, you were drawn into this reality because you pictured an escape into heaven. It is their way of luring you into the lake. Take a moment, Rodger, and look at where you have stopped."

I looked down and could see only sand at my feet. Elohai laughed and touched my forehead. I was no more than three feet away from the lake. I was being lured into her deceptive trap.

Smiling, Elohai said, "All my children, past and present, are very special. Although these children were lost, they were born of this world, which makes them still a part of me. These children were lied to, and while Lucifer has great power, his power lives on through the memory of stories. His power is drawn from people who believe he is right. Rodger, you need to fight the temptations and free these children.

"The Tower of Babel was made by all the people of the world. The reason I destroyed the Tower of Babel, was to ensure diversity and the separation of all languages. It created separation between every type of people but created something more—culture, heritage, and greater knowledge throughout the world along with the language barrier. It was designed to show the differences of each people, and what this does is determine how society and the world will put differences aside to learn from life experiences and to understand and communicate with each other to make the world a better place.

"But this is not the time or place for that. Rodger, you have been possessed, and you must break away from Mala Mujer's deadly grasp in order to proceed farther up the mountain."

I looked at Mala Mujer and turned toward my daughter. I could now see that the beast Vesuvius was playing my daughter. He was using her body, but he emitted a glow, somehow making the experience seem real. With a quick glance at Mala Mujer, I turned back to Elohai and said, "I know what I must do."

CHAPTER 15

TOO GOOD TO BE TRUE

Elohai nodded and disappeared. I now started to walk forward toward the lake. Mala Mujer was laughing sadistically, as this was exactly what she wanted me to do. The lake boiled and bubbled, filled with all the people under her control. Irene tried again to divert me away from the lake, but I pushed her away. Irene stumbled but managed to keep her balance. I quickly grabbed my gun and shot multiple rounds into the mala mujer plant holding Mala Mujer up above the boiling, bloody lake.

Mala Mujer looked confused at first, but my shooting the mala mujer plant pissed her off. After I shot the first set of plants, I quickly moved toward the next set of plants. The legs and torso of Mala Mujer's body landed in the boiling lake, and she screamed in pain as the boiling, bloody lake started to burn her skin. The lake around her was on fire.

"Rodger!" she screamed. "You will not defeat me here!"

Her eyes were on fire, burning a deep, bright purple. She called out to the mala mujer plants and pulled many of them toward her from the shore, and they latched on and grabbed her body. I again started to shoot at the plants. This time Mala Mujer fell face first into the lake. Her screams were deathly. I could see the lake boiling faster now as she disappeared beneath its surface.

I took a deep breath and gasped in shock as I looked down. Reyna was pulling at all the combat gear in my belt.

"Daddy, what happened to the bad lady?"

I gazed down at the image of my daughter and started to laugh. She looked back at me, confused. I could still see Vesuvius using her form, acting the part. I smiled as I looked her dead in the eye.

"She has been destroyed by the lake, baby, and she is no longer going to hurt anyone else."

I picked her up, and as I walked with her toward the lake, I started to laugh. I was beginning to enjoy beating these creatures.

Looking into Reyna's eyes, I said, "It's too good to be true."

Vesuvius noticed that I was acting out of character.

"Irene, come here," I said. She was still in shock from my pushing her.

I took one last look at Reyna, gulped a huge breath, and threw her into the lake. Irene gasped as I threw her, punching me in the face and kicking me in the stomach with all her might.

"What the fuck are you doing, Rodger?"

I coughed and started to laugh. "Irene, that is not our daughter. Look."

Irene turned toward the lake and gasped as the form of Vesuvius started to appear, Reyna's image fading in and out for some time before solidifying into the creature's true form.

"Rodger, you think you have won, don't you?" Vesuvius asked.

"No, I have not won yet," I replied.

I grabbed my gun, loaded another round, and let the son of a bitch have it. He was weakened as the shots went into his body, but the lake was taking its toll on him. Irene's eyes were filled with anger and hatred. Coming to my side, she grabbed the gun and also let some anger out.

"You son of a bitch!" she cried. She shot the gun multiple times and then dropped it to the ground.

"Irene!" Vesuvius cried as he fell into the boiling lake of blood.

I walked over and picked up the gun, peering into the lake. Two rings of fire were burning brightly, almost in the shape of an infinity symbol.

Without another word, Irene grabbed hold of me and gave me the biggest kiss I had ever gotten from her in all the years I'd known her. This was nice. I felt whole again, as if my whole world had come back together. I held her in my arms and did not want to let go.

We were startled by a loud scream coming from the lake. It was Vesuvius. He was wrapped in the mala mujer plant, and he was rapidly making his way toward us. I put my gun to use again, unloading it once more in a series of concussive bursts. Vesuvius started to fall into the river, grasping at one of the mala mujer plants, but he screamed out in pain as green liquid fell from his hand. He was snagged on the plant. I chuckled—he was no more than six feet away from Irene and me.

As we watched, the creature used the sharp claws of his other hand to cut the plant away. He started to fall into the lake, and the splash sent a wave of boiling blood toward us. We moved quickly but carefully backward to avoid being hit by the acid bath and falling onto the mala mujer plants.

Vesuvius seemed to be disintegrating in the boiling blood. His body looked completely different. We stepped back to the shore and saw bones floating out in the distance. I sighed in relief.

"It is—" Before I could complete my sentence, we heard a sinister laugh behind us. I turned to find Vesuvius glaring at me with animosity, blood and gore dripping off his body. He was extremely angry and ready to kill. Raising his arms into an attack position, he started to run toward us. I had two, maybe three seconds to react.

I pushed Irene away, and as Vesuvius rushed me like a pro football player trying to sack the quarterback, I dodged him, and again he landed in the lake. He screamed out in pain, cussing and yelling in a demonic voice. The splash of boiling blood that landed on my leg really burned—it felt like the mala mujer plant's poisonous, venomous sting.

Vesuvius now lay motionless in the lake of boiling blood. Irene started to scream as another one of the lost children grabbed hold of her and started to carry her off. It was the mamba.

"Rodger!" she screamed.

I pulled my knife out and went for the mamba. Her scaly body was quickly moving through the mala mujer. I ran as fast as I could toward Irene and the mamba, but I was too slow. My leg was badly burned, and I knew it was hopeless. She had taken Irene from me.

I could tell where the mamba was going, as her tracks were obvious. I thought of what I was about to go up against. I was going to come face-to-face with the entity and the other lost children. I again started to think of the old tale of the lost children. She was going to the lair where the devil had used the image of God to create his own image. This place was the darkest and hollowest of all places on earth. It was the place where every deathly creature on earth dwelled, not on its highest point, but deep within the mountain.

This dark place had not been seen by man in a long, long time. Irene and I would be the first to witness this dangerous land of fallen angels, damned souls, and of course the many lost children.

The mountain was treacherous and dangerous. At every twist and turn of my pursuit, I could feel the sharp, jagged barbs of the mala mujer penetrate my skin. Every two miles, I had to heal my body by thinking of all the good things that had occurred in my life. The rate at which I was healing my body made me feel stronger and wiser.

The trail of broken mala mujer plants made it easy to track the mamba. But she was extremely fast and super strong. Her animosity had been extreme in the hospital, and she had been able to defeat me, ending up by throwing me down a flight of stairs. She'd made it seem that I was going to have to face the entity in the hospital, but apparently the entity had other plans. He had taken Irene from me, and she'd somehow ended up with me on the staircase.

The entity of Camp Devils Lake was the source of all evil. This was where the fallen had risen and from where they were causing havoc upon the earth. As I walked through the forest, I could see all the evil statues and wild animals staring at me in the distance, their eyes the same as those of the camp director, the boy, and all the people in the city. They had all been taken over by the entity and its siblings.

If I could give this a road a name, it would be the Mamba Road of Destruction. Blood was spattered all along the way where the barbs of the mala mujer had dug deeply into the mamba's reptile skin. It must have hurt her, but she was relentless in getting Irene deeper into the mountain. Little by little, I began to notice that the uphill battle was becoming easier on my legs and back. The burning feeling started to disappear.

The mala mujer plants blocked my view, so I didn't know which way I was really going. I could still smell sulfur in the air as I made my way through the forest. I came upon a man lying on the side of the road, his eyes on fire—he was surely possessed by the entity. The man reached out to grab me but failed, and I easily maneuvered around him, pulling my gun up and pointing it toward him. His face just continued staring in my direction as I walked slowly away. He said only one sentence: "He comes to feast upon your soul."

I looked at him and felt chills creep down my spine. The man collapsed and fell hard back to the ground. I gagged as the mala mujer plant wrapped itself around his body, squeezing him so hard that the blood splattered all over the place, some landing on my shoes. The man did not squirm—he just fell to the ground and screamed in agonizing pain. The mala mujer was now being controlled by the entity. I was shocked, unable to believe my own eyes. The man was alive and trying to hang on, but the entity destroyed him.

A question kept popping up in my head: "When will the entity destroy me? *How* will it destroy me?" As I had witnessed so many people dying all around me, my heart no longer raced at the sight. Sixty feet in front of me, I could see a mala mujer plant wrap itself around a woman and lift her into the air. The barbs speedily overwhelmed her, killing her within seconds. The blood drained to the ground, and as I came upon her body, the blood was at a slow, steady *drip, drip, drip*.

"Rodger!" I heard in the distance. I looked all around but did not see anyone. A split second later, I could hear something in the distance, running around me and growling within the screen of the mala mujer plants. Somewhere out there, I could hear toddlers laughing and giggling. It was starting to drive me insane. The constant noise was making me angry, distracting me from devising a plan to rescue Irene. I felt the world start to spin. Shock was sinking in, and so was the effect of all the screaming people being killed in the distance. The noise was constant and consistent.

It was the entity. I knew I was getting closer to its lair. I now recognized the hellhound's growl, and my heartbeat raced as I heard its thunderous crashing as it ran. I continued to follow the path the mamba had plowed as she'd made her escape. I could see many timberland rattlesnakes coiled up along the side of the path. Their eyes were swirling with fire, and they would try to attack and bite me as I passed, but I dodged and avoided their strikes.

I thought over everything that was currently happening. The mala mujer plant killing the man, the constant sounds of the lurking animals, babies giggling and laughing, the timberland rattlesnakes. What was next?

I'd spoken too soon. Damn. I couldn't believe my eyes. I was gazing upon a giant fortress in the middle of the mountain. My heart sank as I saw creatures walking all around the grounds of the huge lair, and they were killing and slaughtering men, women, and children. These creatures were ruthless and showed no mercy—and the screams were deathly.

"Help! Help! Help!"

"Please, no!"

"Stop! Aghhhhhh!"

"Why? What did I do?"

I could hear the yelling and screaming of all the people, their eyes burning bright. The entity had possessed them all and was having all the fallen creatures wreak havoc on them. The number of people lined up and shackled was greater than our town's population, though. The entity had possessed other places through television and struck fear into all of mankind. It was now in control of the fate of the world. I did not see any bombs falling on the mountain or anyone taking any offensive action toward the entity.

"Rodger, snap out of it," I told myself. "Think of Irene and getting her back. Think of a way to beat the entity and end all this suffering."

Just then, I heard laughter coming from behind me. I turned but saw nothing. When I turned back around, I found myself face-to-face with Vesuvius. His deathly sharp claws were now coming down toward my face. Gathering all my strength, I punched Vesuvius hard in the stomach. His body must have been very, very weak, because he let out a throaty growl and fell to the ground, his hands and arms enfolding his stomach. I watched the mala mujer plant wrap itself around his body and start to squeeze.

Vesuvius started to laugh hysterically as the plant crushed him. The plant grew huge barbs, which broke Vesuvius's skin as they ravaged him. I almost felt bad for him, but he did deserve it. All of a sudden, the plant disappeared, and I was staring at a dead, lost child, the second child that had died by the mala mujer. I thought for a brief moment and saw that the mala mujer plant was still alive, still working to suck the life from the mountain. This must mean that somehow Mala Mujer was still alive. Vesuvius had been very strong and sadistic. He could have easily killed me in a flash, but he'd played Mala Mujer's little game. They were both planning on killing me. They almost did kill me, but I lived on to endure this version of hell on earth.

I started to walk toward Vesuvius. His body was limp and dead, not moving at all. His mouth was wide open. Walking right past him, I focused my attention on the huge fortress. Behind me, I suddenly heard a baby crying. I turned around, trying to pinpoint where it was coming from, but I could not find the child.

"Where is it?" I wondered.

I looked at Vesuvius and realized the noise was coming out of his mouth. Squinting my eyes, I walked back over to him. Sure enough, the cry of a baby was coming from his mouth. The baby that bears no mark. It sounded as if the baby was inside Vesuvius. This mountainous creature was crying like a baby. Looking down at his body, I could see the image of a baby within the monster's belly. The baby was thrashing at his stomach, trying to get out.

I pulled my gun forward and started to shoot Vesuvius in the stomach. The body just moved from side to side as the blood splattered all over my face. I was covered in green blood. Yuck. I wiped my face with my sleeve and gasped as I looked down at the body. There, still moving, was a baby, completely naked and crying—but it was a hideous-looking baby. As the child started to thrash and scream, I turned around and walked away from it. I left it there on the ground.

It was the baby that bears no mark. It was trying to make me pay attention to it.

"Rodger! Huh! Ha!" the baby said.

I turned to look at the baby and realized it was now standing up. Its eyes were pitch black. The mala mujer plants enhanced the feeling of chaos and destruction behind it. The baby's eyes started to change from black to a deep, dark red. The crows in the trees flew up into the air, circling me. It made me think of vultures circling dead prey. The baby was in complete control and power. Its eyes were solid dark red. The baby in my dream had been even more sadistic and scary looking.

I thought, "Is the baby a lost child? How did it come into the world? What was its power besides eating a person's soul and sending it to hell?" This small, lost child looked angry at the world and felt no remorse as it wreaked havoc on those who crossed its path.

"Rodger," the child said.

I looked briefly at the child and then turned back around. The child spoke again.

"Rodger, look at me when I am talking to you."

I continued to look away and felt the air change as the child continued to say my name.

"Rodger! Rodger, look at me!" the baby yelled.

I turned around and looked into the baby's eyes. I smiled.

"What is so funny, Rodger?" The baby was speaking in a child's voice. Its teeth were super sharp and looked demonic as a dark, viscous fluid dripped down its cheek onto the ground. Its face looked like that of a young child crying out to the world, asking for attention. The child was very demonic. The child knew I was thinking and was getting very impatient.

"Rodger, why are you stalling? You must be scared. Do you want to play a game?"

I kept looking up as the crows circled me. They had to be at least a hundred feet above me, and their swirling darkness had turned the sky completely black. The eyes of the crows were all the same color as the demonic baby's. It was controlling the crows, and they remained twirling around me in sync with each other. The child kept its position and stayed poised. It did not move—it just stared.

"Rodger, look at me," it said loudly, this time in a demonic male voice. "Ah, I got your attention now!" It sounded surprised. "You seem to be thinking about the crows above. Let me tell you, they are the least of your worries. Rodger, do you know why you were given the dream of the man who was a truly cruel badass? He was a ruthless man who would kill anyone who got in his way. He did not give a fuck until I gave him a reason to."

The child stayed still for a moment. I looked at the baby in front of me and could not believe my eyes. It was so small but so extremely deadly.

"Rodger, do you want to see what happened to the man? He is here right now."

I looked at the child and could see the shadows of all the crows circling up above. I looked at it and smiled.

"Is this another one of your tricks to try to lure me into another trap?"

The child looked at me with pure anger and screamed at the top of its lungs, "Rodger, you fucking little prick! Pay attention!"

I chuckled and said, "You sound like a little girl."

The child quietly stared at me briefly and then screamed, "Rodger!"

"What?" I asked.

"You want to repeat that last comment?"

"What?"

The baby smiled and started to laugh. "Ah, I like you, Rodger! You are a funny man. You like to make fun of me, don't you, Rodger? Well, I see you will have to witness my power in order to be scared."

Actually, I was more worried about the damn crows than the baby. I kept looking up into the sky because the birds were everywhere.

"Rodger! Look at the ground in front of me."

I looked down, and the baby was moving its arms high above its head, its palms upward. The baby was reciting a chant.

"Demons down below in the pit, your yellow eyes aglow. Bring forth the man who was a real badass. Show Rodger what lies in wait for him deep down below."

I looked on incredulously as a multitude of demonic creatures now pushed up the man in my dream. His face had a blank look. His soul had been eaten and taken from him. He was truly gone from this reality and stuck in the deep, dark pit of hell. His evil had caused him to be put into this situation, and the baby that bears no mark devoured every scrap of soul.

The baby commanded the man to get up. The man listened, but it took quite a while before he got up. He was frail and looked as if he had been severely tortured. There was no life in the man, just pure, utter terror and anguish. The baby, getting impatient that the man was taking his time, snapped its fingers loudly, and the crows started to attack the man, biting and tearing his flesh open and leaving gashes that remained gaping. The cuts were deep and looked awful.

The man screamed in agony as the baby continued to enjoy itself. It snapped its fingers again, and the crows flew up into the sky and started to circle around and around above me again. The mountain started to shake and quake as the baby raised its arms. Watching in amazement, behind the baby in the distance, I could see the mountain start to rise. The baby had broken the laws of gravity—the mountains behind us were floating above the ground.

The baby's eyes were smoldering-hot red at first, and then as time progressed, they turned blue. It was ripping apart a big portion of the mountain. I looked at the baby and gasped. It was no longer the image of a baby—it was a small, demonic creature. It had razor-sharp teeth and razor-sharp claws.

"Rodger!" it said, startling me. Its voice was no longer a child's voice but a demonic, evil voice.

"What?" I asked.

"Look at my teeth. Look at my teeth."

I was starting to feel I was going insane. The man in front of me had been torn to shreds, and the baby had changed his appearance. He was now ready to attack and devour my soul. I thought of Irene and gathered all my strength. As I looked down at the child, the mutilated man quivered as the child moved its hand. It actually made me laugh—the body still reacted to danger even though it was already dead. There was a precedent to this, because at one time I'd had some plants in my house that were always under a light source. Deciding I did not want the plants anymore, I put them outside. The plants could not distinguish between night and day. The danger they were in was the stress of not knowing what was going to happen. They continued to grow and be the best plants they could be—they were extremely lush and beautiful. But like all plants, animals, and humans, we all at some point will find ourselves in survival mode, trying to endure the different conditions life has to offer. If the circumstances change, the plant, animal, or human will survive. This is true, because the plants grew and grew, but when winter came around, the plants died. They did not know when to lie dormant for the winter. The plants continued to try to survive.

This was what I was witnessing with the man who'd been a real badass. Although he was dead, he was still attempting to survive. The meaning of life. He was going to try to adapt, no matter the circumstances. It was written in his cells and his genetic code. It was apparent that the man had suffered for a very long time in the depths of hell. The child that bears no mark had devoured his soul, and now his shell was all that was left. The baby's bite marks were incredible. The child was no bigger than a foot and a half, but he'd made the man suffer in the extreme. The man looked lost, as if in shock.

"Rodger," the child said. "You know what happens next, right?"

I looked at the child and could see the glow of its burning eyes, the light of pure hatred, of sheer evil. Surely it could cause mass chaos in the world.

I nodded to the child and said, "Let's see your true power."

The child smirked, but as it did I could see its deadly, razor-sharp teeth. Its mouth was slit deeply back into its jawbone. Its face was turning red with anger. I was seriously pissing it off. I kept my composure and continued to ignore the facial features of the child that bears no mark. Its face was beginning to turn dark red with black wrinkles. Angrily, it looked at the man who'd been a real badass, and what it did next was brutal.

The child drew its razor-sharp nails and clawed at the man's eyes and face. The shell of a body instantly fell limp. The child expelled the man's energy completely. The meaning of his life now switched to his body's decomposition on the now-barren mountain among the mala mujer plants.

Now the child turned its attention toward me, walking slowly in my direction. I took a few steps back. Its attitude had changed—it had turned into a perfect killing machine. Its body still resembled a baby's, and I could see now why the man who'd been a real badass had died when he encountered the child that bears no mark. Since he'd been a boy, this man had been in trouble with the law and his parents. His family could not stand the sight of him, and now the only one who'd witnessed his demise was me. I felt remorseful toward the man and could not believe it when he was destroyed in front of me.

The man who'd been a real badass had accepted the end quietly. He had not reacted or screamed out in pain as the child destroyed his shell of a soulless body. The child was trying to make a powerful impact on my fears and worries, but what it did not know was that I was now officially fed up with the constant torment the lost children had brought upon me and my life. They'd continuously tormented me with the death of my daughter and the fact that they had kidnapped my wife for the second time.

The mamba's speed and agility had led me to the lair of the lost children and the fallen angels, the realm of the fallen and the lost. This was the portion of the earth no one wanted to venture to because the creatures here were not of this world.

CHAPTER 16

SLAYING THE LOST CHILDREN

The child that bears no mark now came up to me and remained three feet away. I could see its sinister smile and smell the old blood dripping from its fingertips. As night began to fall, the child glared directly into my eyes.

"Look at my teeth. Look at my teeth, Rodger!" the child screamed at the top of its lungs.

I could see the razor-sharp teeth but looked instead toward the child's sharp fingers. The child was obviously trying to somehow take control of me. I knew it would try to bite me. Thinking back to the dream of how the man had lost control of his instincts made me feel better about how I was going to deal with the child. If I were to remain calm and rely on my parenting skills, I could win the child.

The child, growing impatient, moved toward me. I moved back cautiously, knowing the mala mujer plants were right behind me. If I fell down, this would not end well. I stepped back, and the child began to laugh in a sinister child's voice that quickly changed into an adult male voice. Its eyes closed as it laughed, its head tilted down to the ground. I had to be cautious of what it was going to try next.

The child looked up as I stepped hard onto a mala mujer plant. The milk from the plant landed on its right shoulder and arm. The child opened his eyes, looking deadly serious. I gasped as the child let out a growl that sounded like that of a ravaged, caged animal. Its claws grew longer, and it started to make its way toward me. It was not going to stop.

I pulled out my knives and held them out in front of me. The child started to run around the mala mujer plants.

"Rodger! Look at my teeth! Look at my teeth!"

I couldn't help but look at the damn child's teeth. They were right in front of me. My body felt frozen in fear. I was still moving slowly back but could feel the child's control taking over. My arms felt like boulders. I could hardly move. Then the child slashed at my leg, tearing deep into my leg muscle. It was climbing up my body, gripping with its sharp claws. I could feel the energy in my body starting to fade.

"Is this it?" I asked myself. "Or will I find a way to beat this child?"

I tried to think of all the good moments in my life, times when I'd been happy, and I gradually felt my energy coming back. The child had climbed almost up to my neck when I felt my full energy return, and I put my hands on the baby's face just before it could bite down on my neck. It was like a blood-sucking vampire trying to drain my life away.

The child was extremely strong. It was close to my neck now and continued to try to take a bite out of me. I pushed it hard to the ground and kicked it smartly in the face. It seemed almost in a daze. It kept trying to pick itself up, but it couldn't figure out which way was up or down.

I remained on the offensive now. Picking up the mala mujer plant, I wrapped the child up tightly with it, the barbs cutting deeply into my own hands. I wrapped the child up so tightly that I thought it was dead. As I got up, I noticed a large amount of heat coming from behind me. Turning slowly, I was dismayed to see the enormous burning dog. It was here to destroy me. I could feel its radiant heat hitting my body.

The dog growled and looked into my eyes. Behind me, the child was tied up and not moving. I'd ensured the child would not take a bite into my soul. I'd felt strength as never before when I pushed the child off me. It had no chance. I didn't know where this strength was coming from, but I knew I was now in control. But now, this huge dog towered above me, threatening to take control back.

The canine put its head down toward the child. I moved away slowly as the child lay there motionless with no signs of life. The dog growled as I went for my gun, turning its huge head toward me and growling hellaciously. I was no longer near the lake, so I could not use it to my advantage by luring the dog into it and putting its flame out for good. The dog moved toward the child once more and put its nose on the mala mujer plant. The plant lit on fire, and the baby started to scream as the flames burned it.

The dog turned toward me and started to growl again. I tried to make my way toward the huge fortress, where many creatures were torturing and killing the townspeople and others whom I did not know. As I hastily made my way down to the fortress, the mountain fell into a deep kind of pit, making the ground more and more dangerous as I made my way down toward it.

Defying my belief, the child that bears no mark was extremely pissed off and now started to come after me. Remarkably, it still had control of the crows flying high overhead. The child screamed my name.

"Rodger! The scavengers shall feast upon your pathetic body, and I shall feast upon your soul."

Looking at the enormous dog, the child snapped its fingers. The crows started to fly down toward me, but luckily I got to the bottom of a huge concave hole in the mountain and was able to continue toward the fortress. Following right behind me, the crows scratched and bit at my face and arms. I was trying to maintain my composure and get inside the huge fortress when I came upon a statue of a horned creature. The statue was made in the image of Lucifer. I gasped—the statue had idolized him as a beautiful creature. At the statue's base was a message: Turn Back.

Slapping and punching the crows as they attacked me, I ran down a flight of stairs toward a large black door. The crows were relentless. I looked back in the direction I had come and could see neither the child that bears no mark nor the dog. I got to the door and pushed it open.

The door was cold to the touch and felt very heavy, but I was desperate to get into the building so the crows would stop their attack. I slammed the door hard the moment I got into the building. The room was dully lit, and at first it was hard to see. I first focused on the walls and ceiling, looking for crows. The room was huge, with white marble tiles on the floors and halfway up the walls, and a picturesque collage of beautiful angels and demons going up to the roof. To my surprise, not a single speck of dust appeared on the furniture in the room, which seemed to have been well maintained for the many thousands of years it had been here. The art on the walls consisted of picturesque images of the most beautiful angels I had ever seen. In the corner of the room, a lamp flickered. Outside, I could hear the crows still cawing. I kept my back to the door.

From a nearby couch came the sound of a baby crying. I leaned the back of my head on the door and shut my eyes in dismay.

"What the fuck? What the fuck?"

I was exhausted and completely drained of energy. I could not believe the amount of stress I had put myself through so far. The baby was still crying loudly, and the room was cold, dark, and mysterious. It made me feel as if every dead person that had ever lived had walked through these doors. It seemed to embody the anguish and remorse of leaving this life to go to the next, imparting the feeling of carrying a casket to its final resting place. The body gets heavier as it knows its last and final place on this earth. This room felt extremely heavy on my heart. I tried to think positive thoughts, but instead I was filled with emotions of anger and regret. The room felt evil, and the amount of anger my body and emotions exhibited was extreme.

I looked down at my hands and examined the cuts the crows had made when they'd taken chunks of my skin off. I tried really hard to heal myself as I had done before by thinking of the good things in my life, but I failed every time I tried. In the background, the baby cried nonstop as I continued to stare at my hands, feeling the warm blood drip down my fingers onto the white marble floor.

The baby continued to wail as I walked toward the sound. The anger that had built up in me started to weigh heavily on my heart. The closer I got to the baby, the heavier my heart felt, which led to the buildup of even more anger. I then came upon the baby—it was small and crying as loud as its little vocal cords could let out the sound. I sat down near the child and looked at the coffee table in front of me. It was covered in magazines and a series of books whose text I could not make out. I assumed they were written in Arabic or something. Ignoring the books, I noticed all the specks of blood all over the white floor.

I decided to relax and try to clear my mind. I closed my eyes and let everything out of my system, ready to heal myself. I sat near the baby but did not pay attention to its cries. I just let the child be. As I cleared my mind, I could feel the healing process begin. It actually hurt to heal myself. I marveled at all the scars I had on my body. The mala mujer had torn up my legs pretty badly and left a lot of third-degree burn marks where the milk had splashed them. My skin was turning black like Mala Mujer's body. I no longer felt the uncomfortable coolness of the room. My body felt good. I finally looked at the child crying on the couch and discovered the reason it was crying. A bunch of ants were crawling around the baby, biting it every so often.

I got up and walked around the room, noticing a staircase leading up into a long gallery. But I was still interested in the room I was currently in. I looked down at the floor, surprised, not realizing I had bled so much. My cuts were healed now, but I still could not figure out the purpose of this huge fortress in the middle of the mountain of Camp Devils Lake. I suspected this would be where I would encounter the entity and finally end my journey in this world.

I began to sense the presence of a spirit in the room with me. It was the boy, Julian. He was communicating with me. I could hear his voice.

"Who are you, Julian?" I asked. "I know you are a boy from the town, and your mother had to drive you to school every day, but who are you? Why did the entity make its grand entrance into this world through you?"

From somewhere above me, I could hear Julian state, "It used me to find a way out into this world and the other worlds. It came to this place to find Lucifer to destroy humanity. It wants to do what Lucifer cannot."

"What do you mean?"

"Lucifer cannot hurt humanity, because of the sacrifices made, but the entity can hurt the world and wreak havoc upon it. The issue of Lucifer is that he fell and became the hideous creature you saw out front, the statue of a creature with horns and hooved feet. His wings were clipped from his body, and he became a monster, the same monster we all know today."

I thought for a second about all the different stories I had heard in my life dealing with good versus evil. Lucifer always lost, and memories of all the Bible stories reflected back into my mind and made me think about how he had remained on earth—but where on earth did he stay and lurk? I was guessing here. No man had ever ventured here before, and if one had, he'd never returned to the town or the lake. Mala Mujer had made the mala mujer plants grow rapidly throughout the mountain, suffocating the vegetation and killing off all the living creatures. The only creatures able to survive were the birds possessed by the child that bears no mark. It seemed the contaminated air and the animals had suffered the horrible fate of death. I started to wonder now whether this would be the end of the world.

I started to gather the guts to go up the stairs. I took one step and heard laughter coming from behind me. It was the baby, and it was laughing at me, taunting me. I turned around and went back to the couch where the child lay. Summoning what little sanity I had left, I picked up the child. It instantly morphed into the child that bears no mark. I'd known this was going to happen.

"Hello, Rodger. Are you ready to die?"

I gasped as its claws dug into my arms. The pain was excruciating. Every bit of anger and hatred flashed back into my head.

"It's time for you to die, Rodger."

The child was sadistically penetrating my arms to make me feel desperate and angry. All the emotions burst out in my head with colors of black, red, and purple. My anger tore at the inner depths of my soul. I could see everything happening and felt powerless. I thought about Irene and felt the anger spike once again. This time the child looked stunned. It could not believe I was intentionally trying to suffer more.

Looking into my eyes, the child slowly said, "Look at my teeth. Look at my teeth."

I looked into the child's eyes and smiled. Gathering all my strength in my right hand, I punched it hard in the mouth. Its teeth started to fall out, and all the black and yellow ooze as well as the red blood dripped onto the white floor. It looked as if I was starting to win. Then the air in the room got extremely hot, and I felt the breath of the huge dog on my neck, a hot *swoosh* that made me look up.

The dog went airborne, and he descended fast, leaving me no time to dodge or anything. I looked directly at the dog and felt it go into my body. I felt I was on fire. The child, having remained in my arms, bit down on my neck and caused me to scream out in pain. I could not believe it. I was on fire!

I looked at my hands and felt no pain. In fact, I felt stronger than ever before. I could feel the pain, though, of each bite the child took as it continued to gnaw at my neck. It was doing major damage. Trying to calm myself, I focused on healing. The dog inside my body started to whimper as I began the healing process. I was focused on winning against the entity and killing these two troublesome creatures out of this world.

I healed myself in a matter of moments and then gathered all my energy to attack the child. Grabbing it, I started to slam its head and body hard against the marble floor. This was no ordinary child— this was one of the lost children. This child would have killed me had I not snapped myself out of its trance. I could hear the voices of self-destruction tearing me apart from the inside, but at this moment, I had the upper hand. I was in full control of my body and my mind. But I could feel the hellhound's power growing within me. It was trying to cook me from the inside but was failing as long as I focused on containing its power inside my body. I was draining the hellhound's power and using its power to augment my own strength.

I again went after the child that bears no mark. The child's face started to again change into that of a demonic creature. The child laughed as I pummeled it, slashing and clawing at my arms and face. It was trying to kill me, but now it was on the run, scared. I had the upper hand, because the dog was on fire inside my body, making my body somehow on fire, but it was doing no damage to my body or my clothes.

In shock, I turned against everything I had ever learned about children. I knew it was not right to hit the child, but this was no ordinary child. This was a demonic monster ready to kill me, stopping at nothing to get the job done. I was ready for the end and to meet my maker, but for some odd reason, I felt in my heart that I had already met my maker on the mountain. He'd been trapped in the mala mujer and had restored my strength and healed my body, as I knew the maker would be able to do. He'd shown me how to beat Mala Mujer.

I felt the child's claws rip deep into the skin of my right leg. I screamed as it thrashed and clawed its way up my body. The child was not of this world. The child that bears no mark was now trying to slit my throat and end my life. I closed my eyes and imagined that I felt no more pain stabbing at my very life. This felt like a horrible dream, a never-ending dream. Opening my eyes a bit, I noticed the child had opened its mouth wide. The sharp, jagged teeth were now going in for the kill. It was going to bite me in the jugular if I didn't react in time.

The fire burning around my body was now penetrating the baby's skin. I pulled my fist back and punched it extremely hard in the forehead, snapping its head back with the force. Moving its head slowly back to where it had been before, the child dug its claws deeper into my skin. Its forehead was not even hurt. Gazing at its eyes, I knew I had pissed it off.

"Rodger, you little prick. I am going to kill you—slowly."

I gasped. Its teeth were getting longer.

"Rodger, look at my teeth. Look at my teeth."

I looked into the child's eyes, gathered all the fire around me into one of my fists, and punched the little demon in the mouth. It clamped down hard on my arm and then started to scream as all the fire started to cook the baby from the inside. A roaring howl rang in my ears. Then the hellhound went completely went silent. The child's eyes squinted down and then shut completely.

The child's razor-sharp teeth had done a lot of damage to my left arm. Burn marks showed where the venomous acid had seeped through and hurt me badly. I heard a thud on the floor but continued staring at my arm in amazement. It had turned black where the child had bitten me. I was not in pain, because the bite had been so fast. Everything had happened so suddenly. I could not believe the child was dead.

I looked down at the child and wondered how I'd managed to summon all the fire into one hand. The fire was now gone. The dog and the child were no more. They had both seemed to torment my life, and they'd both tried killing me. I sighed in relief and focused all my energy on healing my body and my arm. I could feel my body healing as I focused, but for some reason, my arm remained injured. I could not heal it no matter how hard I tried. In my healing trance, my heart suddenly jumped as I heard a tortured scream coming from Irene. And another. They were coming from upstairs.

Irene's screams kept repeating in my head as I mounted the stairs two steps at a time. Her cries got louder and louder with each step I took, and they were daggers stabbing my heart. I knew she was suffering and in danger. I couldn't stand the torture, the agony, and the constant dead ends to figuring out why this boy had been the start of the entity's reign of power on earth. I understood that it had had its chance at living and ruling the universe for itself, but this reign of power had to stop. It was tormenting the lives of everyone for its own evil purposes. It had managed to take my family and use them against me as a form of redemption. Its mission had caused me to feel the power of the entity. It was a lost child that had no heart. Its domain was nothingness.

"Rodger! Help me, Rodger! Please help me!"

My heart sank as I heard those words come out of Irene's mouth.

"Stop!" I yelled as I came upon a long hallway full of rooms. The staircase was a long way up, but as I reached the top, in the middle of the gallery stood a table full of the most beautiful flowers I'd ever seen. But although their beauty distracted me for a moment, I then noticed a long hallway in back of the table. There was no one in the room. The walls were hollow sounding, as in a cave.

I focused on the rooms behind the table. I'd taken several steps when I heard a voice coming from behind me. I turned around in fear, shaking. I was on the verge of a panic attack. The mamba stood before me, looking into my eyes.

"Hello, Rodger," she said. "I see you took care of my brothers downstairs."

I gulped at the sight of her exposed body. She was a magnificent creature.

"Rodger! What are you staring at?"

I looked down guiltily. She knew I'd been looking at her voluptuous curves.

"Rodger, you are a married man. You know better than to be looking at another woman. Then again, you haven't had any in a long time. Do you remember the luscious lips of your wife, Irene? She always made you tingle with excitement. Isn't that why you created Reyna? Your daughter, who was killed by your actions? She was so young when she died. Right, Rodger? She was your heart and soul in this life. You loved your daughter so much that you led the man right to your family's house. You were a real go-getter, weren't you, Rodger? It's your fault Irene is in so much pain and is suffering so much from your inability to stop working. It's your fault that your life went to hell. I wonder if you thought of putting your family into protective custody. Then you would have been able to save your fucking family!"

The mamba continued to stab at my heart with her words. My anger swelled as I listened to her speak.

"Rodger, you are not an outstanding communicator. How long did it take for you to break open the door? Perhaps if you'd loved your family, you would have reacted much faster. You're a fucking poor excuse for a husband and father."

"Mamba?" I said as I looked down.

"What?" she asked.

I replied softly as I continued to watch the floor. "Look."

The floor was white, but as the mamba stayed still, I could see a green fluid flowing in my direction. It must have been from her taking Irene in the forest. She was bleeding from the mala mujer plants' barbs still stuck in her scales. I smiled, knowing I would have a chance of defeating her and the entity.

"Look at what?"

"Look, mamba, I understand you are a lost child living in a cruel, cruel world. It is apparent that you and your brothers have all fallen victim to the power given to you, even though you were all once children and had families."

The mamba looked confused for a moment. She seemed to be trying to remember her family.

"How long has it been, mamba, since you've recalled your mom's facial features and hair—or don't you remember them? Did she have your hair or your eyes? You were so young when the devil chewed you up and spit you out of this world. He has reigned supreme while you've done all his bidding. Mamba, why has the devil come to me in my sleep? He is a part of me just as he is a part of you."

The mamba looked confused. "Rodger, shut the hell up! You are a fool."

"Why am I a fool? Is it because I'm asking you why he has come to me?"

"Rodger, your wife will die slowly."

The mamba looked extremely confused, as if she were questioning the statements she'd just heard me say.

"Rodger, your daughter is burning in a pit. Her soul has almost depleted all of its energy. You have come to investigate the cause of a little boy's death. The boy is significant to you because you are just as dead as he is right now. You are living apart from the world just as he is. You have many things in common with this boy. Think about it, Rodger. You lost your daughter and your wife, Irene. You've become separated from the world. This boy was living with his mother and father, but although he was living with them, he was trying to find a way out of the constant fighting and pain. This boy is you and your family. Julian is a boy who is similar to you. His death caused you to investigate and dig further into his case, but what you have found is that your own problems keep coming into your head. You have found the purpose of the boy and the entity. The entity is a form of you. It is the darkness of your life and everyone on this planet, the same darkness you saw as you bore witness to his black, burned bones. The very core of your existence. The boy, Rodger, is your investigation. He is your problem to solve."

"What?" I asked, looking up into the mamba's eyes. Her facial expressions gave me the sense that she was extremely pissed off. When she spoke, her words slithered out of her mouth. She did not have teeth at all but snake fangs. Her teeth were extremely long. They looked seductive and deadly. I knew defeating her was going to be a battle. She had thrown me down a flight of stairs, and here in this room was another flight of stairs. She could easily kill me, but the mala mujer plants had weakened her. She seemed fatigued.

"Mamba, where is Irene?"

The mamba came face-to-face with me, put her tongue on my cheek, and very deliberately licked my face. I wanted to take a step back but became mesmerized by her attractiveness. She was gorgeous but deadly. I remember reading about a character named Medusa who would cause her victims to become statues if they gazed at her. The mamba was incredibly beautiful and looked fantastic as she drew closer. I fell in a trance as she licked my face. I could feel her saliva drip off me, warm and amazing. I had no control over my reactions. I could see her incredible figure as she moved in closer.

"You like that, don't you, Rodger? You like what you see. Do you want to touch me, Rodger? I know you do. You are a very sinful man, aren't you, Rodger?"

I could not help myself. All the hormones in my body started to go crazy. I could not believe my eyes as I looked at her again in amazement. She had me in a trance somehow. I told her I would like to touch her. I even went as far as dropping my guard, letting my hands fall to my sides. She was very sexy. I looked down at her torso and at her lower body, noticing her scales as I gazed downward. She was an amazing creature. I could see an opening appearing in her lower torso. She was ready to start mating.

"This is too good to be true," I thought.

I grabbed the knife that was inside my pants pocket. I was prepared to attack this fucking bitch. I was going to stab her in that opening and slide the knife all the way up her body to her face, slitting her open, gutting the bitch. At this moment, I started thinking about my family and me, but I knew this was just a distraction. She was trying to lure me into her grasp.

"She's right—I am a married man," I thought, "and I do love my wife very much, but like with any guy, she's toying with a man's brain. The other, so to speak. But while a man will look at another female, he knows in his heart that he is loyal and loving to his family. This is true for all men. We will look at the other woman but can draw the line between love and fantasy. I wonder if she thinks she is going to kill me while we are having sex."

I was having a hard time pulling the knife out of its sheath.

"Oh, Rodger," she said as I fought with the knife in my pants. She came closer. "I didn't know you were badass. Let me see."

She started to slither her way toward the knife. She rubbed her breasts on my face. I still had my hand in my pants pocket, trying to release the blade from the sheath. I started to smile as I knew this would be taken out of context, but I knew this was the greatest moment of my life. The mamba became excited as she noted the smile on my face.

"Oh, Rodger, you *are* a naughty boy."

She was not even human, but she was extremely turned on.

"You have to keep your hand in your pants to calm him down, Rodger. Damn! Irene must have really loved you. How big is it, Rodger? I want to know. Can you show me?"

The pants were military grade, and the pockets were incredibly huge. I knew the knife was long, but I'd put it there just in case I needed a contingency plan. My gun was still on my back, but I no longer had enough rounds left to shoot this bitch, so I had to make every second count. She was highly seductive, and she wanted what was in my pants. The hole in her body was getting wet—I could see fluids dripping down her snakeskin and scales. It was great. I was leading her on, and she was falling for it.

I finally released the button to the knife. I waited as the mamba came closer to me. I was ready to slay the snake. She came to me, grabbing at her breasts and slowly running her hands down to her lower torso.

"Do you want this, Rodger?"

"Yes," I replied.

"Yes, what, Rodger?"

"Yes, I do."

"Oh, Rodger!" she replied. "You *are* a dirty man."

She started to rub her body up against mine. I leaned in and hugged her with my left arm, and as I did, she was trying to go in for the goods. She gripped my belt buckle tight. I could feel her breasts rub against my chest. She succeeded in pulling my belt off and unbuttoning my pants.

"Slide it into me! I can't wait any longer!" she screamed.

Obligingly, I pulled out the knife and stabbed her right in her sweet spot. She moaned a hellacious moan. She even screamed my name.

"Rodger! Oh, you dirty man!"

I caressed her as I quickly sliced up her body with the knife. She started to cry, saying, "It feels warm!" It was the massive amount of blood dripping onto the floor. She dug her fingers into my back, thinking we were making love. But the pain she was experiencing was the feeling of losing her life. She was going to die, and no one was going to be able to stop me from killing her.

I finally made it up to her throat, from which she was now gasping for breath. She was almost dead, but I knew that to kill the snake, I would have to use the knife to cut her head off. I felt her body go limp, and she was now leaning on me. She was heavy, but considering that all her organs had started to spew out of her gut, it made it easier to start cutting her head off.

"Rodger! What did you do? How come it felt so good and now I feel nothing?"

She seemed scared. I pulled the knife out slowly and realized I was drenched in her blood.

"How?" she screamed out.

I eyed her and said, "Mamba, before I came up here, I soaked all the knives in holy water. The funny thing about this is when you were screaming for me to slide it in, you were too busy looking into my eyes and licking my face and watching my hand in my pants. You thought I wanted to have sex with you. You were way too busy wanting to get down to business. I set you up, and now you are going to die. I am going to get rid of all the lost children."

She tried to get up, but the damage to her body was too severe. She could barely move her arms. I grabbed the knife and started to go to work on her neck. The knife easily cut through her scaly skin. I finished the rest of the cut and made my way to the cartilage portion, which was rougher to cut.

I watched her body hit the floor as I held her head up in my hand. The lost children had driven me mad. I had killed a child and now beheaded a mamba.

"Rodger!"

I looked at the head and realized it was talking to me.

"What the fuck is going on? You are dead."

I looked at the mamba and realized the head had morphed into Irene's face.

"Rodger, why did you kill me?"

"This is not real."

I looked down at the massive snake's body and felt reassured that I had not killed Irene.

"Nice try, mamba, but you're not going to make me fall for your stupid tricks any longer."

CHAPTER 17

WHY KILL THE BOY?

I dropped her head to the floor and started to walk toward the screams coming from one of the doors in back of the huge, long table. Still gripping the knife, I pulled the sheath out of my pocket and slid the blade into it. I smiled and said, "My lucky charm." The knife had saved my life, allowing me to go on living and find and rescue my wife, Irene. I had been through hell in the last couple of hours. Daylight was starting to disappear. The sandy look of the sun began to wane as I walked toward the back rooms.

This house, a quite-impressive mansion, was ancient but very well kept. There were no cobwebs on the floor or the lamps. Figurines molded into the walls hailed the devil, and statues of half-goat and half-human creatures adorned strategically placed pedestals. I could hear grown men screaming from behind the first door. As I proceeded, step by cautious step, I could still hear Irene screaming at the top of her lungs. What was happening to her? Was she being hurt by the entity? As I thought this, the screams stopped. For a moment, I was engulfed in pure silence.

Then the lights started to flicker on and off, and I wondered what was going on. I took one step and then another, and I realized I could hear my own footsteps echoing off the white statues and the walls. Suddenly I heard the entity speaking. Its words were loud and clear.

"I want your soul. You cannot escape me."

Just then, Irene started screaming again in the background. I ran to the farthest door down the long stretch of hallway, and I no longer heard her screams. I gathered my courage, put my hand on the doorknob, and turned it.

The door creaked open with a moan that took an eternity.

"Ah, look, Irene! Rodger has come to see you die!"

The entity bore a sinister smile as it swiped its hand quickly across Irene's face. Fire burned in my soul as I watched it punish my wife.

"You bastard!"

"Now, now, Rodger. Is that any way to treat a person who has a father? You know, Rodger, you will have to speak correctly if you wish to talk to me. I am the being that has managed to trick the devil himself. I will rid the world of you puny, pathetic little creatures."

I looked at the entity and asked why it had killed the boy.

"Rodger, I killed the boy to get to you. The best part is that I would have gotten to you sooner, but the boy's death was sweet. His courage to endure after seeing all his friends disappear right before his very eyes was intriguing, but there was no escape from my power. I will reign supreme here for a long time. The boy was the start of your discovery of our world. He drew your attention to the mountain and the many great powers it has to offer. Rodger, would you like to know what happened to the boy the night he died?"

"His name is Julian," I replied.

"Good job, Rodger. You are much smarter than I thought."

"How did the boy die?" I asked.

The entity smiled and said, "Very well, Rodger, but before I start telling you, I must get you excited about the story. Hear Irene scream for me."

The entity grew claws that looked like those of the baby that bears no mark. It slashed at her leg, and Irene screamed in agonized pain. I took a step toward them both, and it turned around with fire in its eyes.

"Rodger, stay where you are. I will let you come to Irene in good time. Rodger, the boy was stronger than all the people at the camp. He wanted to see me. He embraced the challenge of beating something that was more than he could ever be. And it happened, Rodger! The loudspeaker came on and said in my sadistic, eerie voice, 'You all shall see!' The speaker then went silent, and all the staff and students stayed quiet. They could feel my presence in the room! The room got terribly cold, and the lights started to flicker on and off. Then the light was no more, and they all screamed. I thought it was pathetic, Rodger."

"Why?" I asked.

It smiled and said, "These were the people brought up near Camp Devils Lake, and they were all cowards. The high school students' bodies cooked from the inside out, Rodger. Their eyes burned bright, and as the staff and students in the room looked at them, the fire in their eyes shot out, up into the air, and formed an enormous ball of fire. While the streams of light shot up out of their eyes, the boy could see the flesh start to cook faster and faster until their faces were burned to a crisp. But I didn't stop. I continued to push the flames until their heads exploded and their lifeless bodies disintegrated into the flames. I remained in place, circling, gathering power and strength. The children and the rest of the staff still alive ran out of the quarters down to the lake, where it was extremely dark. They couldn't see a thing until I destroyed the quarters and started to roll down toward the lake.

"It was dark and cold that night, and the children and the adults could hear the creatures of the night lurking in the shadows. The night was still, Rodger, and everyone there could hear wolves howling in the distance and leaves scraping the ground, causing them to jump. The only thing they could see was the dense fog and the creatures of the night staring at them in the distance, passing judgment. The reason they could see these creatures was that the animals' eyes were on fire. They too were being possessed. The remaining staff and students were all extremely scared of the eyes staring at them, but they were moving around, and no sounds were coming from the forest floor. All they could see were the eyes hovering in the distance. The animals began to cry out in pain as I started to cook them from the inside, and as I did, bursts of fire shot from their eyes directly over the remaining lives.

"The fog cleared, and everyone at Camp Devils Lake was now doomed! The power I'd gained was ten times greater, and as the children screamed, they could hear the screams of my brothers and sisters coming from the inside. Rodger?"

"What?" I asked.

"At this point, Julian was watching as all his teachers and friends stared at the huge ball of fire. He looked on as streams of light shot down into their eyes, cooking their bodies from the inside out. He could see their bodies shaking, the pus and blood shooting out of their mouths! Then their heads all began to explode, and all their bodies ignited into flames. As their lifeless bodies were still being cooked from the inside out, they were being pulled up into the huge ball of fire—where they became a part of me!

"Julian started to run as fast as he could toward the road. I don't know why he ran—perhaps he was a coward. At this point, I knew he could feel the real power of evil all around him, but he just kept moving as fast and as hard as his legs would go. He ran to the where the buses had dropped them off. He got extremely lucky, because a man had been trying to call the camp to check up on his daughter, and when there was no reply, the man had driven up to the mountain himself. Julian got into his car and hid in the backseat. Shortly afterward, the owner of the vehicle got into the car and started to drive. The man was extremely scared and hit the gas, making the tires screech as he hauled ass out of there.

"The man was driving extremely fast and picking up speed. Julian started to wonder why it kept getting brighter and brighter. He looked up and could see a huge ball of fire. Julian did not move—his body was trembling with fear. He couldn't talk, and he couldn't scream, because he would scare the driver! He knew there was no hope. I started to change the radio stations in the car."

The entity began to smile as it continued the explanation.

"The driver of the vehicle started to panic. I began to try to get the boy's attention. In my best demonic voice, I stated clearly, 'I want your soul! You cannot escape me, boy!' Then I lost my focus, and the song on the radio switched to an old Michael Jackson song called 'Thriller,' and the owner of the vehicle turned the radio off. The man in the car was extremely scared. Rodger, he pushed even harder on the gas pedal. Julian could not believe his eyes. He was gazing into power.

"They were halfway down the mountain when I used my brother's powers to burst into the form of a huge dog. When I did this, I was able to gain speed, running faster and faster toward the car. I kept hitting the back of the car with my nose, trying to flip the car over. I bit the trunk of the car, tearing a big chunk off, but as I did that, I lost my balance and fell hard to the ground, flinging the piece into some trees—but that evidence is in your investigation. You already know about the car. The man in the car continued to drive away from me as fast as he could. I got up and started to run yet again after the car, gaining speed, but as we neared the bottom of the mountain, I began to shrink, and the farther away they got, the more control I lost of my brother's powers until finally they disappeared.

"It didn't matter, though. I'd burned the mark into the man's eyes as he was looking into his rearview mirror. When he did that, he became possessed. The man started to fight an internal battle as he drove. He slowed to a stop about nine hundred feet away from the mountain, and his eyes began to burn. Julian thought he was safe, but then the man in the car turned to the boy and smiled. Seeing the fire in the man's eyes made the boy scream. His screams still intrigue me, Rodger.

"I used the man to beat the shit out of Julian. I beat him senseless. I then proceeded to punish the boy. I shot the stream of fire from the man's eyes into his. He screamed like a little bitch when I swallowed his soul whole. I left his body burned to a crisp. But Rodger, I could not figure out why his eyes remained on fire."

I gasped as the entity concluded the story. The thought of how it had tortured the boy made me weep. The entity was pure evil.

"Rodger, what are you looking at?"

"I'm looking at your face," I said.

"You have balls, Rodger. I hope you used them against the mamba."

The entity started screaming for its brothers and sisters.

"Mamba! Mala Mujer! Vesuvius!" it called.

I looked at him with a smile. "About that…" I began.

The entity's eyes shot up quickly. "What did you do?" it asked. Its voice was deep, its vibrations threatening to shatter my bones. I could see the entity's wings start to elongate as it became more infuriated. "What the hell did you do?" it screamed.

I looked at it and smiled. "I have killed off almost all of the lost children."

Its demonic eyes burned with fury. "A mortal could not kill off my brothers and sisters. You would have needed help from someone. But who?"

I started to think back about what had happened in the hospital. Why had I not thought of this before? I was being possessed, possibly by the entity's creator. The entity had told me it wanted to get the demon out of me. Its creator had been helping me, but why? If this were true, why hadn't he killed the lost children himself? These questions swirled in my head. It couldn't be that the devil would not hurt his creations.

"Rodger," the entity said, "Irene will surely die if you have managed to kill my family. I will make sure of it."

The entity then flew up into the air of the room and smashed through the glass ceiling right above Irene. Bits and pieces of glass rained down on her, cutting her head, arms, and legs. Outside, the entity began screaming as it found no sign of Mala Mujer.

"Where is she?" it screamed.

I ran to Irene and started to untie her from the chair.

"Irene? Talk to me. Are you all right?"

She remained with her head down toward the floor.

"You son of a bitch. If you've killed her—"

But then I heard a gasp of air escape Irene's mouth.

"Irene!" I cried.

She mumbled incoherently for a moment and then asked, "Where am I?"

I looked into her eyes and told her she was in a room inside an enormous house in the middle of the mountain. Irene tried to focus but was very feeble. I pulled her up from the chair and helped her walk into the hall. She was extremely confused and disoriented. As we walked past the rooms of torture, I could still hear people screaming on the other side of the many doors. I walked over to the huge table and pulled a chair out for Irene to sit on. She was frail and tired.

Irene looked at the ground and saw blood streaming toward us, and this caught her attention. With her eyes, she followed the trail to the mutilated mamba and started to scream. I turned around and saw the mamba's head where I had left it, but its eyes were moving back and forth. The mamba was staring at Irene, and she became mesmerized by the snake's eyes.

"Irene? Irene!" I said.

She snapped out of it and looked up at me. Irene's eyes began to tear up.

"Rodger, he killed Reyna in front of me—multiple times! He made me scream and beg for her life. I was utterly helpless. Rodger, your face is different. Your body looks different—your hair and face make you look old, Rodger."

I looked at Irene and said, "I feel fine." At her smile, I said, "It must have been the way I killed the lost children."

She sighed and stood up. I was amazed that she had the strength and ability to do that. She smiled and gave me a huge hug.

"Rodger, my legs are on fire."

I looked down and noticed the cuts the entity had inflicted when she'd been sitting there helpless. I looked into Irene's eyes and told her that everything would be all right.

"Your hair is all white," she said.

"My hair?" I asked as I ran my fingers through it.

"Ha-ha-ha-ha!" I heard the laughter coming from behind us, from the room we'd just been in. The entity was laughing.

"Ha-ha-ha-ha-ha! Rodger, you dog. You were able to weaken the lost children, to pick them off one by one. I congratulate you!" it screamed. "But you are far from being victorious!"

Just then, the door opened, and an incredibly strong gust of wind made the table fall over. Irene jumped up and hid behind me as the entity strode out of the room. Its body had changed into its ultimate form. It was now even more terrifying. It had long horns protruding from its head, and its body was covered in dark, blackened skin. Its eyes were a combination of red and yellow, and they were swirling around and around, but in opposite directions. Its mouth exhibited extremely sharp teeth, similar to those of the baby that bears no mark. The entity's chest was stabbed by the mala mujer plant, and its claws were as sharp as Vesuvius's. Its body was extremely muscular, and its legs looked exactly like a goat's, the hoofed feet loud against the floor. This demon child of the lost children had to be the oldest of the group. It looked similar to the devil himself. It was remarkably calm.

"Rodger!" the entity said. Its demonic voice was deep and harsh. "Who the hell do you think you are? How did you kill them?"

I smiled as I looked at it. The entity moved its hands around in a circle and crafted a small handgun. The entity walked over to the table that had fallen over when it had made its entrance and righted it with ease, placing the gun on its shiny surface.

"Rodger!" the entity yelled. "When are you going to answer my question?"

I looked at the entity and remembered what the boy wrapped in the mala mujer plant had said: that I would not be able to defeat it but that I could trick it. I could feel the power the entity possessed. I'd just opened my mouth to speak when the entity stopped me.

"Wait! Rodger, didn't I tell you the last time we met that you would end up killing yourself?"

"Yes," I responded.

The entity smiled. I could see its sharp, jagged teeth. "Rodger, you thought you were cocky when you told me that all of my brothers and sisters were dead, but what if I told you their power is eternal? They cannot die. They will eventually come back stronger and faster than before. It is the way we were made. Unlike you, we will live on forever in both worlds. I could open any one of these doors, and my brothers and sisters would come out. They, of course, will take on different forms than the ones you know. This will continue to happen forever in a never-ending, continuous cycle. Rodger! Pull up a chair. Have a seat."

The entity pulled up a chair for itself and sat down. It was extremely upset now that it knew of the destruction of its brothers and sisters. I pulled up a chair and sat next to the entity. It flicked its wrist, and every type of liquor appeared before my very eyes, three shot glasses sitting before the assorted bottles. I looked around and noticed that Irene was still behind me. The entity looked extremely pissed off and depressed.

"Irene," the entity said, "why don't you have a seat next to us and join us for a drink?"

The entity flicked its wrist again, and a chair rose up and plopped down on the floor.

"Irene, bring the chair and have a seat next to Rodger," it said calmly. Its demonic voice was so deep that it made the hairs on Irene's arms rise.

"Well, then—what will it be?" The entity looked directly into my eyes as it spoke.

I looked at the fire burning in its eyes, but at the same time, it was burning in different directions. It was incredible to see this magnificent creature sitting before me and my wife.

"Rodger, what will it be?"

I looked at the entity again and asked for a scotch on the rocks. Smiling, the entity said, "Excellent choice." It pulled up a bottle from the right-hand side, and while it was doing this, ice appeared out of nowhere in three larger glasses behind the shot glasses.

The entity smiled again and said, "I am sorry, Irene. Scotch is a man's drink. What would you like to drink?"

Irene asked for a double-shot margarita. Delighted, the entity smiled and nodded. It crafted the mixture, but before it finished, it asked, "Patrón Silver tequila? Is Gold better, or Silver?"

"Gold," Irene answered. She wanted a drink. I could tell she was weak and extremely exhausted.

"Rodger?" Irene said.

The entity and I both turned our heads toward Irene.

"What's wrong, baby?" I asked.

She looked into my eyes and said, "I am bleeding badly."

The entity smiled with delight.

"Rodger, she will die if you do not stop the bleeding."

The entity did not seem at all concerned. It turned to the other side of the table, where a number of broken chairs were arrayed. It was drinking its scotch. I turned my attention to Irene's legs and was surprised to see that her legs were deeply cut from where the entity had slashed at her. I noticed multiple cuts, all bleeding profusely. The entity grabbed the margarita and handed it to Irene, smiling as it looked into her eyes.

Taking a step back, it asked her, "Any last requests?"

Irene looked down into my eyes at this point, and I realized I was not going to be able to stop the bleeding. I looked around the large room and saw that all the walls were white, but there was no sign of a fireplace. If there had been, I would have used the fire to seal her wounds and the ashes to cover the burns. The entity watched as I pulled my belt off and wrapped it around Irene's leg.

"Irene," I said, "you stay up and looking at me, OK?"

Irene slammed the drink. She did it like a pro, showing no sign of disgust or anything.

"Rodger?" she said.

I looked into her eyes and knew she was going to die. I looked back at the entity, who was drinking multiple shots. The entity started to laugh sadistically as I worked on trying to save

Irene. Irene moved slowly from her chair to the floor, and she began to convulse on the ground. I got the belt and tightened it even more around her leg. She was about to die. I cried out in agonized pain, my heart throbbing as I watched her die.

The laughing in the background continued as I sobbed over the loss of my wife. I could not believe that throughout all the years and all the fights, I felt this so strongly in my heart. I still to this very day love my wife. The separation had caused us not to remember what had happened to our daughter.

"Reyna, baby, your death was not my fault, but we did not intend on the bastard coming into our home and killing you. I blamed myself because he got hold of my wallet in the scuffle somehow."

The laughter was driving me insane. The entity had said it would make me want to kill myself. Now I knew why it had made the gun and placed it on the table. It knew I couldn't live without my wife, but I knew in my heart that she would always be with me in spirit. It had known I was going to react this way. It was a clever being that knew what it was doing to hurt people. It had been hurt when it was a child and stripped of its chance to live. What if I could have it tell me the story of when it had become the entity? Surely I could find some information in its background that would help me end the entity for good, how to trick it and trap it for forever. Ending the entity would help me stay at ease for the rest of my life. It had made me watch my wife die before my very eyes, and because of this, I was no longer happy with the world. I could not find a reason to stay and fight, to live every lingering day until finally I died of sorrowful old age. I was intent on ending the entity and its reign of power once and for all.

CHAPTER 18

THE ORIGIN OF THE ENTITY

The entity smiled as I looked at Irene lying there dead. Her last words had been "I love you, Rodger." My heart was almost crushed as I'd heard these last words escape with her dying breath.

"Irene," I'd said, "I love you too." Tears had rolled down my eyes as I spoke these last words. I thought of trying to heal Irene with my newfound powers, but I found she was too weak for the process. The sinister laughs came from behind as the entity's cruel intentions were now clear. It had attacked me and hurt me internally. I became torn—did I choose life and my family's revenge, or did I pull the trigger of the gun and end my life?

"Rodger," the entity said, "the gun is ready for you to end your suffering. It will take a mere few seconds. If you would like, I could pull the trigger for you. I will watch as you put the gun to your head, and you could shoot yourself, or I could pull the trigger. At this point, it does not matter. You're completely defeated in this life. Your entire world has died right before your eyes. Your job is no longer available for you to hide your fears and anger in. You are the reason for you family's downfall."

The entity began to laugh hysterically. I could see it smiling as it shrugged, as if it had completed an epic saga. I stood up and walked over to the table. The gun lay on its side. I paused in contemplation. The sinister laugh continued as the entity watched me and tried to guess my intentions.

"Come on, Rodger, you can do it. Pick up the gun and pull the trigger. You will be at peace."

I heard it say, under its breath, "And so will your head. It will be in pieces."

It again started to laugh. I grabbed the gun and pulled it up slowly.

"You are absolutely right. In my life, I caused Julian's, Angela's, Irene's, and Reyna's deaths. I put them in these situations. But now they are in a better place."

The entity stopped laughing as I said that last line and turned its demonic body toward me. Its face was pitch black, its teeth razor sharp, its nose pointed. Its eyes were, of course, burning bright, the spirals swirling in opposite directions. I felt hypnotized by the continuous swirl of its power. Its wings were magnificent, and its body was etched to perfection.

"What did you say, Rodger? I heard your thoughts just now. What did you say?"

Its voice was dark and demonic.

"Answer me, Rodger! Hell, you'd better answer, or I will devour your soul rather than allow you the alternative."

I thought for a second and then smiled. Looking into its demonic eyes, I said loud and clear, "They are all in a better place."

The entity clenched its hands into fists and held them for a moment. It glared at me and then said, "Rodger, they are not in a better place. They're in a scary, dark place filled with demons and other dark, sinister creatures devouring souls till they extinguish their existence in hell. Rodger, you can join them on the other side if you use the gun."

I smiled again and put the gun to my side, looking at the entity. "What is your story?" I asked. "You must have been a snot-nosed kid to deserve this kind of fate. You are the strongest of all of your brothers and sisters. You show no mercy, as if you have no ounce of remorse."

The entity started to laugh. "You do not get it, do you? I have been fucking with you. Rodger, you are stupider than I thought. Watch! Who do you want me to be? Mala Mujer?"

It transformed into her easily.

"I have all of their powers. They are all me. I am the being that will destroy the human body and destroy you all! I have tricked the devil himself, and I will do what he cannot! I will destroy what was created by dirt and make you feel my wrath!

"Do you want to know what I have done to trick the devil himself? I have gained his knowledge of all beings on earth and in hell. I have tricked him and caused havoc on earth. I will never bow to his pathetic attempt to please he who cannot be pleased. Although the devil thought he could make your society better, he has corrupted it and molded it to his purpose. But when I was born, I was designed to see differently than my creator. He was already corrupted by his ego and greatness. It is like the scorpion knowing it is the baddest motherfucker in the world. The devil knows he is this throughout the entire universe. The scorpion could kill with one flick of its tail and reign supreme. Rodger, I will kill every man, woman, and child and watch as they all fall victim to my power. *I* am the baddest motherfucker on earth and in hell!"

The entity laughed as I watched. Suddenly, I felt power surge inside me. It was faint at first, but then I could feel the overwhelming strength of the being taking over inside me.

"Hey, badass motherfucker. How come you don't just kill me right now? I have been a problem for you, but you continue to prolong the inevitable. I am ready, but before I go, I want to know one thing."

"What do you want to know, Rodger?" the entity asked.

"Who are you? What is your origin? How did you come to be the entity?" I asked slyly.

The power I felt was coming from inside me. I could feel it growing. It was him, the devil himself. I'd found my trick. How could I make this work to my advantage? I started to heal myself rapidly. The entity smiled and flicked his fingers. As I stared at what it was doing, it created a mirror.

"You see, Rodger, the world you know has always been a world of war. The world has been in constant destruction to find the truth. Is there a God? Religions all over the world have fought to say their religion is supreme. I was created from this type of destruction. The devil found me in a cave, trying to find a divine purpose in this world, but when I asked him about the divine one, he said *he* was divine. *He* was the path. I believed him, and I confided in him. He did things I had never seen before, and he did them with ease. He healed my hunger and thirst. He asked me if I loved him and if I would follow him. I said yes. He was delighted with my answer and continued to show me all the things I could not have imagined. He started to think of religion and war and how he could make the different factions in the world turn against each other. Many religious scriptures were written in honor of the one supreme religion, but the twist was that everyone who was not a follower of the religion was against us and the religion. Thus, the world was constantly at war with itself. Good versus evil all over again.

"The chessboard was set. It was up to the kings, queens, rooks, bishops, and pawns in religions all around the world to turn against each other and cause war, and sometimes the war was waged within a single religion. I was serving a higher purpose, but unknowingly and for all the wrong reasons. I was a child and a fool—my heart did not know any better. The world's religions all point in the direction of one God. The path to war still continues today, and now the chaos has caused the entire destruction of buildings and constellations all across the world. My presence has caused Armageddon on earth. The world's leaders are now going to launch an all-out attack on each other, which will end the world. If you were to defeat me, the factions in the world would eventually kill each other off. Which religion is supreme?"

The entity smiled and gestured.

"The one created by the devil and myself, of course. Which other religion could trump darkness? Evil comes in many forms, but you know this, Rodger. You want to know how I became the way I am now. I was tricked by the devil. He used me to build a false religion to cause war and destruction in this world. I was eating his shit, and he made it taste delectable. I ate it with pride, thinking I was making the world a better place. But as he tricked me, I also tricked him by adding my own spice to this world. I was devoured and spit back out into the darkness of the world. The devil made me in his image. I am sorry to say, but I am enjoying my power of the text I have written. The text inflicts pain in the souls of the people believing in the religion, eating the same shit I had to. I was the creator of the book and am proud to say that with the devil's help, I have become dominant. The wars of the world have caused great joy in my existence, watching people blow themselves up for their beliefs.

"The devil asked me if I would like to have a higher power in my final hours on earth. I looked at him, confused, but I saw greatness and beauty at its finest. The devil grew into a serpent. The snake in the Bible is known as the deceiver, but somehow I knew I had received my purpose of enlightenment, and I found myself face-to-face with the king of darkness. His body was a serpent that looked like a prehistoric dragon. The dragon laughed sadistically and asked if I was ready to do his bidding on earth. I looked into the serpent's red eyes and turned away. I tried to run, but with great speed, he chomped down hard on my body and flew here to his home. I stayed in his mouth, dying. He was delighted I was still alive as he spit me out. I slid onto these very hallowed grounds. This was my final resting place. I died slowly, but when I died, I started to go for a higher purpose, but the devil stopped me before I could leave. He stopped me from transitioning to the afterlife and dragged me back down to earth. He said, 'Would you like me to reward you for your efforts on earth?' I willingly accepted his offer. He devoured my body, swished my bones and skin around in his mouth, and spit out my remains. He told me, 'Put on your new body.' I looked at him and gasped. At first I did not understand what he meant. I picked up the pile of black sludge and put it on. I looked similar to how I look now, Rodger. I was impressed with the power I now had. I was greatness. I had wings and looked incredibly beautiful in the world. I flew around, getting used to my new form. But something was different.

"I turned to the devil and asked why I felt empty. He told me I was soulless now and indestructible. I could not be killed. This is when the other children were brought upon the devil as an offering. The devil did not care about the offering—he wanted to cause chaos in the world. He did the same thing to the other children but could not make them as perfect as me. His powers were starting to diminish. He was becoming weaker. His children all stood before him, looking for love from their creator. But he showed no love or care for his children. This was because we were not his children. We had all been deceived by the devil. He is a coward and a follower. His greatness is measured by the number of souls he torments in the world—which is the reason we were all created. We caused havoc on earth and covered up our presence to take over the world. The world's influences were always one of the lost children taking on a political role, causing destruction and ruining a person's image in the world."

The entity was ancient, but when it had made the book it had described, it was basically making a false prophet in the world. It had caused war through religion, the bias of fundamental religious beliefs questioned by the church causing war after war, the war among men, when the answer had always been present. One supreme religion defined all in the world. This meant that no one religion was right or wrong—faith was the beliefs of the people, who in turn chose the religion. The key to fighting the entity was right in front of me. It was war and destruction of the world. It wanted the world to end so that the darkness could win. "Is this how it wins and rids the earth of what was created from dirt?" I wondered. The destruction of the earth would end the torment it had lived. It was lost, soulless, and was the greatest creation of the lost children.

I looked at the entity and smiled. It smirked back at me, its sharp teeth making me feel intimidated.

"Rodger, your time to die is now. Pick up the gun, and put it to your head," the entity said as it looked into my eyes.

I told it no.

The entity looked surprised.

"Why have you given me the story about you and the devil making plans for an endless war in the world? What is the purpose?"

The entity, still surprised, looked at the gun in my hand. It stared at the gun for a while.

"Rodger, you're trying my patience. How about I give you a little incentive? But you did ask a question. The endless war is to cause the destruction of this world."

The entity started to laugh. Its deep voice and evil, sinister smile made it hard for me to concentrate. I could still feel the power growing inside of me. I felt as if I were going to explode. I felt anger and rage, but I also found peace in my heart and my soul. I had been through hell trying to solve this case. I knew now that Irene and Reyna were in a better place, but I kept telling myself, "Just a little longer."

The power of the devil was incredible. I could feel it surge as he boosted my strength.

"Rodger, look into my eyes, you little shit," the entity said.

I could feel the inner power surge again as I looked up. My stomach became tight, and I felt I was about to puke. I started to feel extremely hot in my chest area. So much energy was surging through my body that it felt as if I were being electrocuted. The entity looked at me questioningly.

"Rodger, what has happened to your hair and your body?"

I looked at it and squinted. "What do you mean?" I asked.

It smiled. "When you were in the thick of the mala mujer plants, what happened to you?"

I looked at it and said, "I walked through the mountainous terrain and the dangerous mala mujer plants. I came upon a boy who was trapped, wrapped in the mala mujer. I rescued the boy and let him escape. The boy has come to me several times as I have been trying to save Irene."

"Poor, poor Rodger. You were so hoping to rescue Irene, weren't you? I ruined your plans to become the hero. What else?"

"I noticed something in one of my dreams. You were not there, but since you said you *are* all of your brothers and sisters, it became apparent."

"What became apparent?" the entity asked as I continued looking at it.

I smiled and positioned the gun toward the entity's head.

"It became apparent that you were hiding in my body. Who you were hiding from is the question I want answered."

"This was a dream, Rodger. You are a silly man. Did you hit your head too hard in the hospital?"

"I did wallop my head, and my body took a lot of damage, but I was able to heal myself and make my body feel good again."

"Rodger, do you want to see how you look? You look ridiculous."

The entity looked down at Irene and spit on the floor. As it did so, I pulled the trigger of the gun, and the whistling bullet halted right in front of its two horns.

"What the…" I said in my head. The entity smiled.

"What did you think would happen? Rodger, let me show you how stupid you look."

I put the gun to my side again, as I felt helpless. The entity flicked its wrists, and a mirror appeared out of thin air. It positioned the mirror in front of me, and I gasped.

"Rodger," the entity said, creeping to the side of the mirror, "what is wrong? Do you see something you don't like?"

"You are a monster!" I yelled. "And you are going to get what is coming to you. I will make damn well sure of it!"

"Now, now, Rodger, let us be civil. I am giving you the chance to end your pathetic life, but you keep on and on about your wife and kid. How you love them and want to be with them, but here we are—waiting!"

The entity's patience was beginning to thin as I looked into its eyes. I became mesmerized. It was almost hypnotic, the sense of my becoming possessed. I could still feel the power of the devil brewing in my body, but I could also feel the entity's presence. It was trying to take over.

The entity smiled and said, "That is much better. Rodger, put the gun to your head."

I felt my arm start to move. The entity began to laugh as I started to lift my arm, the gun in my hand. I could feel the entity starting to take control of my body.

"Rodger, how does it feel to be controlled? It must feel great," the entity said. "I am tired of our little game. I want to make this interesting."

The entity lifted up my body and flung me across the room. I hit the wall and was surprised when I did not hit the ground. The entity was keeping me up.

"Rodger, your wife is here with us in the depths of hell." Its voice now changed into Irene's.

"Rodger, help me! Please! They are ripping me apart!"

The entity's voice landed on the word *apart*. Its voice sounded even more sinister than the last time.

"Well, if you're not convinced…here, we will make it even more attractive."

The entity's eyes started to burn brighter as it stared at me. Suddenly, the chair where Irene had died shifted. I looked on in shock as Irene's body began to move toward me. She was alive, but how? I watched as she used the chair to help herself up. Pushing herself the last few inches, she sat down in the chair.

"What are you doing?" I asked the entity. I felt as if wind were hitting my body at seven hundred miles per hour. I could hardly move. I could barely breathe. The entity moved its arm, and I fell hard to the floor. The entity looked really angry. My head spun as I tried to regain my composure.

"What in the hell was that?" I asked.

The entity started to laugh. "You said *hell* as if you knew what the word really means. You are not in hell, but you can have a taste of it if you like."

The entity smiled as I stared in horror at Irene sitting on the chair.

"Irene?" I said as I picked myself up and started to walk over to her. "How are you alive?" I asked out loud.

The entity did not move but just watched as I made my way over to the chair. Irene was slumped in the chair, her left hand dangling as her head fell back on the chair.

"Irene?" I said again. She did not move. She remained quiet.

"Irene?" I said, now four feet away from her. The room was huge, and the wind against my body was unlike anything I had ever felt.

"Irene, are you OK?" I said, touching her shoulder. She still did not stir. I walked around her and moved her body so I could see her face. Her eyes were closed, and her mouth was wide open.

"Irene!" I called out her name again. The entity did not move. It just continued to stare at me.

"What do you want? What do you want?" she repeated.

I told her to look at me, but she moved her head from side to side.

"I can't," she cried.

"Why not?" I asked as she continued to evade my gaze. "Irene, look at me."

"You want me to look…aaat…yooouuuu." Her voice was starting to change. "I…wiiiillll look at you. How do you want me to look at you, Rodger?" She began to scream at me as she pulled her head around in my direction. "Here, you wish to see me, Rodger?"

She opened her eyes, and it scared the hell out of me. Her eyes were the same fiery tornadoes as the entity's.

"Who the hell do you think you are, Rodger? You think because you got me killed, I am going to be happy to see you?"

"Irene, what is wrong with you?" I asked. She thrust her arms up quickly and grabbed my head. She was not supposed to be this strong. She seemed to have superhuman strength. I pulled at her hands and her arms and finally managed to escape.

"Damn you," I said, turning my attention to the entity.

"Why, Rodger? It's already been done." It started to laugh. "Ah, Rodger, I would watch your back."

I turned around, and Irene was waiting for me. She punched me hard in the face. I fell backward and landed on my butt. I checked my jaw before getting up again. This was the final straw. I moved my body up to stop Irene. This was not my wife but an imitation of the real thing. I knew the entity would attack my heart again. It would somehow make this situation my fault. I gathered all my strength, and as Irene came to punch me in the face again, I dodged her attempts. I made sure to keep an eye on the entity as well to make sure it was not going to attack me from behind. The entity looked on from a distance.

"Look, it's the two lovebirds fighting again."

I could not stand the way the entity was talking about us. I knew in my heart that Irene would never have hit me. Now, she scratched my face hard and tried taking a bite out of my arm as we scuffled. The fight was short because the entity had severely damaged Irene's body earlier, slashing her leg. She went in for a punch and hit the chair with her foot. Her bones shattered, and she fell to the floor. But even though she was on the ground, she was still trying to attack. I kicked her hard in the face, and Irene, in her evil, zombie-like state, was now out cold.

"Ah, Rodger, you found a way to defeat your wife." The entity was now excited. "Here, let me help rearrange your face."

The entity punched me hard in the face. I stumbled backward and felt the blood start to flow. I regained control as the second punch came toward my face, maneuvering my head down to miss its strike. It smiled and again pursued. I continued to dodge as fast as I could, but its next blow hit me on the shoulder. I felt the sharp claws tear at my deltoid and fell hard to the floor, right next to Irene. The entity stood above me, smiling.

"You know what, you little shit? You can dodge my hits and still manage to stay alive. Fuck you!" The entity spit on me, pissed off. With interest, I started to feel pain on my leg where it had spit on me. I could see the mala mujer's acidic blood start to bubble. I began to wonder about the power building up inside me, the intense, burning heat. Steam was starting to come off my body. The entity backed up for a second and smiled.

"Rodger, what is going on with you?"

I smiled and then started to laugh. "You think you are supreme, don't you?"

I could see everything, but I was no longer in control of my body. I could feel the unbelievable power surging and instantly felt secure. I felt no pain in my arm or my leg.

From my mouth came, "My child, you are unyielding, but you lack a soul. You are a very dark shadow in this world that can torment the living and do my bidding. You have no soul. Why try to gain power in the universe?"

I floated up and landed on my feet. I could feel a burning sensation on my forehead as blood shot down my face. Something was growing out of my head. I knew the king of darkness was now in control. The entity again tried to punch me, but the power of the lord of darkness blocked each shot and answered with his own mighty blows. It was my trick to end the entity, but how had the kid wrapped in the mala mujer plants known this would happen?

The entity, surprised, backed up and started to speak.

"Rodger, you dog! How did you—"

"Stop!" I felt myself say in an even-darker voice. "You are addressing me as this puny human?"

The entity smiled. Rage filled my body in a multitude of colors as the devil became incensed.

"How dare you! I created you!"

The entity smiled again and then started attacking my body. The devil was swift as lightning and as agile as the turtle is extraordinarily patient. The entity slashed and clawed at my body but had no luck hitting me. Changing tactics, the entity started spitting acid again. It hit my body and remained on my skin, bubbling. The entity was pleased with the results as we came to a stop.

The entity said, "You are a wounded father."

The devil glanced down toward my body and realized the entity had done severe damage to my stomach area. I could see all of my insides. I did not want to look, but for some odd reason, the devil was making me watch. The entity began laughing as the devil did not look up. I was trying to put my body back together but could not do it.

"Ha-ha-ha-ha-ha! You got me!" the devil said. He snapped my fingers, and instantly my body was healed. The devil looked up and rushed the entity, transforming my arms into weapons, using many different forms of arms. He would spit on the entity too, and the entity would scream out in agonized pain. The entity hit the wall several times before the devil finally picked up my hand and pulverized the entity into the wall. He remained looking at the entity.

"Demon, you hid inside this man's body. You hid from me as I tried to capture you."

The devil smiled. The entity was bleeding from the massive number of blows and punishment the devil had inflicted. The entity was weak. I could feel it, and the devil felt it.

"Shadow, you're weak." The devil became pleased as he remained in control.

"Aghhhh, fuck you!"

The devil smiled. "Pathetic Shadow!" he said, continuing. "The darkness engulfs the shadow like the sunshine lighting the way."

"Shadow?" the entity asked as it looked up in pain.

"Yes, your name is Shadow. You are the lost children, but you, Shadow, have done incredible things in your time here on earth."

"Shadow?" the entity screamed. Its eyes now opened in my direction. "You cannot stay in Rodger's body forever. Your powers will weaken."

But I felt strong. I knew the entity was lying. The devil's power was dangerous. I could feel all the demonic souls surrounding my body.

"Shadow, you have been extinguished from existence. The entity is now a mere memory in the world."

The entity started to laugh. "You are wrong, Rodger. Your wife is here to see you."

The devil was surprised by Irene's attack. She stabbed me in the heart. I felt the broken piece of chair puncture my skin. The devil took his eyes off the entity and focused on Irene, who was running around the room, pulling at her skin, which had started to bubble. I watched her tear her skin from her bones. The devil watched, as he knew it killed me to see her destroy herself. It was as sinister as a serial killer watching his victim take his last breath before dying. The entity disappeared from the devil's grasp. The devil put his hand down and smiled.

"So you are hiding behind another human. You are using their bodies to remain in existence."

Irene was breathing heavily as the entity's body transformed into its perfect form. Irene's skin shredded as the mala mujer plant wrapped itself around her and ripped the rest of her flesh apart.

"Here is where you created the lost children. Here is where we were spit out to do your bidding." The entity dropped its arms down, and the ground began to quake. The lost children of Camp Devils Lake—Shadow, Vesuvius, the mamba, Mala Mujer, and the baby that bears no mark, along with the flaming hellhound—stood before me. The devil smiled.

Shadow began, "Blood, guts, and Rodger's head on a silver platter, and as for his newfound power, it's nothing, because ours is greater overall."

The devil started laughing as the entity finished. I felt my soul separate as the devil pushed me away. I hit the floor of the mansion. I was now back in my body, healed and completely healthy. The devil stood before the lost children and turned into the massive ancient serpent. The lost children started to attack the beast. The fight did not last long, because the devil swallowed all of the lost children one by one.

Shadow walked toward the devil and smiled as the devil chomped down on the entity. The devil disappeared, and I was left alone. Existence was the entity's key to power. I walked over to the gun on the floor, picked it up, and maneuvered it toward my head. I thought about Shadow and realized it was a student devoted to the study of right and wrong in society—specifically, how evil had been defined and personified throughout history and time.

I tried to pull the trigger but then dropped the gun to the floor. I walked over to the mirror and looked at my hair and face. I was old and looked destroyed. I turned my head from side to side to get a good look at the man I had become. I noticed that the mirror looked warped. I focused on the ripples moving.

"Am I seeing things?" I thought to myself.

I touched a portion of the mirror, and it did nothing. Shrugging my shoulders, I turned around. I walked through Camp

Devils Lake and noticed that everything had gone back to normal. The trees were all vibrant and alive. The fortress was deep within the mountain. I knew I would have to take action to ensure the entity never returned.

I walked over to my car, hit the unlock button on the remote, opened the door, and got into the driver's seat. Putting the key into the ignition and starting the car, I drove down the mountain, looking at the forest and the road.

"Rodger, you did it!"

I looked into my rearview mirror and found Julian smiling at me from the backseat.

"I did, kid. I figured out what the entity wanted."

Julian looked at me and asked why I looked so old. I told him it was a long story.

He smiled and said, "Rodger, the coroner will call you tomorrow and tell you my eyes have extinguished. You can act surprised, but you did it!" He yelled, "I am free!"

I arrived home and walked into my empty home. In the bathroom, I sat and stared at my face. The mirror started to ripple and move again. I ignored it and turned around. But then I heard laughter coming from behind me. Goose bumps crept up my arms, deep into my neck, and down my spine.

"Ha-ha-ha-ha-ha!"

I turned around and looked into the mirror. The ripples got bigger and bigger, and as I focused on my image, my heart began to sink, as I knew what was about to happen. The entity came out of the mirror and grabbed me by the neck. Laughing, it said, "Rodger, I've come to feast upon your pathetic soul!"

It then dragged me into the mirror, laughing.

About the Author

Anthony Gurule was born in 1986 in Albuquerque, New Mexico, to his mother, Janet, and his father, Anthony Sr. Anthony's passion to help students learn and to encourage them to read is ultimately what pushed him to write *The Entity of Camp Devils Lake*. His passion to serve as a public servant for the school system has pushed him to inspire any students willing to read to pick up a book and learn something new or read for fun, and he always encourages students to use their imagination. This volume is the start of a new line of horror/fantasy books. Anthony is currently working on the sequel to *The Entity of Camp Devils Lake*.

COMING SOON: THE ENTITY PARALLELS

ANTHONY GURULE

www.ingramcontent.com/pod-product-compliance
Lightning Source LLC
Chambersburg PA
CBHW050724180626
46814CB00002B/591